TRANSFORMATIONS

FIC King

King, J.
Transformations.

PRICE: $13.17 (3620/af)

ALSO BY JAMES KING

FICTION

Faking

Blue Moon

NON-FICTION

William Cowper: A Biography

Interior Landscapes: A Life of Paul Nash

The Last Modern: A Life of Herbert Read

William Blake: His Life

Virginia Woolf

Telling Lives or Telling Lies?: Biography and Fiction

The Life of Margaret Laurence

Jack, A Life with Writers: The Story of Jack McClelland

Farley: The Life of Farley Mowat

CO-EDITOR

The Letters and Prose Writings of William Cowper

William Cowper: Selected Letters

Early Voices

TRANSFORMATIONS

JAMES KING

A CORMORANT BOOK

Canada Council
for the Arts

Conseil des Arts
du Canada

ONTARIO ARTS COUNCIL
CONSEIL DES ARTS DE L'ONTARIO

The publisher gratefully acknowledges the support of the
Canada Council for the Arts and the Ontario Arts Council
for its publishing program. We acknowledge the financial support
of the Government of Canada through the Book Publishing
Industry Development Program (BPIDP) for our publishing activities.

Printed and bound in Canada

National Library of Canada Cataloguing in Publication

King, James, 1942–
Transformations : a novel / James King.

ISBN 1-896951-57-0 (bound).   ISBN 1-896951-74-0 (pbk.)

I. Title.

PS8571.I52837T73 2003   C813´.54   C2003-904234-0

Cover and Text Design: Tannice Goddard/Soul Oasis Networking
Cover image: Too Early, 1873 (oil on canvas) by
James Jacques Joseph Tissot (1836-1902).
Image Credit: Guildhall Art Gallery, Corporation of London,
UK/Bridgeman Art Library
Printer: Friesens

Cormorant Books Inc.
215 Spadina Avenue, Studio 230, Toronto, Ontario, Canada M5T 2C7
www.cormorantbooks.com

For Heidi Woodhead

PART ONE

LONDON

CHAPTER ONE

BROKEN HEARTS

On the morning of the twelfth of April, 1855, Daniel Home receives a letter summoning him to an urgent meeting that afternoon. He has been in London less than three weeks and is again importuned by a person in distress for assistance.

He looks at himself in the full-length mirror that graces his luxuriously appointed hotel room. He sees a tall, spindly young man who looks as if he could be pushed over by the slightest breeze. His hair is an unpleasant, gaudy shade of red, his small blue eyes watery, his mouth thin, his small nose is the only part of his countenance of which he feels even momentarily proud. Daniel does not like to see his reflection. He is reminded of what a miserable specimen he is, and of his increasingly poor health. He is what physicians call tubercular; he may not suffer from tuberculosis, but he has a weak constitution and has the malnourished look of those who suffer from the disease.

Disgusted with his body he may be, but Daniel is even more dissatisfied with his soul. Unlike other young men, he does not have the luxury of rejecting things of the spirit. Since early adolescence, he has been haunted by ghostly presences who confess their secrets to him. They insist he communicate with the living — an inconsolable parent, a sweetheart left precipitously behind — to offer them assurances about the continuation of life beyond the grave. Then there are the bereft, who knock constantly at his door, beseeching him to help them get in touch with their lost ones who have shed their mortal coils.

Truth to tell, Daniel would like to rest. His long sea journey from Boston to Southampton has fatigued him beyond endurance. Yet he cannot bring himself to say no to a mother who has lost her only child. His walk will not be a long one, but he is not certain he can be of any use. He takes one last look around his new habitation, picks up his hat, opens the door and sets out on his promenade.

The main streets of London are filled dirty cheek to filthy jowl. Daniel is immediately part of a mob, a pulsating assemblage of all types of humanity. There are beggars whose clothing barely covers their arms, legs and even private parts; their stench, a mixture of sweat, tobacco, gin and urine, greets all those they approach. There are the merchants clad as in uniform, black being the only colour they favour. There are the servant girls in pale blue and pink ginghams; their modest hats have no feathers adorning them. There are the women dressed as if they are quality, but a close inspection of their garments reveals that they are hand-me-downs or tattered discards. These are prostitutes disguised to look like members of the middle class. Every so often, Daniel sees an elegantly dressed woman, discreetly accompanied by a servant, entering or leaving a shop. These ladies follow the exacting standards of society's dictates; they are the customers whose attendance the merchants crave. Then there are those the shop owners uniformly despise: the countless children, obviously orphans, who clamber about everywhere, swearing, crying, fighting, jostling. Some of these unfortunates are paid to carry garbage away; some are sweeps; some are beggars. Most are idle. All the hubbub in the street comes from these little castaways, upon whom Daniel bestows a tender eye as he weaves in and out among them.

At precisely twenty minutes before four on the afternoon of the same day, a handsome young man walks briskly to a rendezvous. Day after day in London the spring has consisted of a thick, molasses-smelling yellow fog followed by heavy, petulant rain. His appointment at 12 Half Moon Street is at half-past three, but on that day he quits his lodgings in Piccadilly late. He walks quickly down Regent Street, but his path is blocked by layabouts, dustmen, packmen and a huge collection of sweeps who obviously cannot ply their trade that afternoon. Although he breaks into a trot when he reaches Green Park, he is at least ten minutes late when he raps on the door of Number 12.

In an instant, Millicent lets him in. "Mr. Wilson, how nice to see you." A tiny scrap of a woman, she is dressed in a maid's costume made of the finest black Indian silk. Without further ado, Millicent strips him of his greatcoat and, in the process, her own clothing becomes drenched. Seeing the look of concern on his face, she reassures him: "Not to worry, Mr. Wilson. We are delighted you were able to make your way to us this afternoon. Some of the other members have succumbed to the influenza sweeping the capital. A deadly peril, it is." As she takes his hat in one hand, she uses the other to push the door open. "Mrs. Sinclair will be delighted to receive you. You are a great favourite of hers."

As usual, it takes Julian Wilson a few minutes to adjust his eyes to the darkness. The walls of the large room he has stepped into have been painted a sinister dark brown. The serpent-entwined Gothic columns, two on each side of the room, are the first objects Julian becomes aware of. In this very chamber, he thinks, Samuel Johnson called upon Boswell, and from this room Lola Montez, once the mistress of mad King Ludwig of Bavaria, sallied forth to celebrate her bigamous marriage to Gerald Heald. He then notices four figures inhabiting the cavernous space. Two elderly grandees are seated in chairs on his right; further away on the left is an enormous sociable, one of those button-back sofas where the occupants face each other. There a man and woman are engaged in earnest conversation.

The woman, of middle age, wide of girth and clad in a dark green velveteen gown to match the light green damask of her settee, rises and walks in his direction, bowing ever so slightly as she reaches him. "Julian, my dear," Mrs. Sinclair declares, "I am happy you are here. We have had many illnesses with which to contend this fortnight." After he assures her that he is well, she asks if he knows her companion, a tall, freckled, red haired, loosely put together fellow of his own age. When Julian replies that he does not have the pleasure, her spectral companion stands up to take his hand and mumbles: "I am Daniel Home, the medium."

Having exchanged commonplace remarks on the dreadful state of the weather, the two are interrupted by their hostess, who turns to Home: "I must get Julian settled." She assures her companion that she will return soon to resume their conversation.

That was Julian's first meeting with Home; in that darkened room the spiritualist's deep-set eyes, wispy beard and emaciated thinness conspired to make him look like an emanation. Daniel Home was never — Julian will later remind himself — mere flesh and blood.

"As usual, Julian, Rachel is prepared to your exact specifications." With those words, Mrs. Sinclair pushes the door open and withdraws. Julian is overwhelmed by the scent of the lilies that clutter the large secretaire opposite the bed. His painter's eye scans the orange-brown tulipwood from which that piece of furniture is constructed; he studies the elaborate floral marquetry. The large assortment of Turkish cap lilies in the vase on the secretaire boasts all the shapes and shades of their genus, but their deathly, waxy odour vanquishes any comfort he takes in their purples, pinks, reds and ochres. At the foot of the bed is a gilt wood table inlaid with marble; he studies the countenance of the gilded sphinx that forms the base, but she, remote creature, looks away from him, lost in her own thoughts.

Head down, Julian sits in the room's only chair, a small upright one made of mahogany. In the shadowy recess behind him, he does not see the crouching female figure. Costumed in deepest black so as to blend into her surroundings, she studies what little she can see of the visitor: his hunched back, the top of his shoulders.

After a quarter of an hour, Julian finally raises his head to look at the woman who occupies the bed, which is covered in deep red silk. Only her head is visible. Her eyes are closed, as if she is taking an afternoon slumber. Julian fixes his eyes on the abundant auburn hair that flows down to her waist.

I wish, he reflects, I had asked Mrs. Sinclair for a prie-dieu so that I might truly worship the creature before me. I am torn between adoration and lust. This young woman is a saint, fully worthy of veneration. A creature best kept away from vile creatures such as myself. And yet, I should like to rip that protective sheath away and have my way with her.

The sacred and the profane wage a mighty battle within him. His troubled heart beats irregularly; he begins to sweat; he can feel his member harden, slacken and then renew its claims. Although her view is extremely limited, Julian's unknown visitor discerns the beads of sweat congregating on his neck. She is wryly amused by the young man's suffering. At the end of the hour, Julian stands, approaches the bed, bends down to inspect Rachel's face and then leaves the room. Not one syllable has been uttered.

Within thirty seconds of Julian's departure, Sylvie rises from her hiding place, walks to the bed and pounces upon Rachel. In repose, Rachel's face has an angelic aspect. When animated, any trace of virtue disappears. "Sylvie, he did exactly as before. I don't know how I kept still. At one point, I felt like bursting into gales of laughter! The absurdity of it all!"

"Be still, my cunning one. You did not have to suffer any intrusion, and you earned a good sum of money. I wish my patrons were so amiable!"

"Mr. Wilson is a well-made man. There is, I suspect, some pleasure to be had from him. I despise playing in a deaf and dumb show. It frightens me to act the role of a dead woman. I am of interest to him only because I look like his beloved, the much lamented Laura. Otherwise, I would be of no value."

"He has never recovered from her death?"

"He wallows in her passing, bathes and perfumes himself in it. I am his accomplice."

"It sounds to me like you are disobeying one of Mrs. Sinclair's fundamental rules: you are pining for one of our clients. You are a very wicked girl to do that." Sylvie's words are mischievous; her dark black eyes gleam. "Perhaps that young blood from Sussex will shake you out of your languor when you see him tonight?"

Rachel laughs, but as she searches her friend's alabaster countenance and marvels at its beauty, she is chilled by her icy composure.

At the very moment Julian Wilson encounters Daniel Home, Abigail Fanshaw, seated at her desk in her boudoir at her home in Mayfair, completes a letter to the spiritualist:

Dear Mr. Home,

I am much comforted from having made your acquaintance two weeks ago. As you know, I have been disconsolate since the loss of little Tom. The death of a child must be, I once imagined, the greatest burden ever imposed on the heart of a mother. To my cost, I now know that sad veracity from first-hand experience.

As I told you, for the last year I have been obdurate in refusing to obtain any consolation from yourself or any other person of your persuasion. In fact, I was convinced that your activities were mere charlatanism. Even my dear sister-in-law's recollection of an evening spent in your company could not persuade me to call upon you.

Why then did I present myself on Albany Street that fateful night? I knew of your meeting with the Smiths and the Curzons, but I had no intention of intruding. Moreover, I had not been invited. At half-past six that evening, I informed my maid that I intended to take a promenade before dinner. Her eyes opened wide in astonishment. Fearing for my safety, she offered to accompany me. I laughed — something I hardly do any more. Dismissing her worries, I said I would be gone only a short while. I simply had to clear my head.

As I strolled down the street, I took no notice of the beggars and other vagabonds I encountered. I did not look out for the pretty little Orange girl to whom I often donate a shilling. I was thinking only of the bright, cheerful two year old my boy had been; I recollected that awful moment when his porcelain white face turned deep scarlet, his dear little countenance distorted by an angry rage. He would not allow even his dear mama near him. The fever that invaded him appeared from nowhere; within a few hours, having tired itself by sporting with him so cruelly, it vanished. When the savage beast withdrew, it took with it the heart and soul of my beloved son. A very rare, acute, fast-acting meningitis, Mr. Melrose the doctor informed me, emphasizing each of his adjectives precisely and dourly. No one could have done anything for him. I did not believe him: a good mother should always be able to assist her child.

Guilt and bitterness. Those two bilious concoctions invaded my every waking moment. Those familiar sentiments filled my heart during that walk. Spring had at last established itself, the rebirth of nature speaking to my own troubled heart. All of a sudden, a force took hold of me. Unaware of my own purpose, I moved along the street like an automaton, much in the manner of Olympia from Hoffmann's tale. My reverie was shaken by the sound of my hand pounding on a door and by the puzzled look on the face of Bowen, the Smiths' butler.

"Madam, we were not expecting you."

"I daresay. I did not mean to be here." Thoroughly confused myself and having further puzzled the manservant, I asked that he summon his mistress. Amelia Smith appeared, completely unperturbed by my sudden presence in her home. "Abigail, how wonderful to see you! I am thoroughly delighted you have decided to join us."

"Decided to join you?"

"To witness Mr. Home's amazing talents. You will be happy you changed your mind."

At that point I did not feel I had any mind left, so startled was I by my discourteous conduct. Mr. Home, I can assure you I have never played the role of the uninvited guest before. In any event, Amelia, taking me by the hand, led me to the drawing room: "I know how difficult it has been for you to attend one of Mr. Home's séances. You obviously had to steel yourself to the task. Perhaps you had to surprise yourself?" Amelia is a large, winsome woman. Her smile and charm are genuine. She looked me up and down carefully and then, in her sisterly way, whispered into my ear: "You are most welcome."

The huge drawing room of the Smiths was familiar territory to me. So were the cordial faces of Samuel Smith and the Curzons. Still deeply embarrassed by my outrageous conduct, I avoided their eyes and, instead, studied that magnificent chamber.

I could almost feel myself transported back to my beloved Florence. The enormous oil by Zampieri of St. John the Divine above the mantle filled me, as it always does, with confidence in the Almighty's abiding presence. Next to that masterpiece, the two Portland vases flanking it seemed trivial attempts at art. Cupid, Paris and Helen may be rendered with the greatest care in white relief against the solid black jasper, but these works by Mr. Wedgwood celebrate the ephemeral rather than the everlasting. Cupid is a mere troublemaker, and Paris and Helen unconscionable narcissists. On the night I met you, I took little pleasure in the lovely Qianlong porcelain pug dogs and all the other bits and pieces of Chinoiserie that have made that Mayfair room so celebrated.

My eyes soon settled on you. You were, you may recall, at the far end of the room. What a strange-looking creature, I told myself — you will forgive me if I speak with an excess of candour? How could he offer me any comfort in my vale of tears? I had resisted you and then, against my will, had been drawn to you. Nevertheless, I told myself, I shall not find anything here of use. At least, I shall take the measure of this man. That was the comforting assurance I bestowed on myself.

"Now that we are all assembled, shall we begin? Mr. Home told us not fifteen minutes ago that we should have a visitor present herself at our doorstep. Did you not, Mr. Home?" Mrs. Smith inquired.

"I did, Madam. Sometimes I have premonitions before my meetings, and they usually come to pass." I noticed the indistinct, gravelly way in which you uttered words. There was absolutely no clarity in the way you spoke. Each syllable was produced with considerable effort.

I was growing more and more discontented, although I had nothing to fear except the loss of my time. I was surprised when Mrs. Smith indicated that we should simply sit down around the ghastly cast-iron table with the life-sized deerhounds positioned at each corner, the only thing out of place in a room of superb taste.

I was startled when the illumination in the room was in no way diminished; I had been under the impression that all mediums worked under the cloak of darkness. The Smiths seated themselves side by side; the Curzons across from them; I sat at one end of the table across from you. So there we were: six sets of human eyes accompanied by four pairs of canine ones.

I must admit that I was repelled by the increasing strain in

*your voice as you began to talk of the powers that might vouchsafe
to visit us. I was distinctly angry when you leaned back as if in a
swoon, showing only the whites of your eyes. I refused to pay
much attention to the guttural sounds issuing from your mouth.
The Smiths and the Curzons seemed bored.*

*There is much smoke and little fire here, I told myself.
Therefore I was completely astounded when a tiny hand grasped
my left one. I could barely see it, such a mixture of substance and
insubstantiality it was. Translucent might be the correct word. I
had heard of the appearance of protoplasmic limbs at spiritualist
meetings, so I was not altogether surprised. I was convinced I was
the victim of some sort of trickery. Then, almost as if the owner of
the hand sensed my doubts, it grasped me fiercely, insisting I pay
heed. It was in that moment that I knew incontrovertibly that it
was Thomas's. I was on the verge of fainting, but I held on,
willing myself not to lose consciousness.*

*Thomas was born with a defect on his right hand; a small
bone spur between his second and third fingers that had become
increasingly larger as he grew older. No one else was aware of this
oddity; I had never mentioned it to my husband. I had never even
thought to tell his physician, since I was convinced that the spur
would recede as Thomas grew to manhood. Many had been the
nights when singing to Thomas at bedtime I had grasped his hand
and felt this peculiarity between his fingers.*

*That evening at the Smiths, I felt the limb I had not touched
since the day my little boy departed this life. In that moment, my
own life was restored to me. My little boy might be dead to this
world, but he had moved on to an existence in another plane. I
would one day meet him again. All the consolations of*

Christianity had not offered me such solid assurance of the life to come. My heart was filled with hope. Like Lazarus, I came back to life.

Later, you told me you were simply a portal between the two worlds, as if you merely provide a staircase between the two storeys of existence. In my opinion, only a person of extraordinary goodness would ever be vouchsafed such a talent.

I write today to urge you to visit the English colony in Florence, where we, like the poets Browning, reside for most of the year. We are not like our brothers and sisters in Great Britain. The Italian air is fresher. Sometimes we are baked to a crisp; often our skins take on a darker hue. If you come, I think you will find yourself appreciated far more than you could ever be in damp, sun-deprived England.

Let me know if you will consider this possibility. My husband and I will be delighted to have you stay at our villa. I must confess a selfish purpose: perhaps my husband might be granted an audience with his dead child?

I have written at far too great a length, but I have another request. If the opportunity presents itself, could I ask that you speak with my friend, Julian Wilson, the painter? He has not recovered from the death of his much beloved fiancée. Until I met you, I had no power to overcome the melancholy following the death of my dear one. Julian still wanders in the miasma of despair. If, somehow, he could encounter Laura's spirit, his weary soul might be soothed. I have taken too much of your time.

Yours gratefully, &c &c &c

❧

After Julian takes his leave of Rachel, he is only three streets away from The Royal Academy, where a newly discovered Leonardo is to be presented that afternoon to the best of Society. He has promised to look in, but he is not anxious to encounter his mother who will, as is her wont, attempt to control his every movement once she espies him.

The finest account of that grand event, penned within an hour of its conclusion, was written by Cynthia Wilson, the greatest gossip of the age. Although Julian has no appreciation of his mother's artistry, she has a talent for noting both the profound and the trivial — and never distinguishing between the two.

> *Dear Lady Anstey,*
>
> *Like you, I do not know if I shall ever recover from seeing the Leonardo. Was there ever a canvas that so mixed the beautiful and the repulsive? Leda's face is that of a Madonna, so chaste and refined is it. Her eyes have the delicate blue of all the painter's women. The putti who attend her are such splendid little fellows, their countenances an apt mix of adoration and deviousness. The doves are enchanting. The landscape is paradisiacal. But not only is her nakedness unabashed but she holds the swan's head as if she means it to penetrate her. Like our age, this canvas is a mixture of the sublime, the grotesque, and the ugly.*
>
> *I am glad that I can speak openly to you of such things. The men comment on Stephen Widdicombe's discovery as the eighth wonder of the world. After all is said and done, he simply came*

upon it in one of the countless unused chambers at Arundel Castle. I suspect that earlier generations of Exeters could not bear to destroy a Leonardo but refused to countenance such an abomination in one of their public rooms. The young Duke, who is said to be penurious, rejoices in the identification of a picture he probably never set his eyes on before Widdicombe's arrival.

The kind words of encouragement you whispered into my ear were most gratefully received. Julian's spirits have apparently recovered, but I suspect a subterfuge. He is worried that his poor old mother frets herself too much on his behalf and so he now takes great care to conceal his real feelings from me.

Just before we briefly encountered each other today, I exchanged some pleasantries with Sir George Markham, the president of the Academy. As you know, he is a man of a flirtatious turn of mind and most of our conversazione was trivial in nature. "I am delighted to see, Mrs. Wilson, that Mrs. Montagu's penchant for bird feathers is being revived by you. Those yellow and black offerings from that American bird, the so-called Baltimore Oriole, have found, as it were, a perfect nest in your new bonnet. A most exquisite piece of millinery." Only when he espied his wife approaching us from the other side of the exhibition room did he change subjects.

"Julian's art took an altogether new direction in the past two years. Why then has he stopped painting so abruptly?"

Before I could say anything, he went on in his tiresome way: "I had been prescient about him; his achievements were quite distinctive for his tender age. But he was merely one of a hundred young men who painted very competently. His sudden reappearance at the exhibitions brought him to the fore of his generation with that remarkable series of portraits." Sir George frowned. "A profound sense of humanity inhabited every portrait of that young woman who had become his sitter. His new work brought tears to my eyes."

I decided to be direct: "Perhaps Laura transformed his work?"

"I had not considered it in that way. I had only thought Julian's mechanics vastly improved in a short space of time. Then, once again, he cast his talent aside. Does he think he has nothing more to achieve? The arrogance of youth."

I did not know what to say to Sir George. I hesitated to tell him of Laura's death last year. As you know, my poor boy has again abandoned picture-making in favour of picture-collecting in the service of the wealthy. He claims that the tricks of the artist's trade no longer interest him and that he takes greater pleasure in selling art than making it.

How like Sir George to speak of mechanics to explain the change in my poor son's work! If Julian has become a better artist, he has paid a heavy price for the privilege. Indeed, I wish my boy was still in the middle of the pack of a hundred would-bes. A man is always happier if he has something to strive for. Having reached the highest level of accomplishment in his profession, he now rejects it in favour of becoming a trader in those same commodities. The vulgarity of his calling is beyond my reckoning.

After your departure, the reception soon became one of those tiresome occasions to which we have long accustomed ourselves. From across the room, I could see that the obnoxious Mrs. Osborne, clad in a hideous brown frock, had put in a rare appearance. She must be accustomed to being snubbed at such events. A completely tiresome woman, more burdensome still because she refuses to realize she has no place in Society. Her fortune should provide her with a ticket of admission, she must reason; but she is simply an imposition rather than a desired acquisition. The woman is as vulgar as the tailor, Robert Baker, who, acquiring a fortune selling picadels, those obnoxious stiff collars, purchased the land that derisively was named Piccadilly. She is sniffing out the Leonardo because she recently sold one; likely she wants to know the price the Leonardo will fetch so that she can compare it to the amount she received. I could tell by the look on her face that she found nothing unseemly about the painting. Perhaps Mrs. Osborne approves of such licentiousness.

The recently widowed Lady Rhonda also roamed the room. Though she is about to reach her fiftieth year, many men still consider her bright red ringlets the height of fashion whereas women universally despise her. Her beauty is of the coarse kind and even I, unthreatened by her, find her loathsome. Her bearing is aristocratic, her conversation not unenlightened, her smile conveys benignity, and she never speaks ill of anyone. Yet one feels that she easily could, especially in private. Her eyes betray her. There is a hunger in them that is appalling. I am certain, as she studies the canvas, that Lady Rhonda considers herself on the same plane of existence as the loathsome Leda. Arrogant creatures, both of them.

That braying laugh of hers is as distracting as ever. Many a gentleman who has flattered her with his attention flinches when he hears that sound and withdraws from the conversation. She is reputed to be a close friend from childhood of Elizabeth Barrett

Browning, and I have heard tell she assisted the flight of Miss Barrett from Wimpole Street into the arms of Mr. Browning.

Now resident in Florence, the poets are to be in England soon. I have it on the best authority that they will be in attendance at a séance to be conducted by that strange man from America, Mr. Home. The poetess's delicate health is evidently sustained by a precarious mix of laudanum and morphine. Perhaps her husband hopes that the pursuit of spirits will replace those dangerous opiates?

Stephen Widdicombe and Lady Smythe paraded around the room with the Duke of Exeter in their wake, as if he were a pig led by a string. Mr. Widdicombe's American accent announces him well before one sees him. As always, he is costumed in the height of fashion: his cravat of the purest silk is a bright orange, his afternoon coat of fine Peruvian wool a virulent red.

Overdone. That is my assessment of Mr. Widdicombe. He might be a great connoisseur, but, like most of his countrymen, he will never be a gentleman. The diminutive Lady Smythe accompanies him everywhere, so completely besotted with him is she. He is the male bird in dazzling bright plumage, she the dour hen.

The Duke is a true gargantuan. His youth — he cannot be more than four and twenty — is lost in enormous masses of fat. Although his eyes sparkle a bit, they are small and stare at one rudely. His carrot red hair, which cascades down his back in a most unseemly way, has not been washed in months. Would that the fashion for wigs might be revived to spare one the sight of those locks!

I must halt. My little pocket watch tells me Julian will probably be here in less than ten minutes, and I have dropped, *forgive me, a tear or two on this scrap of paper. I shall have to repair my face, and you must perforce forgive this abrupt conclusion.*

Yours faithfully, &c &c &c

Mrs. Wilson's mysterious reference is to the death of Laura Bennett one year before in the small Sussex town of Saxe-Mundy. For a number of years, the small Tudor cottage in the centre of Saxe-Mundy, conveniently positioned between a small hotel and the Anglican chapel, had been let by its owner, Mrs. Conway, who had removed herself to the nearby countryside to minister to her ailing sister, Lady Bennett. Members of the Bennett family often took their holidays at their very elderly relative's abandoned home, and she looked forward to the occasional rent from their visits.

When Laura asked to stay at the cottage, she gave her great aunt no reason for the sojourn. She simply inquired if her proposed dates would prove convenient. Since no one had ever expressed even the remotest interest in occupying the cottage in the middle of winter, Mrs. Conway's assent was conveyed back to London by the first return of post.

A remarkable boon gained by Mrs. Conway in letting to relatives was that they had, over the years, without extracting any contribution from her, repaired the cottage's thatched roof. Altogether, The Wayside was a more elegant affair than it had been during the years its owner had occupied it.

Its two rooms, a sitting room and a small bedroom (a tiny

kitchen was haphazardly attached behind the sitting room) contained some remarkable pieces of furniture, articles of a quality of which no other cottage in Sussex could boast.

Mrs. Conway, a widow of extremely limited means, had not collected any of the objects found in her former abode. In fact, everything she had once owned had been distributed free of charge to the villagers by Laura's father, who now used The Wayside as a place to store the overflow from his London collection. Mrs. Conway had no objections to this practice; indeed, she had been delighted to be of service.

Why Laura wanted to escape to the Sussex countryside had puzzled everyone. She was, after all, supposed to be in the midst of her wedding preparations. From early childhood, she had been declared a great beauty and great beauties were expected to marry young and produce handsome offspring. After all, that was the least they could do to repay the advantages bestowed upon them. As a child, Laura had been perfectly happy to play the role assigned to her; as a young woman, she grew doubtful, even though she tried to conceal those reservations.

Julian Wilson seemed the answer to this young maiden's prayer. A young artist of great promise who had turned to the selling of artwork, Julian had quickly established an enviable reputation. He spoke to her candidly about his ambitions; he told her that she should have ambitions of her own; he nurtured her interest in writing; he educated her in the renewed interest in Greek and Roman antiquities; he promised her they would travel as far as India in the pursuit of the ideal landscape.

Laura's parents were not certain they wanted a family of their wealth and standing to be allied to the Wilsons, who were, when all was said and done, a merchant family whose fortune had been acquired in the past decade. To the Bennett's consternation and recurring embarrassment, their daughter's behaviour had grown erratic, with displays of temper and excessive high spirits at inappropriate occasions. In Julian's company Laura seemed mostly content. Perhaps a love match was the solution to their daughter's high-strung personality? They did not wish, as Mr. Bennett said, to marry her off, but they wanted her to settle down. Julian Wilson, as long as he did not get up to the high jinks of the Rossetti clan, might offer the ideal solution. Mr. Bennett consented to the union the moment Wilson asked for his daughter's hand; his wife, listening in the adjoining room through a tumbler, raised her hands in such unbridled joy she almost hurled that piece of crystal to the floor.

Laura's decision to spend a week by herself in Sussex remained a sizeable bee in her mother's bonnet. Young women, she reminded her, did not travel from home unaccompanied. Her old governess, Winifred, would go with her. Nonsense, her daughter countered. She desperately needed to get away from everyone: Julian, her family, London. She would be gone a mere week. She needed time to "collect" herself. That was her very word.

Laura's parents uttered a few more imprecations, but, within a few days, they had begun to agree that perhaps their daughter was doing herself a good turn. For one, she obviously needed a rest: the dress fittings, the interminable discussions about the reception, the detailed planning for the Italian honeymoon, all had obviously robbed Laura of energy. A stay in the country would be a respite. She would return full of vigour, eager to fit in all the remaining pieces of the jigsaw that constituted a perfect wedding day.

Mr. and Mrs. Bennett — in a show of family solidarity — accompanied Laura to Marylebone station. Although Laura's complexion remained highly flushed, she was in excellent spirits. "I am going to sleep for the first day or two. After that, I may visit my aunts in an afternoon. I shall see you in a week's time." She kissed both her mother and father most affectionately before stepping into the first-class portion of the rail carriage.

Laura's arrival in Saxe-Mundy on a bright Tuesday morning was observed by a number of townspeople. In truth, they were a bit shocked that she arrived unaccompanied, carrying her two large carpetbags herself. One or two even noticed that a piece of clothing — perhaps the hem of a dress — stuck out from one the bags. Had she packed in haste? Laura remained no more than an hour in the cottage before she ventured out to make arrangements for provisions with the various tradespeople. Laura, long known to the locals and much beloved by them, remembered their Christian names, asked after various children and grandchildren. A real Christian gentlewoman: that was the town's unanimous opinion of Laura Bennett. All of the provisions — milk, cheese, coffee, meat — were delivered to her late that afternoon.

After Laura received her delivery from the butcher, she was not seen again. Smoke could be seen rising at regular intervals from her chimney. The only event of note was the arrival on Thursday afternoon of a young gentleman on the London train, who walked up the slight hill to the village, knocked at

The Wayside and was allowed entry. At the time, the young man's appearance attracted attention, in the same way any outsider is an object of fascination in rural Sussex.

The visitor was costumed in a strange fashion, dressed in a bright blue corduroy suit with a peak cap made of the same material. His boots were extremely unusual: a dark but very glossy green. From underneath his cap could be seen a magnificent tuft of curly blond hair, more white than yellow in hue. He could not have been much more than seventeen or eighteen and was painfully thin. He stayed not more than an hour at The Wayside, closed the door after himself when he left, doffed his cap several times in salute to two or three village elders, descended the hill to the station, where he waited approximately half an hour for the next London train. He was not in the village more than two hours. The townspeople, who considered the matter, thought the young man a messenger, carrying an urgent missive from London.

That Thursday evening, no smoke gusted from the cottage chimney. On the following day, there were no signs of any activity. Knowing Miss Bennett's love of the countryside, the villagers assumed she had taken the fifteen mile walk to visit her elderly aunts. On Saturday, Julian Wilson arrived, by appointment, to visit his fiancée.

His knocks went unanswered and, like everyone else, he assumed that Laura, who could be absent-minded about arrangements, was with her aunts and had not yet returned. He set out in the direction of Lady Bennett's estate, expecting he might meet Laura on her way back to the village. No such thing occurred. In fact, the elderly women were much surprised that their niece had not called upon them. Julian hastened back to the village, which he reached only at nightfall. He attempted once again to gain entry to the cottage. Now both perplexed and troubled, he called upon the village magistrate, who accompanied him back to The Wayside. When Mr. Brown could not gain entry, he sought Julian's assistance in breaking down the door.

At first nothing seemed to be out of place in the cottage. The main room was filled with furniture of various styles. The eighteenth-century Italian bombé chest made of walnut and ostentatiously inlaid with ivory and mother-of-pearl flowers always surprised the first-time visitor. The contrast between the black and reddish-brown hues in the oyster-veneered laburnum cabinet set against the far wall made it the most eye-catching item in the room. Nothing seemed disturbed among the many small objects in The Wayside, which included Bow and Lawrence Street figurines, a pair of Meissen hard-paste porcelain eagles, and a Yongzheng punch bowl.

However, once inside, they could make out a faint, acrid odour. The two men, somewhat chagrined at entering a lady's bedroom, pushed open the door and beheld the magnificent carved and gilded bed designed by Matthias Lock. This piece, with its domed top and rococo cornices, dominated the room. On the bed lay a slumbering Laura. Her deep red hair and the scarlet damask of the bedspread was a perfect arrangement of warm, earthy colours. But she only appeared to be sleeping. The scent from her dead body was so overwhelming that the two men knew immediately that they were looking at a corpse.

No blood was visible about the body. Laura lay as if sleeping contentedly. The room was as it should be but for an empty goblet by the side of the bed. When Julian picked it up and smelt it, he instantly detected a metallic scent.

Only a few hours later when the body was being removed did the attending physician see the small wound that had been inflicted into the centre of Laura's heart. He concluded that the murderer, obviously the young man in blue corduroy, had drugged and then stabbed the young woman. However, the knife had been inserted so expertly that little blood flowed from the victim's heart. The post-mortem revealed not a trace of any dangerous substance in the body; the glass was so totally empty of liquid that no chemical analysis could be undertaken of its contents. During his testimony, the doctor marvelled at the economic manner in which the murder had been accomplished. He remarked that it was as if a small steel worm had been inserted into the heart, punctured the organ and then quickly withdrawn.

The coroner's jury came to the not unreasonable conclusion that Laura Bennett had been murdered by persons unknown. Julian had no idea of the killer's identity. The Bennetts were similarly mystified. With the onset of idle, malicious gossip, even they began to wonder if Laura had been murdered by a jilted lover, though such a possibility seemed inconceivable and was dismissed.

Even now, a little more than a year later, Julian finds it difficult to speak Laura's name. He is certain she did not betray him with another man, who became jealous. He becomes even more convinced of this when Mrs. Sinclair informs him of the strange circumstances surrounding the death, two months earlier, of her daughter, Bethany.

Despite her surname, Mrs. Sinclair has never been married. A woman who taught herself to read and has a fine grasp of irony, she took her name from that of the bordello keeper in Richardson's *Clarissa*. "I wanted to be tainted by literary association," she informed him.

Mrs. Sinclair was born at the end of the last century in Bristol to Abraham and Adele Stein. Her father was a Russian-born rag merchant, who wandered the streets of his adopted city in search of goods he could re-sell from his small shop near the wharf. From infancy, Stella was a rebellious child. She had no interest in attending Temple; in fact, she did not consider herself a Jew. "I have always been a close observer of society, and I knew from an early age that to be a Jew is to be a victim. I never fancied being a scapegoat." Her orthodox parents, appalled by their only child's obduracy, were not greatly upset when she disappeared from home at the age of fourteen. They never saw her again and assumed correctly that Stella had gone to London and become a woman of the night. Unlike many of her confederates, she was a crafty person who saved her wages until, at the age of twenty-two, she was able to set up her own establishment in rooms which had begun as those of Mr. Russell, Upholsterer, and through time had become home to Boswell and Montez. "Mr. Boswell and Miss Montez appreciated the pleasures of the flesh," Mrs. Sinclair once commented, "and I carry on a noble tradition within these walls."

For many years, she enjoyed her hard-won status. She received clients in sumptuous surroundings, was pleasant to the girls who worked for her, paid them well, and, in general, reaped the rewards of what she had sown. "But, I later found out," she tells Julian, "death is the real wage of pleasure. My troubles began when I encountered Isaac Minsky, a merchant banker. I had long made it my policy not to mix business with pleasure. In fact, I had refrained from any sexual congress for almost fifteen years when I met him. Minsky was a gentleman of advanced middle age; I was touching thirty-five. At first, he would appear at my house once every three months, selecting a different girl on each occasion. In the third year of our acquaintance, he began to pay court to me, declaring that he came to my establishment only in the hope of seeing me. He flattered me by claiming that he preferred women of substance to mere girls. I succumbed to his charms and became his mistress. I refused his money, but he did provide me with a number of gifts, mainly brooches in which he inserted locks of his hair. Two years after I became his inamorata, I was with child. Isaac was pleased by this turn of events but, of course, there was no question of making the baby legitimate. Isaac was married and the father of four married daughters.

"I was thirty-seven when Bethany was born. From the start, she was very much her mother's daughter: headstrong, wilful, rebellious. Everything I did for her became a source of displeasure rather than comfort. I could never soothe her as infant, child, adolescent, or young woman. We were simply too much alike. Isaac took less and less pleasure in his daughter.

Perhaps in Bethany he saw magnified the flaws of my own character. My lover absented himself permanently from Half Moon Street, although an envelope containing fifty pounds appeared each year on Bethany's birthday.

"The child was a constant source of agitation and worry, but she did take to some of the girls here and allowed them to comfort her in a maternal way. My daughter remained with me until last August, the month she turned twenty. No longer could she stand the sight of a woman who exploited other women for profit. Useless were my observations that I paid my girls well, and that I never abused them or allowed clients to treat them discourteously. By this time, Bethany had become expert on the wrongs suffered by all women and by prostitutes in particular. Many of her criticisms were warranted, but the only profession I knew was bordello-keeping. That August, following a particularly heated exchange, Bethany vanished.

"I had no idea where she had gone — or how she was supporting herself. I wondered if she had asked succour of Isaac and wrote asking him if this was the case. Early the next morning, he appeared at my door. He had no idea where Bethany was; she had not contacted him. Immediately, he engaged a man called Skeffington, a person who specializes in what he calls "private inquiries." Nothing was heard from him for months. On the twelfth of March, a month ago today, a grease-stained, unkempt Mr. Skeffington appeared at my door. He had just been to see Isaac to convey to him the fruits of his search; 'Mr. Minsky has instructed me to give you a full account of all the particulars.' "

At this turning in the conversation, Mrs. Sinclair bursts into tears. "You must forgive me, Mr. Wilson," she says, struggling to control her weeping. "I find it almost impossible to continue and yet I have reached the part that is of utmost importance to you. Give me a few moments to collect myself." She dabs her eyes and cheek, looks herself over carefully in the mirror on her bureau and then continues: "Mr. Skeffington told me Bethany was no more. I asked him: 'You are telling me she is dead?' He nodded his head in agreement. I asked him to give me a full account as possible of what had happened to the poor creature. 'I shall be happy to comply, Madam, but my account is a woeful one.' I nodded for him to continue.

"'Through an intricate network of friends, acquaintances, associates, and, I must own up to it, criminal elements, I determined that the subject of my enquiry had removed herself to Blackheath, specifically, to Newsome Street, a squalid street of warehouses for a wide variety of importers. Some of these firms allow transients to live on their premises. In exchange for a rough-hewn bed, the residents provide a measure of safety for the contents of the buildings. An economical method of obtaining surveillance, I am sure you will agree?'

"I beseeched him to tell me more. 'Well, there is not much more to tell. Five days ago, I ascertained that my charge was living in a building owned by Mr. Chang, an importer of ivories from the Far East. I placed Miss Sinclair under surveillance for four days and, on instructions from her father, was to confront her on the fifth. At two in the afternoon, I had positioned myself in my usual place across the street from her abode. I was about to cross, when I noticed a young man, of eighteen years or thereabouts, approach that very door. He was dressed in bright blue corduroy, a blue peak cap and green boots. His hair was a mass of yellow curls. He knocked and was let into the dwelling. About an hour later, the door opened and the young man walked back in the direction from which he had come. I waited for some time and then crossed the street. When there was no response to my knocks, I became anxious since from my vantage point I could see all possible entrances and exits from the building. I waited about ten minutes, uncertain what step to take. At that point, spying a constable on the street, I approached him and asked for his assistance. Together, we broke down the door to the place where Miss Sinclair was staying.'

"'At first, we could see very little, so crowded was the room with crates. No one was in the front room or the one behind it. At the very back, we came across your daughter lying prone on a chaise lounge, an empty glass by her side. It was immediately apparent she had died only a little while before. There was no sign of a struggle of any kind. The constable set off on foot to summon help and shortly afterwards returned in the company of a physician, who, upon examining the body of the young lady, noticed a small puncture to the heart, obviously inflicted after the victim had been sedated.'

"Mr. Skeffington could provide me with no further information. Later, the police and the coroner concluded that the absence of any sign of struggle meant that my daughter must have known her assailant."

Mrs. Sinclair tells Julian her strange narrative only after he has related his. They are convinced that the same individual, the young man in blue, had killed Laura and Bethany. But who is he and why had he murdered them? What possible motive could he have? Had the two young women summoned him to their sides, and, if so, why? What possible connection could there be between the two victims, who were, as far as everyone knew, unconnected to each other?

On the day Julian encounters Mr. Home, the medium had been summoned to Half Moon Street by Mrs. Sinclair to discuss these sinister, troubling synchronisations.

Spirit babies, two unsolved murders, a bordello, a rediscovered Leonardo, and a motley assortment of strange characters with, so it would seem, little in common. This is a strange prologue. Furthermore, this true story — one centred on an anxiety-ridden medium — will be concerned with a dilettante artist, two rich widows, visitors from the spirit world, the poets Robert and Elizabeth Barrett Browning, the President of the United States, three cities, a grisly killer, and matters of love and redemption. In this account, there will be only necessary digressions, those that always prove real life is stranger than any fiction. Suspension of disbelief is required, for it includes strange congruencies, unlikely associations, murky circumstances, and dark footpaths; again, these are the stuff of real life — they are not literary contrivances.

Quite often in life as in books, heroism is foisted on reluctant shoulders. Although Daniel Home would never accept the distinction, such a designation would not be incorrectly bestowed upon him. At first encounter, though, he is a decidedly shabby, wasted-looking sort of fellow, a person to hurry by on the street. If one has had the misfortune to have been introduced to him, one cuts him on the next meeting. He is certainly not the kind of man accepted into a London club or invited to an important gathering. Yet in the London of 1855 he becomes a much sought-after personality who must perforce turn down many requests for his presence. In order to begin unravelling the meaning of the events already described, the early events in this strange character's life must be inspected closely.

⁓

CHAPTER TWO

A HEART ON A SLEEVE

A semblance of a human being. A poor approximation of a man. That is how Daniel Home conceives of himself. Some would say he is a chronic complainer. He is a man upon whom were bestowed enormous gifts. He has not exactly squandered that inheritance, but neither does he appreciate it. He has the gall to claim that his God-given talent is a burden. Yes, that is the substance of his lament. I was given a gift that made my life a misery, he tells himself on a daily basis.

Some of his detractors attribute his troubles to his abandonment by his parents. Since he was one of ten children, his childless Aunt Cook beseeched her sister to part with him when he had reached the age of four so that she and Mr. Cook could have a child of their own to raise.

Ever afterwards, he has a hazy memory of his early life in

Edinburgh with his parents and brothers and sisters. He recalls being one of many tiny mites squeezed into a small airless bedroom on the top floor of a tenement on a small lane leading off Princess Street. The faces of his parents and siblings elude him, but, he recalls distinctly the grease-stained wall-paper where he rested his head each night before going to sleep. On that surface was drawn or printed a rendition of a peony. The bloom was full, although just about to drop; he fantasized that it would, in a day or two, be deprived of its ruby red colouring. Of course, the flower always remained the same, and the child was amazed by its endurance against all the laws of nature.

He retains one other memory. The stairs on Brooke Lane were a tremendous obstacle, constructed at a dangerously steep angle. One day he advanced steadily out of the flat and then looked down into an abyss that seemed to reach into the centre of the earth. His mother, carrying two of the younger children in her arms, told him to move along smartly. He looked up at her, questioning her command, whereupon she scolded him, informing him that he was an obdurate child forever disputing her instructions. Overcome with fear at the dangerous feat he was about to attempt, Daniel stumbled and fell down ten or eleven steps, stoking the fury of his mother who accused him of having staged a scene in order to distract her from his siblings.

From the time Daniel was very small, he had an excellent memory for the names of birds and plants. This inclination of mind seemed to deeply offend his mother but entranced his aunt, who, when she decided to ask for one of her sister's offspring, expressed an interest in her sister's least favourite child. Mrs. Cook, seven years older than her sister, decided to take advantage of what she perceived an infirmity — more precisely, a lack of taste — on her sister's part.

Mrs. Cook was tall, thin and exceedingly bony, very much the embodiment of the Witch in the Grimm Brothers' tale of Hansel and Gretel. Mrs. Home, short, squat, bulbous-nosed, bore a striking resemblance to the same authors' description of the Stepmother who persuaded the Father to abandon his children. "Betty," Aunt informed her sister, "Daniel is precocious and in need of special attention." Mrs. Home *understood* her sister to say: "Daniel will always be a nuisance, so why not let me have him?" What Mrs. Cook *thought* was: "Daniel is a deeply intelligent child who, with careful management, will become a credit to Mr. Cook and myself."

At the age of five, Daniel moved with his aunt and uncle to nearby Aldgate Street. Since his father and uncle both worked as clerks in the same life assurance company, the funds available to his adopted parents were far greater than those enjoyed by the boy's parents, who still had eleven mouths to feed. Despite the austerity of her countenance, Mrs. Cook was never cruel, but she had little in the way of motherly instincts. She and her husband nurtured the small boy as best they could: he was clothed and fed well. Although the rooms rented by the Cooks were well heated, Daniel always felt cold there. At his new home, Daniel did not share a bedroom and, strangely, he missed the hustle and bustle that had once been a constant in his existence. He did not dare confess to his aunt that he was desperately afraid when he went to bed alone each night and, for a month or two, silently cried himself to sleep.

Being an only child became an impediment to Daniel rather than an advantage. Deprived of his brothers and sisters, an earlier propensity to be visited by morbid thoughts increased; such fantasies lingered more frequently and then eventually became everyday companions.

In those long-ago days, he did not encounter any of the creatures of the invisible world. But his daily activities were grim and unaccommodating: he rose early in the morning, walked by himself to school and endured the torments of boys of his own age, who saw in the awkward, self-conscious child a victim for their robust energies.

Daniel's only companion was Fitzroy, the tiny Italian greyhound who, before him, had been his aunt and uncle's only child. Fitzy, as Mrs. Cook called him, could not have been more than five pounds in weight, was pure grey (his pride-filled owners insisted he was a blue dog) and possessed the long, thin head of the larger members of his type. His soulful dark brown eyes were rimmed with black. Despite its melancholic countenance, the little fellow was lively and graceful, a ballet dancer in miniature. He never barked but would immediately pirouette around Daniel as if the boy's mere arrival was the greatest boon that could be offered him. When the boy returned home in an afternoon, Fitzroy was there. He snuggled close to the child's head when he went to bed and remained there, a sprite guarding his little master's dream world.

Two years after the boy had taken up residence with his aunt and uncle, they announced to him one evening that they had determined to emigrate to the United States, where the future held greater promise and opportunity. They would be sailing in two weeks' time. When the startled child enquired about Fitzroy, he was told the dog would, of course, accompany them. Daniel has little memory of the trip in the crowded and cramped third-class portion of the *Intrepid*. Although the crossing was relatively calm, his aunt and uncle were constantly sick. Daniel was a good traveller and ministered to them.

The only instance of bad weather occurred three days before they reached Boston. Daniel was strolling on the deck with Fitzroy, keeping him carefully protected inside his pea jacket when, of a sudden, the ship was buffeted by huge swells which threw the boy to the deck. In that instant, he let go of the dog, who was thrown overboard. Realizing that nothing could be done to save the unfortunate creature, the distraught child ran below to break the sorrowful news to his aunt and uncle. Though they sought to calm Daniel, he could discern that they might have preferred their other child to have been the one to meet such a sorry end.

Like many who arrived in the New World before him, Daniel was immediately taken with the plenitude of space. In Edinburgh, most streets were just wide enough for a vehicle to pass either way, with room between the curb-stone and the houses for a pedestrian. Nails often projected from the dwellings, and it was not uncommon for clothes to be torn. During the hot summer days, the streets of the poorer quarters would fill with people and the stench could be overwhelming. Layabouts crowded the doorsteps, nursing pipes and downing jugs of beer. Barefoot children played in the gutters, and, in short order, their hands and bodies would be besmeared with mud and even less desirable substances.

Such memories were largely erased by the world of Agawam, the small town in western Massachusetts where the Cooks settled. The houses — of wood rather than brick — may have been roughly the same size as those in Scotland, but they were separated from each other by large lots; the streets and avenues may not have been grand, but they were decidedly spacious.

At his new school, Daniel was a good student, although not an outstanding one. In truth, his studies consumed very little of his time. He had a propensity to daydream. He would lose himself in reveries while taking long walks in the country-side. On his wanderings to the woods and streams, he was often accompanied by Edwin. Like Daniel, Edwin was a cerebral youth, one who examined every strand of existence micro-scopically. He never tired of asking Daniel about Scotland, who, in turn, plied him with questions about New England. Edwin was of a delicate constitution. He could walk great distances but then would be overcome by fits of coughing. A great admirer of Wordsworth, he would recite passages of the poet's work when confronted by a sublime piece of landscape. Daniel supposed his companion a trifle histrionic, but the feelings Edwin expressed seemed genuine enough.

On reflection, it must be admitted, Edwin was decidedly morbid. One afternoon, his triangle-shaped face aglow with the deep crimson of the setting sun, he asked Daniel to make a pact with him. "I should like to think that death will not be a parting of the ways for us." Startled, Daniel nodded assent. "Let us promise," Edwin added, "that whichever of us dies first will appear to the other." Edwin often talked of the spirit world, but it was not a sphere to which Daniel's mind had yet turned. Convinced that they both had many years before them, Daniel agreed to the proposition.

Mr. Cook quickly prospered. He did sufficiently well at his new firm to summon his brother-in-law to assist him. No sooner had Daniel's parents arrived in the New World than the Great Atlantic Assurance transferred the Cooks to the northern part of New York State, to the Homeric-sounding town of Troy. Shortly afterwards, the Homes settled near them at Waterford.

At their parting, Edwin was distraught. When, in the presence of their families, they shook hands good-bye, Edwin embraced Daniel briefly and whispered: "Remember our promise!" Daniel saw the tears forming in his friend's eyes, but, having to get on with the business of making a new start, he paid them little heed.

Daniel's first days at Troy were uneventful. His new home, nestled in the woods, was larger than the one in Agawam, although in other ways nondescript. Three days after they arrived, the night sky was crowned by a brilliant full moon. After bidding goodnight to his aunt and uncle and retiring to his chamber, Daniel did not ready himself for bed. Instead, he looked at that resplendently plump moon through the uncurtained window.

Suddenly, he was enveloped in darkness so palpable that he felt he could grasp its substance. He moved his right hand before his face but could not see it. From the darkness came a voice: "The moon is shining still, but we are on the other side of darkness." Daniel recognized Edwin's voice but was too frightened to respond.

As quickly as it had disappeared, the moon's brightness was restored. At the foot of the bed stood Edwin in a cloud of great brightness. His features were unchanged except in luminosity, and the only difference in his appearance was the length of his hair which now fell in wavy ringlets upon his shoulders. Smiling, he slowly raised his right arm and traced three circles in the air. Then, his hand and arm slowly began to disappear. Finally, his whole body melted away.

Daniel lay on his bed in a state of complete paralysis. After what seemed an eternity but turned out to be little more than an hour, he rang the bell in his room. Mrs. Cook, woken from a sound sleep, was agitated: "What is it, child?" Summoning every fibre in his being, he told her: "I have seen Edwin; he died three days ago." His aunt was furious at such outlandish nonsense and informed him that he was reading too much verse of a morbid kind rather than turning his attention to the adventure stories suited to boys of his age. When, a day later, the letter informing them of Edwin's death by drowning arrived, she took the news without the least display of emotion. Not so Mrs. Home, when she was told the following day. The woeful look she gave her son spoke volumes, but she uttered not a word.

As is their wont, Daniel Home's doubters and adversaries have scrutinized and probed this event mercilessly. What kind of ghoulish young men would make such an eerie pact? Perhaps the two young men were half in love with death? Perhaps Daniel Home knew his friend intended to kill himself? Perhaps Home convinced his friend to take his life at a prearranged time? Reasonable enough speculations given the strange events in his life. Yet both youths were known to be strange creatures by their contemporaries, so, it can be argued, the two misfits formed a bond that unsurprisingly bore strange fruit.

Four years later, another series of startling events took place. A small stream marked the front of the Homes's land, the ground gently sloping from the front porch down to the water. Mrs. Home, crossing the bridge on the way home from town, spotted a bundle of clothing floating in the water that was swollen from the spring rains. As she made her way to the water's edge, Mrs. Home realized that the bundle of clothing was her daughter, Mary. The distraught mother lowered herself into the stream and pulled the child to the bank, only to discover that the five year old was stone cold. With the death of her youngest child, Mrs. Home withdrew into herself, unable to shed the sorrow that enveloped her.

A month later, an overwhelming sense that his mother wanted to see him seized Daniel, and he immediately set out on the twelve mile walk to the home of his parents. As soon as the Homes arrived in America, Daniel had noticed a marked difference in his mother. Gone were her anger and resentment toward him. Instead, she seemed to search his face, at times anxiously, as if looking for the confirmation of something. As mother and son, they had become easier with each other. "What have you to tell me?" he asked as soon as they were alone.

She looked at him intently and then smiled. "Daniel, I must make a confession." He replied that she need not do any such thing. "Child, I must. There is little time left, and you must understand." She paused and then informed him that her coldness to him as a child and her eagerness to part with him had not been done willingly. "I had to steel myself to those acts. Often, I was deliberately unkind to you in order to put a measure of distance between us."

She continued: "I agreed to let Sister have you as her child because I thought you might, if removed from me, be spared the suffering of second-sight." When a puzzled Daniel told her that he did not understand her, she continued: "To some people an unkind legacy is bestowed. They can see into the future. They can communicate with the dead. They behold things best closed-off to mere mortals." At this point she was engulfed in tears: "I am one of those unfortunates, have been ever since my twelfth year. So are you, my dear son. I fear that you have inherited this awful facility from me."

From the time he was a wee child, Daniel had shown a similar inclination. This propensity had frightened her, causing her to believe that separation from her might lighten Daniel's burden.

Daniel's phlegmatic exterior, carefully constructed not to betray any emotion, cracked. He too burst into tears. Now he knew the true reason why his mother had abandoned him. He told her that he cared not a whit for the supernatural. "Daniel, it matters not what you feel. You will soon learn that only a thin veil separates earthly and spiritual existences." His good fortune, she informed him, would be to take comfort from knowing a great many truths hidden from most mortals; his misfortune might be to live in the constant shadow of the supernatural.

"If your experience is at all like mine," she continued, "you will often curse *that* apparent godsend. I rue the day I first became aware of it. It has been a heavy burden." She then explained in considerable detail how she had often known that so-and-so — a cousin, an uncle, a friend — would meet a severe misfortune or die suddenly. Sometimes she knew things of joy but, mainly, she was privy to misfortune.

Edwin's strange appearance from the dead four years earlier had convinced her that she would eventually have to tell Daniel the truth. Now, she was forced to do so because she would be dead in exactly four months. "Pray, how could you know that?" the son, again on the verge of tears, asked. "My dear boy, Mary appeared to me last night to disclose the exact moment I am to join her in Eternity! She held four lilies in her hand, allowed them to slip through her fingers one after the other, till the last one had fallen, and declared: 'Then, you shall come to me.' I asked whether the lilies signified years, months, weeks or days? 'Months,' she answered. She also told me that I shall be quite alone when I die, that there will be no one near to close my eyes."

"You have a large family close to hand. This vision is a false one," Daniel assured her. "Oh, Mother, I am so delighted you have told me this because it shows that this must be an errant message, perhaps engineered by malignant forces." She shook her head in disbelief. When they parted, mother and son held firm to their contrary opinions. On the last day of the fourth month the apparently impossible prophecy was fulfilled.

That evening, at twilight, Daniel heard a voice near the head of his bed. When he turned, he saw by the window what appeared to be a bust of his mother. Agitated, he called out to his aunt. When Mrs. Cook arrived, he told her of his mother's sudden passing. She was nonplussed: "Nonsense, child, your brain is fevered!" When the truth was revealed the next day, his aunt held her tongue. That night, Daniel bit his pillow so no signs of his grief escaped his bedroom.

His most profound experience of the other world occurred at this time. One day, as he awoke from a nap, he was floating in an ocean of silvery light. Then, he could see his entire nervous system composed of thousands of electrical scintillations, which took the form of currents darting over his entire body. Although his extremities were less luminous, the finer membranes surrounding his brain glowed.

In the next instant he realized that a spirit-body was connected to his corporeal one, which he now saw lying motionless before him on the bed. Then a voice, majestic in its cadences, assured him: "Death is but a second birth, corresponding in every respect to the natural birth."

It now seemed to him that he was waking from a dream of darkness to one of light. The voice commanded him: "You will come with me, Daniel." For the first time he looked to see what sustained his body and found it was but a purple coloured cloud. Its movements wafted him upward until the Earth was a small globe far below. He wanted to see more, but the voice told him that he must leave: "Return to Earth, love your fellow creatures, esteem truth and in so doing you will serve the infinite God of love." He heard no more and sank into a swoon. When he awoke, his limbs were so numb that at least half an hour elapsed before he could reach the bell rope to bring anyone to his assistance.

The comfort her adopted son began to take from the services of the Wesleyans and, later, the Congregationalists, increased the friction between Daniel and Mrs. Cook. A devoted member of the Kirk of Scotland, she believed all other sects heathenish. Things came to an awful pass when Daniel's sleep was disturbed by sounds of bumping and banging which could be heard through the small house. At first, Daniel thought someone had secreted himself in his chamber. His aunt was convinced that Daniel himself was the cause of the noises. In her opinion, his attendance at the rival prayer meetings was upsetting his delicate constitution and causing him to ramble about in the dark, upsetting the concord of the entire household.

Daniel was about to seat himself at the breakfast table a few days later when his and his aunt's ears were assailed by loud rapping sounds with no visible cause. Mrs. Cook became enraged: "So, at long last, you've brought the Devil to my house, you ingrate!" A woman of violent temper, she rose and hurled her chair at him.

Things quickly went from bad to worse. Furniture now began to move itself about of its own volition. The first time this occurred Daniel was in his bedroom brushing his hair before the looking-glass. In the mirror he saw his chair move towards him. It stopped within a foot of him and, in terror, he jumped past it, rushed down the stairs, seized his hat in the hall and raced out of the house, all the time wondering what was happening.

Then furniture began to move when he was in the sitting room with his aunt and uncle. When the side table, a valuable one of Portuguese rosewood, was in danger of toppling, his aunt got up, fetched the family Bible and, with a flourish, placed it on the table: "There, that will drive the devils away!" But the table moved even more violently. Not a person to countenance any kind of rebellion, she placed her entire weight on the table. Immediately, she was lifted up with it from the floor and, as quickly, deposited back down there with a violent flourish. The table was unscathed, not so Mrs. Cook. That adventure ended Daniel's stay with the Cooks and began his life as a peripatetic spiritualist.

Daniel never undertook his profession by choice. He always refused money for communicating with the spirit world; in his estimation that would have been akin to sacrilege. No, his calling was thrust upon him by unknown forces and by the kind strangers who chose to give him refuge once he had been expelled from aunt's house. For Mrs. Cook, the rappings and noises had been proof of an alliance with Satan. For others, these phenomena pointed in another direction, indicating that there was a spirit world and that certain persons had ways into it. For every person who believes an action or a belief to be evil, he soon learned, there is an equal number who believe the opposite. During one of the rapping sessions, Daniel's mother spoke clearly to him, uttering a litany of apparent truisms: "Fear not, my child. God is with you, and who shall be against you? Seek to do good. Be truthful and truth-loving, and you will prosper. Yours is a glorious mission: you will convince the infidel, cure the sick, and console the weeping."

From pillar to post. That was Daniel's life in the ensuing few years. Once again, he lost touch with his father, brothers and sisters. Rich sympathizers in places such as Willimantic, Connecticut and Springfield, Massachusetts would take the young man in for brief, sometimes extended, periods of time. These persons would give him the run of their homes, provide him with meals and buy his clothes. In turn, he performed at meetings, providing the spirits of the dead the opportunity to communicate with their living brethren.

A newspaper account in the *Hartford Courant* of March 1851 provided an eyewitness account:

> *At the medium's request, the large table at which the audience was seated was moved repeatedly and in the direction that we requested. All in the circle, the Medium included, had their hands flat upon the table, and we looked several times under the table while it was in the most rapid motion and saw that no legs or feet had any agency in the movement. At one time, too, the table was moved without the Medium's hands or feet touching it at all!*

Daniel, a mere eighteen, shrank from the notoriety that was growing around him. He was dismally aware that he lacked the slightest power over the spirit forces: to bring them on, to send them away, to increase them or to lessen them. I am merely a conduit, he told himself, a lightning rod through which the great electricity of the spirit world speaks to mortal men.

Forced to sing for his supper, Daniel recognized that he was valued only for what he could do. When he read of P.T.

Barnum's elaborate promotion (some said, prostitution) of Jenny Lind, he knew that, like the Swedish soprano, he was esteemed simply as an entertainer. Unable to imagine himself as a person of any value in his own right, he conceived of himself as a mere showman.

Realizing he had to find a profession to sustain himself, Daniel thought of becoming a physician and made enquiries at Harvard Medical School in Cambridge, Massachusetts. The learned gentlemen of that establishment were at first sceptical of his application and told him that they held serious reservations about a person of his propensities. They wrote back: would he be willing to subject himself to their scientific scrutiny? They were startled when he readily acquiesced and presented himself at the school the following month.

One witness to these events, Professor Beale, left a detailed record of the ensuing séance:

A favourite little daughter, not long deceased, of one of the gentlemen present, a stranger from Virginia, announced her presence by a thick pattering rain of eager and joyful little raps; and in answer to the silent request of her father, she laid her baby hand upon his forehead! This was a man, like myself, who was not a believer in spiritual manifestations — he had never before experienced them, but he could not mistake the thrilling feeling of that touch.

Suddenly, and without any expectation on the part of the company, Mr. Home was taken up in the air! I had hold of his hand at the time, and I and others felt his feet: they were lifted a foot from the floor! He palpitated from head to foot apparently with the contending emotions of joy and fear which, I am told, habitually choke all his utterances. Again and again he was taken from the floor, and the third time he was carried to the lofty ceiling of the apartment, his outstretched hand gently grazing the plaster.

Towards the end of the proceedings in that bright room, a hand manifested itself and shook hands with each of us present. I examined the limb closely, grasping it carefully. It was tolerably well constructed and anatomically correct. The skin was soft and slightly warm. THIS HAND ENDED AT THE WRIST.

In our opinion, Mr. Home exerts some control over protoplasm and his ability to manipulate these particles by a form of telepathy is astounding. We are convinced, after perusing the works of Mesmer, that he does not employ any form of mass hypnosis.

After the demonstration, Professor Beale and his associates informed Daniel that they had as much to learn from him as he could possibly learn from them. A place was offered. Daniel would have pursued this path except that winter was exceptionally severe. Daniel became seriously ill and was diagnosed with a tubercular-like condition of the left lung; he was advised to quit America for the milder climate of his native land. So Daniel's nine year sojourn in the New World came to an end when he boarded the *Africa* at Boston on February 23, 1855.

That afternoon, he stood on the deck, broken in health,

watching the coast vanish from view. A sense of utter loneliness crept over Daniel, until his heart seemed too heavy to bear up against its weight. He sought his cabin, prayed to God to vouchsafe him one ray of hope and, a few moments later, felt a surge of joy course through him. That happiness was to be short lived.

CHAPTER THREE

~⌐

HEARTFELT CONFIDENCES

*D*aniel did not have to be concerned about finding a place to live in London. In fact he was provided lodging and food gratis by Mr. William Cox, the proprietor of the hotel that bears his name at 55 Jermyn Street. Even before he set sail, Daniel read of his new home in the pages of *Pendennis*. Mr. Thackeray's hero, Major Pendennis, lived at the very same establishment, which had not changed since the publication of the novel five years before.

Daniel could not have asked for a more magnificent spot. The street lies between St James's Street, the vista of which ends at the Palace, and Lower Regent Street, which concludes in Waterloo Place. Here, he can behold the towering plinth which bears the imposing statue of the Duke of York, and the Athenaeum Club, over whose portico stands the great, gilded rendition of Athena.

Mr. Cox, who, although he has considerable interest in the spiritual life, lavishes all the care he can bestow on the material one. Upon entering the foyer that first afternoon Daniel confronted a tall, dark, heavily carved walnut sideboard depicting scenes from *Robinson Crusoe*, Mr. Cox's favourite book. The proprietor confided to Daniel that he admired that narrative for its depiction of the hero's inner life and not for its portrayal of an exotic locale. He bowed when Daniel applauded his critical aptitude.

The other pieces in the entry room were of the previous century. Mr. Cox was gratified when Daniel took especial notice of the Italian desk or, as the English prefer, bureau. Its swelling, curvaceous lines, reminiscent of the baroque manner as practised on the continent, makes it an item of great beauty.

The appointments in Daniel's quarters, a sitting room opening on to a tiny bedroom, are of a similar exalted calibre. During his time in America, Daniel has become accustomed in the homes of the rich to some marvellous specimens of cabinet making. In his new abode, he is surrounded by masterpieces: a small George II yew wood dresser with three small drawers decorated with a deep arcaded frieze; a Hepplewhite rosewood shield-back chair; his four-poster bed is of the Regent's time; fluted columns, foliate edges, and stars made from fruitwood and parcel gilt adorn the wood.

Daniel is not a person who requires luxury. In fact, he is well aware he cannot afford it. One of the benefits of being in the service of the well-to-do has been to be surrounded by some magnificent artifacts. In such circumstances — his enemies would insert the adjective, pampered — he has acquired a good eye, although he lacks the means to acquire such treasures, and he is unschooled in the art of connoisseurship.

~§~

Even during his brief encounter with Julian Wilson, Daniel hopes to have encountered a kindred spirit. Two days later they chance upon each other at White's, where Daniel is awaiting his host. The two young men exchange warm smiles. Assuming correctly that he knew something from Mrs. Sinclair of Laura's mysterious death, Julian asks the medium if it is possible to get in touch with a beloved one beyond, as he puts it, the veil?

"Of death?" Daniel asks in his annoying, scratchy voice. Julian nods yes, whereupon the medium informs him that this might be a possibility but that in his experience no guarantee could ever be proffered. Julian presses him.

Daniel's reply is automatic, one repeated many times before. "Although I seem to possess some propensity to have spirits appear when I am present at meetings designed for such a purpose, I have absolutely no control over such events. I cannot summon the spirits."

"So I might attend one of your séances to no avail if I wished to communicate with my beloved?"

"I was sorry to hear of your loss when Mrs. Sinclair alluded to it," Daniel responds. "But you are correct. I can give you no assurance that your loved one will make herself known at one of my meetings."

Julian doesn't know what madness pushes him forward, but he confesses to this awkward young man that he does not know if he can go on living without Laura.

Daniel searches his eyes intently before responding: "Yes, I can see the depth of your suffering. I am not sure I would recommend any spiritualist, myself included. Have you read Tennyson's *In Memoriam*, his poem about the death of his friend, Hallam? Since my mother died, no piece of literature has given me such comfort. In those verses, you feel the efforts of Hallam's spirit to reach out to his dead friend." Julian recalls some of the poet's words that chilled him to the bone: "Dark house, by which once more I stand/Here in the long unlovely street. . . . A hand that can be clasped no more."

Abruptly, he asks about the young man outfitted in blue. Who is he? Daniel looks him up and down before confessing his ignorance. "He is a sinister figure — one born in hell-fire. I know nothing of such persons." Just then, as Daniel's host walks in his direction, Julian takes his leave.

Outwardly, Daniel and Julian are opposites. Inwardly, they are subject to the vagaries of their highly-strung sensibilities. Julian is more adept at concealing his vulnerabilities, or so he thinks.

Many are called, few are chosen. So the Gospel informs us. But what about the chosen few who reject the calling? Are they cast into the darkness, an unredeemed and undeserving lot? What about the artist, wounded by a bad press, bored by his profession, and suffering from a broken heart, who breaks from the pack?

From childhood, Julian has been told by his mother that everything comes too easily to him. He was, as she puts it, a natural for the artistic vocation. "From the time you were a tiny boy, you always had a pencil in your hand and a sketch-book close at hand. No one ever really taught you to draw or paint. If these things had come with difficulty, you now would be more grateful for them."

Perhaps there is a germ of truth in what she claims. In 1840, just after his family had moved from Birmingham to Manchester, Cynthia Wilson took Julian, a boy of seven, to London to present him to Sir George Markham, the president of the Royal Academy. At the outset of the interview, that grand gentleman, costumed and wigged in the manner of Sir Joshua Reynolds, his predecessor in the previous century, informed the pair that the purpose of their visit was risible. "Make such a young boy into a painter! Better make him a chimney-sweep than an artist! He will earn more money and be a greater credit to your family."

As was her wont, Cynthia Wilson insisted Markham look at her boy's drawings. Unable to extricate himself from the interview, the elderly artist sneered, adjusted his pince-nez and brusquely seized the portfolio from underneath the child's thin arm. As he inspected the drawings, Sir George gasped once or twice. Abruptly, he put them aside and then stared at Julian and his parent for a minute or two, as if contemplating in what direction to turn the conversation. Finally, he addressed Mrs. Wilson: "You must fit the boy for his chosen profession. As a parent, you must make certain he follows the path ordained for him by Nature." He suggested the boy attend at a preparatory school at Bloomsbury and, after a few years, transfer to the Royal Academy Schools.

✧

In his first years in London, Julian attended the National Gallery in his leisure moments. In fact, he soon decided to create his own National Gallery and painted miniature landscapes in the manner of Hoppner, Ruysdael, Turner, and mythological scenes after Titian, Rubens, Veronese, Correggio and Rembrandt. For each, he made frames out of tinsel; he then varnished each of his specimens to give them the appearance of works in oil.

Julian had a rebellious turn of mind and, when the artistic facility seemed merely a constituent part of himself, he became quickly bored with it. He may have lacked inspiration, but he was filled with hubris. He could copy anything he beheld and, in most instances, could produce excellent versions of what he saw; often, he simply perfected the inspiration he derived from others.

Julian saw himself as a mere copyist, someone who could, in an almost other-worldly manner, imitate others. Bored, indifferent, and, in pursuit of novelty, he stumbled upon the Pre-Raphaelite Brotherhood, of which he became an enthusiastic member.

This strange confederation of Holman Hunt, Millais, Dante Gabriel Rossetti, and Julian Wilson soon became notorious. One of the few critics favourable to the group wrote about Julian's involvement in the Brotherhood: "Wilson sees with a crystalline clearness into those parts of Nature that make a perpetual and brilliant appeal; he has a hand that, even in childhood, was singularly skilful to record the impressions of the eye. His hand has been severely trained by the prescribed academic methods. He is the perfect artist to render in a minutely elaborate manner the spiritual world of the Brotherhood."

Perfect artist; perfect copyist. Julian did not possess the convictions of his confederates that the artist must look through Nature to Nature's God. He did not believe that art must have a great and abiding purpose. He held no strong conviction that by rendering the world in a heightened manner that he could replicate God's divine love that led to the creation of the world and of man. Always attracted to strong, bright colours, to accuracy of detail and to theatrical effects, he was, as it were, a natural Pre-Raphaelite.

He also became a devoted reader of Keats, the group's literary mentor. Julian was also partial to working out of doors and was early renowned for his painstaking rendition of individual details, say, in a face or a dress. He also became a proponent of the use of flat expanses of bright colour and an advocate of the luminosity achieved by employing a wet white ground.

He had little understanding of the reason for the group's name, which implied that only painting done before Raphael was of any value. The designation also intimated that the quattrocento, considered by many the highest achievement in European painting, could be surpassed. The name made the group sitting targets, as Julian soon discovered to his considerable cost.

Although London bohemia was saturated with tobacco, spirits and all manner of oaths, he, like the other members of the Pre-Raphaelite Brotherhood, neither smoke, drank, nor swore. Despite such virtuous behaviour, Julian's mother was perturbed by his new friends and their new creed. She feared lest Julian become mad like poor Richard Dadd, the colourist, who, after suffering sun stroke while visiting Cairo and the Pyramids in 1842, was prone to visions so disturbing that he murdered his father in Cobham Wood, leaving the victim's body, stabbed through to the heart, where it had fallen and escaping to France. Brought home, Dadd was pronounced a criminal lunatic, relegated to Bedlam and, after, to Broadmoor. "Julian, you must protect yourself from mania of the spiritual kind," Mrs. Wilson warned her son. He nodded his head in agreement, not having the heart to tell her he had absolutely no religious convictions.

Julian might have continued as a member of the Brotherhood but for the storm of abuse he endured on displaying his first painting in that manner, a scene from the hidden life of Jesus, at the summer exhibition of the Royal Academy in 1852. He was nineteen-years-old, had shown great promise since early childhood and was just about to reap the benefits. Although the painting sold quickly, almost immediate was the condemnation of all the critics, especially those of a literary persuasion. The novelist Thackeray was unstinting in his condemnation: "Mr. Wilson, who in his picture represents the holy family of Joseph, Mary and Jesus in the interior of a carpenter's shop, has been most successful in rendering his subjects in the most undignified manner. This work is a pictorial blasphemy. In this instance, the imaginative talents of Mr. Wilson have been perverted in the service of an eccentricity both lamentable and revolting. The composition looks as if it had passed through a mangle." Mr. Dickens was even nastier: "Such a collection of splay feet, puffed joints and mis-shapen limbs was assuredly never before made within so small a compass. We have great difficulty in believing a report that this unpleasing and atrociously affected picture has found a purchaser. This work inspires laughter rather than disgust."

Julian Wilson could not stomach such critical savagery, and he began to feel he deserved the censure. "I am a fake and have been uncovered," he told himself. He voiced such sentiments to himself on a daily basis. Having absolutely lost faith in what he was rendering on canvas, Julian suffered such a complete crisis of confidence that he decided to abandon the making of art for the selling of it.

In his young life, he had met everyone of power in that world, especially the collectors who, like coxcombs lusting after whores, are constantly on the lookout for additions to their holdings. So he became a coadjutor to these persons, a middle-man between those who wished to sell high and those who insisted on buying low. His mother was aghast. In her some-what narrow view of the world, the life of the artist might be a genuine calling, but the person who traded in such commodi-ties pushed himself to the precipice of social acceptability. In her eyes, her son became something of a renegade.

To Julian, his new profession seemed simple enough. He acted primarily as a go-between in a transaction between two principles, one of great, newly-made wealth and one of impoverished but noble circumstances. For a carefully negoti-ated amount he would arrange for a Watteau that had been sitting in a noble home in Lincolnshire for a hundred years to suddenly appear in the sitting room of a newly built villa in Chiswick. His aristocratic clients would be spared the embarrassment of having to approach Mr. Christie or Mr. Sotheby, and the purchasers would obtain an object of considerable value at or below the customary London prices.

Some of his clients Julian found troublesome. Mrs. Osborne, the widow of the teaman, asked him to call upon her. A spare, angular woman of fabulous wealth, she lived, improbably, in rented rooms above a greengrocer in Highgate, near the Egyptian cemetery. She herself greeted him at the door and accompanied him up the stairs to her rooms. Her maid was away that day, she explained, and, in any event, she did not mind doing things for herself. Costumed in a blue frock washed so many times that its colours were almost depleted, Mrs. Osborne ushered him into her sitting room, which was filled to bursting with all manner of silver objects — tankards, beer pitchers, ice buckets, tea and coffee sets and ewers. The glare from these objects was so bright that it took Julian a while to notice that the carpets were threadbare and the stuffed furniture in a bad state of decay.

Seeing that he was bedazzled by the silver, she laughed: "These are my children. They are also my wealth. You cannot have enough pure silver. More attractive than gold bars, don't you think?"

Julian felt a wave of irritation. He did not deal in decorative objects, so the long, dusty trip to Highgate had been a waste of time. Before he could say anything, Mrs. Osborne, turned her small ferocious eyes on him: "I am anxious to acquire more offspring and to do so, without breaking into my capital, I must sell something Osborne left me." With that assurance, she walked out of the room and returned a few moments later with a tiny landscape. The framed canvas was small — five by seven inches — but in its minute details every portion of the genius of Leonardo, its creator, lived and breathed. The deep purples, tender mauves and rich lavenders of the sky competed with, and eventually overwhelmed, the bright greens of the grass and nearby hill.

So overcome was Julian by the gentle sadness of the landscape that he was startled when the widow asked him, "Will you sell this for me? It is a small object, but, I am certain, a valuable one. Osborne admired the pastoral; I abominate it." When Julian assured her that he could easily obtain two or three thousand pounds for the painting, she asked him to dispose of it immediately.

Julian had to be on the lookout for fakes, of course, and, on more than one occasion, he had to break the bad news to Lord X or the Earl of B that his much-esteemed Rubens or Correggio was not, as he would delicately put it, as authentic as he would like. He spared all manners of buyers and sellers considerable embarrassment and, in the process, became a wealthy man within a few years.

His most difficult disclosure of inauthenticity occurred at the Twickenham estate of the Earl of Langdon. That old gentleman, nearing the end of his life, was anxious to sell a Michelangelo Madonna in order to assure the financial stability of his much younger wife. The Earl, a man of great height bowed down by a wasting disease, received Julian with great cordiality.

"I am delighted that Mr. Sanders wishes to acquire my

Michelangelo. I am sure he will give it an excellent home."

"Of that you can be assured. He is a dedicated collector."

"Yes, I know that. Will he treasure the picture, esteem it as I have?"

"I hope so. He is very keen to have it."

"Yes, but there is a difference between the pride of ownership and the love of an object. The acquisition of an object can merely be a token of advancement in society whereas these inanimate things, either because of the care that has gone into the making of them or because of what they show us of existence, are worthy of veneration."

The two men had reached the long gallery and were now standing beneath the huge canvas they had been discussing. The Earl nodded in its direction. He waited patiently while Julian carefully examined the painting. The colouring was magnificent, the rendition of the drapery exquisite, the heads of mother and child splendid in their humanity. The Madonna eyed Julian, as if he was the one up for inspection. She was a woman of quiet, assured magnificence. Yet Julian knew immediately, splendid though she and her infant were, the painting was not by the master to whom it was attributed. The colours were wrong, the countenances not sufficiently monumental. Julian was on the verge of informing the Earl of his conclusion when Lady Rhonda joined them.

She walked over to her husband and grasped his arm tenderly. She then offered her hand to Julian. He had heard of her beauty but had never beheld her in the flesh. She is a superb creature, he immediately decided, her soft cream-coloureded skin and its roseate hue competes with the Madonna.

Before her spouse could speak, she asked: "You think the picture is a fake? Or a misattribution?"

She had read his expression perfectly. "Exactly. It is a wonderful quattrocento piece but not from the hand of Michelangelo."

If she was disconcerted, Lady Rhonda did not betray that emotion. Laughing softly, she turned to her husband. "I have always liked that picture. If it is not of great value, we may continue to enjoy it."

Her husband was not so philosophical. "I wanted funds to take care of you . . ." He paused: "After I am gone."

"But, dearest, you have always taken excellent care of me." With that, she bowed in Julian's direction and walked silently down the corridor. The Earl, obviously unsettled, attempted to conceal the extent of his dismay. He invited the young man to take tea and, during that ceremony, not a further word was exchanged about the Madonna.

Exactly a week after their meeting at Mrs. Sinclair's, Julian receives a missive from Daniel Home asking if he would visit with him in his room at Cox's. A surprised Julian agrees and calls at the hotel at the appointed time.

Julian has never visited Cox's and is impressed by its lavish furniture and paintings. He waits cannily for his new acquaintance to broach the reason for the invitation. At first, Daniel is reticent, but he then begins to speak with some ease, although the nasal twang of his accent and the irregularities in his vocal chords distract his listener. Soon, the narrative absorbs Julian's attention.

"One of the disadvantages that I have suffered throughout my existence is a readiness," Daniel begins, "to believe the best of others. Mr. Cox was incredibly kind to the young man thrown up on his shore. I made the same assumption about elderly Lord Brougham, the former Lord Chancellor. I had heard that, as Attorney General, he had defended Caroline, Princess of Wales, against her husband's attempts to disown and divorce her.

"The talk about Brougham was that he was an enthusiast for all kinds of information, that he applied the power of a mathematical intellect to all manner of phenomena. When he asked, three weeks ago, to attend one of my séances, he led me to believe that his mind was perfectly open to discovering the phenomena over which I exerted some control. Never an enemy of healthy scepticism, I welcomed him warmly.

"Two hours before the agreed time last week, I received a message from Brougham asking if he might bring along Sir David Brewster, the inventor of the kaleidoscope. The two arrived early for the afternoon appointment. I had been awake most of the night with a cough, but I dressed myself quickly and received both downstairs. Brougham, a cadaverous, extremely formal gentleman of the old school, introduced me to Brewster, a diminutive, tetchy individual of seventy who spoke in a clipped, affected way. Brougham's smile seemed genuine; Brewster did not attempt the least display of cordiality.

"The three of us, accompanied by Mr. Cox, made our way back to my room, where I asked if they wished to search for concealed machinery. They declined. Brewster sat at my left, Cox on my right and Brougham opposite me at the small

Sheraton mahogany drum table. Some tables of this kind, Brewster pointed out to Brougham, have been known to contain false drawers in the frieze running below the edge. Mr. Cox quickly assured him that these were functional and pulled them out one by one to prove that they were empty except for the tulipwood that lined the insides. Brewster nodded his head sagely.

"We sat for half an hour in total silence when, of a sudden, I felt my mouth fill with blood. I was without a handkerchief and rushed to my bedroom where I found one and expectorated. The discharge was from my troublesome lung. After an absence of perhaps three minutes, I resumed my place at the table. Brewster suggested that we move to the larger table, a Dutch oyster-veneered walnut, near the window. Rather than relate myself what happened next, I can read you from the letter, recently published in the *Times*, that Brougham wrote to his daughter the following day.

"Immediately after we sat at the second table, it began to shudder, the vibrations travelling up our arms. We heard rapping, and the heavy table, complete with its spiral-turned legs, stretchers and bun feet, rose from the ground with no hand guiding it. When we moved back to the card table, it exhibited similar movements. A small accordion, which Home had asked Sir David to hold, wheezed out a single note, but it would not play. A small hand bell was then placed on the Turkey carpet, and it actually rang though nothing visible touched it. Then the bell, placed on its side and still upon the carpet, leapt into my hand. These were the principal experiments, or amusements, of the afternoon.

"We could give no explanation of these phenomena and could not conjecture how they could be produced by any kind of mechanism. Hands were seen and touched; these hands grasped each other and then seemed to melt into air. But, though neither of us can explain what we saw, the evidence before our eyes suggests that the spirits of the dead are able, under certain circumstances, to materialize by manipulating protoplasm — the essential material that constitutes the living part of cells — in order to make contact with the living. That would explain how a bell could be rung or a hand materialize from thin air.'"

Daniel ceases reading. "Lord Brougham was obviously discomfited by what he had witnessed, although he said little. On the other hand, Sir David's terse statements gave way to gasps of astonishment. When he and Brougham took their leave, Brewster declared to me, 'Sir, this upsets the philosophy of fifty years!'

"Sir David attended two further séances. At the last of these, he and Adolphus Trollope, the brother of the novelist Anthony, dropped to their knees and crawled under the large mahogany table when it was elevated, measuring its distance from the floor to be about five inches. Adolphus asked his coadjutor: 'Does it not seem that this table is raised by some means wholly inexplicable?' The answer was immediate: 'Indeed it would seem so.'

"After that event, Mrs. Trollope, Adolphus's mother, a formidable woman unkindly referred to by some as 'Old Madam Vinegar,' clasped my hand, telling me that the séance had given her a pillow for her old age. Sir David declared that although he was not about to recant his scorn for spiritualism, he would never venture to abuse it again publicly.

"Three days ago, in contradistinction to Lord Brougham, he wrote a letter to *The Morning Advertizer* declaring that he had witnessed nothing remarkable. He labelled all my exhibitions, as he called them, farcical and said he had refrained from saying a harsh word at the last meeting in deference to the feelings of a talented woman who had been present.

"In his letter, Brewster concentrates on the events he had witnessed in my rooms. 'There were rappings in abundance, the table actually rose, as it appeared to me, from the floor. This result I do not pretend to explain, but rather than believe that spirits made the noise, I will conjecture the raps were produced by Mr. Home's toes.' He condemns me for retiring when my mouth filled with blood: 'Mr. Home left the room for several minutes, probably to equip himself for the feats which were to be performed by the spirits beneath the large round table that was copiously draped and beneath which no one was allowed to look.' Mr. Cox graciously replied the next day: 'I assert that no hindrance existed to Sir David's looking under the drapery of the table; on the contrary, he was frequently invited to do so by Mr. Home.'"

Quickly Daniel's emotions get the better of him. "I have frequently felt like reminding my detractors of the words of the Saviour: 'Let those who have eyes see, let those who have ears hear.' Sir David clearly demonstrates such an admonition would fall on stony ground. I have invited all sceptics to use their eyes and ears and yet, having done so, they still attack me with the full force of what they call reason.

"Some consider me a creature of such a delicate, fine-tuned propensity of mind that I have put myself beyond the range of normal feelings. Nothing can be further from the truth. I suffer greatly from being labelled a charlatan. I am not a robust man, but I am capable of rage, especially when ridiculed publicly. Sir David Brewster's conduct has mortified me, causing me enormous pain."

His tone turns pleading. "Surely, you can see how the report in the *Advertizer* astounded me. I am used to betrayal but not on such terms!" He sucks in his breath and looks Julian directly in the eye. "Your business is to uncover fakes. I wonder: do you think me one?"

Julian blushes, uncertain of what he really thinks. Home's sincerity is hard to doubt. He sidesteps the question, requesting permission to attend Daniel's next séance. He means to leave the matter there, but the candour of the medium is so affecting that Julian begins to unburden himself.

"I reached my twentieth year in 1853. Rare for a man of my age, I had already thrown over one career in pursuit of another. To my chagrin and considerable surprise, I had become a wealthy man. My life seemed on a settled course when I met Laura Bennett, whose father had contacted me in pursuit of a Rembrandt. He wanted to purchase a Biblical scene, any Biblical scene, by the Dutch master. As it turned out, I knew of a small *Susanna Amongst the Elders* that the Duke of Cumberland wished to part with.

"I brought the small canvas with me to the Bennett estate just outside London. Mr. Bennett, a brusque, self-important man who had made a fortune in the Portuguese sherry trade, was pleased with the painting which he intended to place in the entrance way of his home. I was on the verge of warning him that this would not be the best place for such a fragile oil when his daughter, Laura, joined us. She gave her father an affectionate kiss — much warmer than he deserved — and then shook my hand.

"Laura's father had perfunctorily inspected his acquisition; she surveyed it closely, commenting on the costumes, the rendition of the well, and, even, I was surprised, the ample, beautiful flesh of Susanna herself. 'No wonder she was such an object of desire and curiosity,' she observed. Mr. Bennett informed her that this was an unseemly observation coming from anyone, let alone a young woman. 'But, father, I am merely using my eyes and commenting on the beauty of the picture you have just purchased through Mr. Wilson's kind agency.' Her father told her that she must learn to hold her tongue.

"Having obviously determined to say nothing further on the dangerous subject, she inquired if I had been invited to take tea. Mr. Bennett intervened: no such invitation had been extended because he had business later that evening in the City and must soon be on his way. She then offered to attend to me if I wished to stay.

"As we sat together that first afternoon, I first took note of the ringlets of strawberry red hair that covered her head and dropped down over her shoulders. Then the beauty of her sapphire-coloured eyes gained my attention, followed by the perfection of her bow-shaped lips. Her complexion, her bosom, her liveliness of movement, each gained ascendancy but, in turn, each was vanquished by yet another weapon in her arsenal. Not least of her accomplishments was her learning. Although she had never attended school, she was an avid and intelligent reader. Within ten minutes, I was hopelessly in love.

"Here I was, a youth of twenty, who had very little experience of the world or of women, although I had attended houses of pleasure in Mayfair since the age of sixteen. That day, I knew I had met my match because lovemaking had been heretofore a merely physical act of little consequence. When Cupid's arrow wounded me, I was devastated.

"Strongly desiring to see Miss Bennett again, I asked if I could call upon her when she was next in London. She told me she would be delighted if I would do so and expected to be at her family's Mayfair residence within the fortnight.

"That was the beginning of my pursuit of Laura. She always seemed to be fleeing from me, even as she readily granted me her time. There was always something unreachable and remote about her and, in a vain attempt to subdue her, I unthinkingly employed the best weapon I had in my reserve. First, I asked if I could sketch her. When that privilege was granted, I pleaded that she sit for a portrait. After the first was complete, I zpersuaded her to model for another and then yet more. She always acquiesced to my requests, sometimes with a wry smile. Without realizing what I was doing, I began to devote all my time to drawings and oils for which Laura served as my model: Laura as Aphrodite, Laura as a shepherdess, Laura as the Old Testament's Judith. I gave up my second career and resumed my first. The renditions of Laura, done in a naturalistic style which owed little to the Brotherhood of a few years before, made me celebrated. The critics commented on the freshness of design in my compositions, on the perfect rendition of drapery and costume, of the exquisite flesh tones of the young woman who was the subject of my compositions. I insisted in rendering her again and again because I could never fully capture her beauty on paper or canvas. For the first time in my life, I had found a subject which eluded me and thus spurred me on to do my best work. I was constantly dissatisfied with the results, yet I was doing the finest work of which I was capable.

"I was a new man, transfigured by love. But my beloved did not return my affection as I hoped. She began to complain of her role as model. I saw her, she lamented, as a commodity. She accused me of being cast from the same mold as her father. Men, she informed me, only wished to manipulate women to their own ends. Her father wanted her to marry into the aristocracy and thus further ennoble the Bennett family; I was simply using her as a means to renew my artistic career. I told her the truth: I was a man metamorphosed by an enchantress, but she rejected this claim, observing: 'My own experience of life, limited as it may be, convinces me that men have nothing but ill will towards the female.'

"I could not dissuade Laura from her conviction about the malignity of men. To prove my devotion, I asked her to marry me. She agreed, perhaps in anticipation of her father's disapproval. Shortly after our betrothal, she retired to the countryside, where she was, as you know, murdered. Once again, I stopped working as a painter and resumed my career as a coadjutor to collectors."

Daniel's eyes are moist as his friend's narrative comes to a conclusion. "You tried to rid her mind of her fear of men and then she was murdered by one?" Julian nods his head in agreement.

Julian next encounters Daniel Home three months later at the Rymers. July 23, 1855 is the evening of the great debacle, although Julian does not know at the time that the events he is about to witness will prove so controversial.

The Green at Ealing, where the villa of the *nouveau riche* Rymers is located, is a rectangle of lawn surrounded by trees. The newly built houses share common features: wrought iron balconies, round-headed windows, massive front door steps and fanlights. The neighbouring premises consist of the better sort of milliners, confectioners, and boot-makers. There is even an academy for young ladies nearby. The homes and shops, monuments to refined prosperity, are served by the Great Western Railway which runs a line to Ealing from Paddington. Mr. Rymer, a solicitor who practises at Whitehall and in Chancery Lane, returns home each evening to a large household: his wife, four sons, three daughters, a governess, a cook and three housemaids.

Although not as adept in the spiritual world as the merchant princes Daniel Home had known in the New World, the Rymers are keen to enter fully into that sphere because one of their sons, Watt, had died at the age of thirteen four years earlier. It was first on the evening of May 8, 1855 that the grateful parents once again communicated with their child. The accordion played "Home Sweet Home," and the shadow of a hand hovered over the large dining table at which fourteen people sat; the hand wrote a brief note — *Dear Papa, I have done my very best* — which, when compared to a sample of Watt's writing, was declared by a graphologist to be identical in every respect.

Julian's carriage deposits him at seven on that hot, sticky summer night and, just as he is making his way to the front door of the villa, he hears sounds of great merriment. Home, pursued by three of the Rymer children, appears, galloping in his direction. Surprised, Home halts suddenly as do the children behind him.

Absent from his acquaintance's face is all the weariness Julian had witnessed in London. For the nonce, he is simply a tall, pale, somewhat stooped young man enjoying himself. Daniel asks if Julian knows the children, but they interrupt in a chorus that they have known Mr. Wilson for an exceedingly long time. At that point, Daniel bends down and lavishes each with a brief kiss.

Julian can still hear the annoying falsetto in Daniel's voice as he inquires of the children where "Papa" and "Mama" are, a strange usage he thinks for a guest to bestow on his hosts. At that moment, Mrs. Rymer steps out the door, whereupon Home presents her with a clematis wreath which he and the children have woven. Delighted with the gift but distracted by the guests she is about to receive, Mrs. Rymer hands it to one of the serving girls.

Julian occupies the next hour in the small sitting room on the main floor talking with Bendigo Rymer, a man of his own age, until they are summoned into the candlelit dining room. Bendigo informs him that the Brownings, who had arrived in

Ealing just that afternoon, will be in attendance. Apparently Daniel Home had joked with the poetess that he would endeavour to have the spirits crown her with a wreath during the séance. Julian is again struck by the change in Home since their last meeting.

Mrs. Osborne is seated next to Julian. Further down the table he catches a glimpse of the elegant profile of the recently widowed Lady Rhonda. Across from him are the celebrated poets. Julian admires the poetess's short, frizzy, black hair, but he is most attracted to her eyes, which glow green in the candlelight. He can see little of her husband except that he is of medium height, but he can tell that he is in an agitated state. The poet bends now and again to speak to his wife, but then pulls himself up abruptly, sways and squirms in his chair, which seems to have little chance of containing him for very long. At the far end of the table Julian can just manage to make out Stephen Widdicombe, the Duke of Exeter, and Lady Smythe.

The séance commences when Home, in what is for him a deep voice, asks the group to maintain silence and join hands. For ten minutes or so, nothing happens. Then, vibrations emanate from the table, although the cloth, the heavy candelabra in the centre and the other ornaments on the table move not a whit. Then the Rymers, husband and wife, announce that they can feel the presence of their dead son.

Julian has a good view from where he sits. Then, there are a series of loud raps. Home translates these: the spirit will play the accordion and show Mr. Browning his hand. These two events are not of great interest because Home holds the accordion under the table and only a screeching note is produced. When Home hands the instrument to Browning, all that can be heard are some hard pushing noises.

Then, after Home resumes his seat, a hand appears from the table just behind Julian, withdraws and then appears again. The hand is draped in white muslin, but its fingers and thumb are clearly outlined through the cloth; the muslin reaches down to the floor, from which it is never separated. Then, the hand withdraws; a few moments later, it reappears behind the poetess carrying the clematis wreath, which is dashed to the ground, then retrieved by the same hand. As the wreath moves toward Mrs. Browning, her husband rises and stands behind his wife. The hand ignores him and places the wreath on her head.

Home sinks into an even deeper trance and mumbles and mutters for about five minutes. Mr. Browning, who has sat back down, again becomes restive. Suddenly, Home is restored to consciousness and asks that all those present, with the exception of Mr. Rymer senior, leave the room. "The spirits have a message for our host of a private nature." The assemblage does as it is instructed and moves into the antechamber. Browning is furious. He approaches Mrs. Rymer, declaring that he had been promised to see the table levitated by invisible forces.

After about a quarter of an hour, the door is opened by Mr. Rymer, who invites the company back into the room, which is now brightly lit. As soon as the guests settle down, the table tilts without the objects on it sliding except for a silver pen that Mr. Browning places on the sloping surface.

Mr. Browning asks the medium: "Have the spirits no power to prevent the pen rolling?" Lady Smythe is exasperated: "Do not ask childish questions. Have you not seen enough?"

After ten minutes have passed, Home invites Browning and Julian to stand, bend down and look under the table. When they do so, they can plainly see that the entire table is lifted at least a foot above the floor. At the same time he beholds this phenomenon, Julian clearly observes Home's hands and those of every other person in the room. He is astounded at beholding such a contradiction to the law of physics, but the only emotion Browning displays is that of rage. Home asks the two men to resume their seats and a few moments later the entire audience feels the table settle to the floor. Home shows no elation at the conclusion of the séance. He remains slouched in his chair, as if a heavy burden has been lifted from him. He is bereft: the spirits have sucked all the air out of him. Within the next half hour, all the guests take their leave.

Julian is astounded by the events of that July night. Never before has he entertained a serious belief in a world hovering at the edge of the flesh and blood one. He is, he reminds himself, a materialist. He is also a bit of a trickster. He knows all the sleights of hand used to bend the real world to the two dimensions demanded by canvas. Like him, Home goes against nature. In raising the dead back to life, however, Home proclaims the existence of a spiritual plane. Julian always considered men such as Home fakers. Yet his eyes did not deceive him: the huge table floated in the air. Julian, an expert in sniffing out impostors, cannot affix this label to Home. Must he now alter all his ideas about the nature of existence?

CHAPTER FOUR

A HEART IN
THE RIGHT PLACE

*T*here were several other keen-eyed observers at the home of Mr. and Mrs. Rymer that humid summer night of the now infamous séance. Miranda Osborne, Julian's former client, is perhaps the most disinterested among them.

Relique. A hand-me-down. A discard. A woman left behind. A female person of absolutely no value who has had the bad luck to be abandoned through death by her spouse. This is how the Widow Osborne sees herself. In the terminology of the law, she is, simply, the fifty-year old remains of her husband.

Miranda Osborne is accustomed to being overlooked. Her mother, a servant girl who succumbed to the pecuniary advantages offered her over the course of several months by one Matthew Blake, a butcher from Newcastle, died giving birth to her. She has no idea who chose her Christian name,

Miranda, but she doubts it was Mr. Blake, of whom she has no early recollection.

The first thing she recalls is being found destitute at the age of four on Newcastle Quay by Mrs. Brown and being pressed into service to sell sand for the cleaning of stone floors. Mrs. B, as the small girls called her, fed only those of her charges who managed to sell four pence of sand on a given day. If Miranda did not meet her quota, she went to bed hungry. From that experience, she learned the value of hard work, perspicacity and diligence.

Her living quarters were not salubrious. Often, four or five of the girls, the sum total of Brown & Co, Purveyors of Cleansing Supplies, slept in a small crowded room behind what their employer had the effrontery to call her boudoir (she pronounced the word, booh-dwarr). They had no bedding, bed clothes, or straw mattresses. But, often, during the night a child would grasp another around the waist and feel a semblance of human warmth.

Mrs. Brown, customarily clad in either a pale green or bright pink frock with a straw bonnet firmly pushed into her scalp, would purchase her sand near the Quay, hire a man with cart and donkey to take it to the city centre where the children assembled precisely at six o'clock in the morning, and then consign supplies to each girl. Sometimes, householders were gracious enough but many were belligerent or cruel. A few tried to cheat Miranda; none ever did.

Her hectic childhood was interrupted at the age of seven when Mr. Blake appeared one evening and reclaimed his daughter from her employer, who demanded compensation for the loss of an excellent worker, though no word of praise had ever escaped her lips before. Blake quickly paid the three guineas demanded, and father and daughter were on their way. From the fact that he did not quarrel with her keeper, Miranda surmised correctly that her father was now a wealthy man. On their journey, he explained to her that he had prospered through an investment in the coffee trade and was now the proud owner of an estate and a young wife.

When Mr. Blake arrived at Binchester Hall, Miranda was introduced to Elizabeth, Mr. Blake's wife of three years. She greeted the youngster warmly and then instructed her maid to provide the child with a warm meal, bathe her, and prepare her for bed. That evening Miranda overheard the domestics saying that Elizabeth Blake was barren, very much desired to have a child and had therefore insisted her husband reclaim his illegitimate and previously unwanted daughter.

Miranda wishes that she had been a loving and dutiful child to her new mother. She was always pleasant to Elizabeth and she to her, but no deep feelings of affection developed between the women. Miranda's early existence had hardened her, making her suspicious of all acts of kindness. Within a year, she was sent away to boarding school, where she was a tolerable student. When her education was completed at the age of seventeen, she returned to Binchester Hall, where she was soon courted by Mr. Osborne, a widower more than thirty years her senior.

Osborne, born in Calcutta but raised in Darjeeling, had made his way to England at the age of twenty and quickly established himself as an importer of tea. Although she did not follow his business affairs, Miranda gradually became aware that her husband's fortune was not directly attributable to the leaves he imported from China, Ceylon, and India. Rather, having purchased a great quantity of, say, gunpowder-green he mixed it with blackthorn leaves and, in the process, obtained ten pounds of *saleable* tea made from six pounds of *genuine* leaves. Mr. Osborne was deeply hostile to the likes of John Ruskin, who, fully aware of the frauds being committed by merchants of Osborne's type, opened a shop in Paddington Street to sell pure tea to the poor.

During the years of her marriage, Miranda's obligation was to look after the household, the servants and the grounds of their large home in Manchester. In turn, her husband never touched a penny of her dowry. From the time of his youth, she later learned, her husband had been a frequenter of brothels and other establishments that cater to the appetite for flesh of the male creature. He never troubled her in that way.

They lived as man and wife for sixteen years before he was carried off by a cancer of the throat. At her husband's passing, Miranda received his entire estate. Within a year, she sold his firm, placed the entire amount in fixed Consols and moved to London, where she and Smith, her maid, took lodgings over a greengrocer in Highgate.

Like most widows, she wears a mourning brooch of rubies in which a lock of her dead husband's hair can be seen under glass; in fact, Osborne had chosen the object himself. Some relatives assumed the widow chose to live near Swain's Hill and the cemetery as part of her observances following the death of her spouse. Far from it. She reckons the rooms in which she resides spacious and attractively priced. She does enjoy walking through the serpentine paths and roads leading through the burial grounds and often pauses to admire the columns and obelisks that comprise the Egyptian Avenue, the Circle of Lebanon, and the Catacombs. Having little inclination to travel to the Near East, she partakes of some of its exotic pleasures.

Miranda's choice of residence caused much concern among her husband's family. Why, her nephews and nieces asked, do you choose to live as if in reduced circumstances? Calmly, she explained to them that she was indeed living in reduced circumstances. After all, her husband had passed away. "No, that is not what we mean. You are a woman of considerable wealth and should conduct yourself accordingly." In reply, she told them the truth. She did not care for a grand house and most certainly was not willing to pay for the upkeep of one. This reply checked the tongues of her interrogators. After all, they all hoped that on her death, they might inherit all the more money because of their aunt's addled, frugal ways.

A few of the more clever relations are convinced their aunt is determined to spend her fortune to satisfy her collecting mania. Again, they are incorrect. Despite the amount of money she lavishes on silver, Miranda's fortune has remained largely intact. Though she is lenient in the dispersal of the interest, she never touches the capital.

A favourite pastime of Miranda is travelling throughout London on those most wonderful modern inventions, the omnibus and the *cabriolet*. Two or three days a week, she is a member of the crowd in the Waterloo Road, jostling and shouting and pushing at the portals of the Royal Victoria Theatre. The cost, only three pence, pales in comparison to the antics of the two thousand patrons: women with tiny babies, tousle-headed boys, businessmen on holiday. Fisticuffs are frequent. The noise is so resounding that the orchestra frequently cannot be heard when it begins to play. Many of the patrons have to stand and demand silence of their colleagues: "Order! Ord-a-a-a-r." Before the entertainment commences and during the intervals, ham sandwiches, pigs' feet and porter are hawked to the hungry. On stage there are a wide variety of marvels: dances, comic songs, acrobatics, Highland flings and reels.

She rejoices in being part of these audiences, where she can mingle and yet remain anonymous. From the time of childhood, she finds it easier to be a solitary; she takes no great pleasure in human companionship and is happiest in her own company. Miranda does not think of herself as a misanthrope. When she converses, she listens carefully and judges reluctantly.

She does not know why she chose her strange style of life. She does not fear that spending money will, of necessity, deprive her of her resources in an unexpected crisis. That fantasy never presses itself upon her, although she fervently believes that she who wastes not will want not. I must have, she sometimes tells herself, the mentality of a gypsy. I wish to be ready at any given moment to pack up all my possessions and be on my way. True, nowadays I would have to hire several, sizeable wagons to cart away my holdings.

Miranda and her husband had never ventured into society. Since her rooms make it impossible for her to receive those of similar status, she does not have the worry of entertaining. Instead, she takes comfort from her inanimate companions, the objects of silver with which her apartment is filled. They do not remonstrate with her, or call attention to any deficiencies they might discern in their mistress.

The collecting mania has only fully asserted itself during widowhood. Before Osborne died, the couple owned a few good paintings and a scattering of silver objects. Now she owns more silver pieces than any other individual in Christendom. Why silver?, she often asks herself.

Silver has the advantage of being unbreakable. It can wear down, be dented, and suffer other indignities, but it will, unless it meets a particularly ferocious fire, survive intact. Battered it might become but seldom torn asunder. Although some pieces are large, they are easily transportable. A large collection of silver gleams even in shadow; in sunlight, the owner catches refractions of herself, as if she inhabits the surface of the objects and is part of their souls. "Yes, they have souls, each of them," she assures herself. Not their own souls she wistfully reflects, but a portion of their makers' souls survives in each.

Her first purchase, a French sugar castor, was made as a kind of memorial to her husband. Made in Paris in 1723 by Nicholas Berlin, this piece, only ten inches high, is decorated in the Régence style with strapwork, female busts, birds, baskets of fruit; the pierced cover is topped with an artichoke. It looks like a small memorial urn in which one might reasonably deposit ashes instead of sugar.

Once bitten, Miranda was not shy. Her second acquisition was a gravy boat in what is termed the rococo style; the floral and fruit swags, paw feet, fish-head terminals on the handles, and lion masks just above the tiny feet entranced her with their frivolity. Then a George III candelabrum with owls, dragons, and lions was added to her collection. And so on and so very on until, according to Smith, her mistress has four hundred and seventeen items in her inventory. Even the Queen, she has Smith's assurance, does not have so many sumptuous pieces in all her residences. Eagles, Chinamen, vines, and all kinds of creatures inhabit her ice buckets, chocolate, coffee and tea pots, ciboria, chalices, communion plates, claret jugs, tankards, and rose bowls.

Of necessity, Smith, sharp-eyed but soft-spoken, has become an expert in all the hallmarks (London, Sheffield, Chester, Edinburgh, Exeter, Dublin, Berlin, Madrid); like her mistress, she is careful to note the scratch weight embedded on the base and an object's actual weight, knows a good patina, and how to spot pieces that have been repaired using lead rather than silver solder.

Both women are sufficiently versed to know the real from the sham. Fake punches are usually easy to see. The alternative scam — cutting genuine hallmarks from worn-out pieces and then inserting them into freshly-made ones — is just as easily detected. More difficult to spot, except for the connoisseur, is the method whereby a relatively common object, such as a spoon, is converted into a fork. The bowl of the spoon can be hammered flat and then turned up at the edges to form a rectangular tray; additional silver is poured in and the filled tray is then beaten to the correct profile; the prongs are cut out, filed and polished.

Very few women are collectors. Of that small number, even less appear at the auction houses or haunt the vendors' stalls. Mrs. Osborne is not loathe to inspect objects for sale at Mr. Christie's or Mr. Sotheby's, but it is Smith who bids on her behalf and removes the purchases.

In fact, the only woman Mrs. Osborne ever sees habitually at the sale rooms is Lady Rhonda. For a year or two, when they chanced upon each other, they simply bowed in the other's direction. The noble woman's cream-coloured complexion and deep auburn tresses cause every eye in the room to turn to her. Like everyone else, Miranda fell victim to her beauty but found her manners outlandish. Lady Rhonda always spoke clearly and elegantly, but her constant high-pitched laugh was maddening. She habitually concluded all her sentences with a whooping sound. She was also too generously learned.

One day Miranda overheard Lady Rhonda telling a German gentleman that Englishmen liked their wives to consume, not collect. She then quoted one of the *Spectator* papers wherein a husband laments that his wife has set herself to reform every corner of his house, "having glazed every chimney piece with a Looking-glass and planted every corner with heaps of China, I am obliged to move around my own house with the greatest Caution and Circumspection."

Lady Rhonda introduced herself to Miranda by observing that they seemed to share an obsession for collecting, one for silver, the other for figurines. Miranda agreed that they suffered a common frailty. Lady Rhonda responded with uproarious laughter, as if her acquaintance had uttered a particularly choice *bon mot.* "William of Orange's Mary and the Duchess of Portland have also partaken in what you dare label an impediment!"

Lady Rhonda then confessed that she was a second-generation collector. Having inherited a large collection from her father, she felt obligated to maintain it. On making this observation, she screeched and then contradicted herself. "Really, I am always hungry to acquire more Meissen, Chelsea and Bow." Looking around to be certain they were not overheard, she added, "I have read somewhere that collecting is libidinous, a substitute for sexual activity." Gleefully, she asked if Mrs. Osborne agreed. A bit too primly, Miranda informed her that she had no opinion in the matter. From that time onward, they would always, when encountering each other, exchange only pleasantries.

Miranda's presence at the Rymers for Mr. Home's séance is the result of serendipity. For some time, Mrs. Rymer had been trying to obtain some rare George III large-bowled caddy spoons. A dealer told her that Mrs. Osborne probably owned such curiosities, and she came calling to plead with her to sell one or two. Miranda would not have consented to sell a piece from her collection except that she knew Mrs. Rymer owned several Charles I Apostle spoons. She proposed an exchange, a George III for a Saint John? They made the trade and, shortly afterwards, Mrs. Rymer wrote asking if Miranda would give her the honour of attending a séance at The Green.

Mrs. Rymer may have thought that Miranda's interest in Saint John showed spiritualist leanings. In any event, she was trying to repay a kindness. Ordinarily, Miranda would not have even considered presenting herself at the Rymers. She had been reluctant to attend the London debut of the Arundel Leonardo, but her curiosity got the better of her. Yet she felt drawn to the séance, some part of her obviously aroused by the possibility of communicating with the spirit world. In the end, she informed Mrs. Rymer she would attend the séance but not the supper beforehand.

As the carriage she has hired for the evening approaches The Green at Ealing, the vastness of the Rymer villa shocks Miranda. She cannot imagine paying the wages of the servants required to attend the interior and exterior of what looks to be a mausoleum consecrated to Mammon. Although she has vastly more capital than the Rymers, Miranda could never display her resources so ostentatiously. Nevertheless, she admits to herself that the display of great wealth sends a frisson down her spine. She certainly experiences a strange sensation as the manservant greets her, informs her that the supper is in progress and shows her to a sitting room where she might await her hosts.

The long, burgundy coloured chamber dwarfs a single person. The many portraits on its walls stare accusingly at Miranda. Attempting to make herself comfortable, she sits on the settee near the mantelpiece — no doubt imported from some seigniorial home in France — and studies the few interesting bits of silver displayed. She takes satisfaction in the fact that all these pieces are of considerable value but of no great rarity. She begins to wonder anew why she eschews most of the trappings of wealth as vainglorious whereas, she is well aware, all her possessions will in the end be sold by her heirs.

Miranda's reverie is interrupted by the sensation that she is not alone in the enormous room. She looks around but sees no one. Not convinced, she rises and walks to the end of the room. Gradually, in the evening dusk, she beholds a woman slumbering. Above the woman is an enormous canvas, in the manner of Mr. Rossetti, of a fierce archangel, his sword drawn as if he had spied an intruder. The face of the angel is rendered in a whirl of creams, blacks, and reds, but it is his enormous blue eyes that hold Miranda rapt.

"One of Mr. Wilson's finest creations, don't you think?"

Startled, Miranda realizes that the woman has awoken from her sleep.

"Mrs. Osborne, how wonderful to see you! I never expected you to be here this evening."

Only then does Miranda recognize her interlocutor as Lady Rhonda. Her husband having died about six months before, the countess is in deepest black, including the veil which covers her face. Without thinking, Miranda curtsies, causing Lady Rhonda to whinny with laughter. "No need for such formality, my dear. We two widows must join forces." Miranda supposes the presence of a worldly person such as Lady Rhonda at the Rymers should not have surprised her.

"Are you in hopes of establishing communication with the Earl, your late husband?" Miranda finally inquires.

Lady Rhonda smiles warily. "I am not certain why I am here. I am intrigued by what I hear of Mr. Home's supposed powers and wish to witness them for myself."

Before Lady Rhonda can ask, Miranda interjects: "Exactly my sentiments."

The woman begins to laugh yet again but then takes control of herself. "I suspect we are both sceptics but sceptics able to be persuaded by good evidence."

Miranda bows her assent to this declaration as the man-servant enters the room to fetch them for the séance.

The dining room at the Rymers is Brobdingnagian. Many more than the fourteen persons invited could be accommodated at the prodigious mahogany table. Although the table is lit by a wide assortment of candles, the room is dark, perhaps because its doors to the outside are flung open and a thick fog encroaches upon the guests as they take their seats.

Lady Rhonda is seated three down from Miranda. Mr. Wilson sits next to her and politely engages her in a variety of chitchat. Suddenly, shadows hover over her as a tiny woman accompanied by a stolid, well-made, bewhiskered gentleman take their places opposite. The woman's tightly-curled tresses of raven black flow down and meet the rich, velvety green of her dress. She has a button for a nose but an exceedingly large mouth, one suitable for a much larger countenance. Her face is etched with lines, her complexion is dark and sallow. Her eyes are of a greenish brown hue. The stranger looks about her modestly, but her eyes seem to scoop up everything in

their path. She is a person of great intelligence, Miranda decides, but she is overly compliant to the gentleman, who is presumably her husband. Although he is hardly of medium height, the man bends down to his companion, answers her questions with great deliberation and then raises his head and cranes his neck about, watching the arrival of others. He speaks to the woman as if conversing with a child of prodigious gifts. He is the caretaker, she the parcel on which he dotes.

Miranda makes her interest in the newcomers known to Mr. Wilson, who whispers: "The Brownings."

She looks again at the famous poets whose romance is known to all and sundry. "Indeed. I did not know that they partook of spiritualist things."

"The gentleman does not, but I understand the lady is desperate to make Mr. Home's acquaintance. In fact, she has travelled all the way from Italy to see him."

"She is an invalid, is she not?"

"Very much so. I have been told that she wishes to get in touch with her favourite brother who has been dead some years."

The Brownings do not overhear them, but just as Mr. Wilson finishes speaking, the poetess bows and smiles in Miranda's direction. At first, her husband takes no notice. Then he stares at Miranda. When she catches his eye, he turns away, as if he had completed the inspection of a mundane piece of furniture.

A few minutes after the arrival of the Brownings, a curious trio enters the room: a red-haired youth of enormous girth, a middle-aged man dressed correctly but ostentatiously, and a small slip of a woman. Mr. Wilson nods in their direction and informs Miranda that this group consists of the Duke of Exeter and his constant companions, Stephen Widdicombe and Lady Smythe.

Miranda's attention is soon riveted on Mr. Home as he takes his place at the head of the table. He reminds her of a thin willow that follows every whim of the wind. He is unkempt. His jacket has a number of holes in it, and the knot in his cravat is extremely loose. But the strangest thing is Mr. Home's voice. Often as he begins to enunciate a phrase, his voice rebels and brings him to a complete stop. He does not stutter; it is as if his voice box has lost all power to propel his voice outward. Finally, after several tries, Mr. Home tells the assemblage that he is only the poor instrument of the spirits and that the audience will have to be patient with them — and, especially, him. "Some nights the spirits do not assemble round me; on others, a few of them wish to make their presences known. We shall have to be uncomplaining and follow their dictates."

The assembly waits in silence for ten long minutes. Every so often Mrs. Browning glances in the direction of her spouse, who gently holds her small hand in his huge paw. Then, the rumblings begin. Strange noises emanate from underneath the table, shaking it. After an interval of about five minutes, the accordion next to Mr. Home begins to play in a desultory way. When these uninteresting sounds conclude, Mr. Home asks if Mr. Browning might like to play a duet with the spirit? Mr. Home picks up the accordion and hands it to the poet. The poet seems uninterested although he does touch the instrument; Miranda can clearly see a hand, near the poet's, playing the instrument. Again, the sound is of no consequence.

At this point the events of the evening take a momentous turn when, of a sudden, a wreath that Miranda had noticed at the side of the table begins to move in the direction of the Brownings. At first, she thinks that the wreath is floating in the air, but that observation proves incorrect. When it is about four feet behind husband and wife, she can see it is being held by a perfectly formed hand cloaked in muslin. She looks at Mr. Home, who is at least twenty feet away. Miranda hears herself gasp.

As the wreath moves closer to the Brownings, the poet leaps to his feet. He assumes a standing position behind his wife's chair in order, Miranda is certain, to be crowned with the greatest possible flourish. But the hand quickly moves around him and gently places the wreath on Mrs. Browning's head.

The members of the audience are pleased by this dramatic turn of events; Mr. Home, now slouched in his chair, seems to be rendered unconscious. Suddenly, the medium begins to speak in a garbled fashion, at which point Mr. Rymer bends over and converses with him. Restored to consciousness, the medium asks all of the audience to leave the room immediately; Watty Rymer wishes to speak privately with his father.

Miranda is behind the Brownings as they leave the room. The poet, now enraged, speaks accusingly to Mrs. Rymer. He has been told that the table would be lifted from the floor through the agency of Mr. Home. Is he to be deprived of that entertainment? She apologizes and says that she will intercede with Home. After about fifteen minutes, a flustered Mr. Rymer opens the dining room door and asks the group to rejoin him and the medium.

Since the doors to the outside are now closed, no evening vapours can block the company's view in the brightly-lit room. The guests resume sitting for about ten minutes when the huge table lifts itself at least a foot from the ground. From where Miranda sits, she can see that the great claw foot nearest to her is completely elevated without any apparent assistance. Then the table begins to move up and down in the manner of a see-saw. Mr. Browning places a silver pen on the table, which, unlike the candelabra, responds to the movement of the table and falls to the ground. Sensing that the poet is in some distress at what he is witnessing, Home, in his faltering voice, invites him and Julian Wilson to inspect the space between the table and the floor. They do so and cannot account for the phenomenon they witness.

Miranda views the evening's events as an entertainment. She does not know if in Mr. Home she is beholding someone truly in contact with the spirit world or a very enterprising magician. What is more, she does not really care. Well pleased by what she has witnessed, she considers the money invested in hiring the coach for the evening well spent. She takes her leave of the Rymers having enjoyed herself enormously.

A fortnight after the séance at Ealing, a messenger from Mr. Browning calls on Miranda. Would she be prepared to receive the poet at three o'clock on the following afternoon? Although a bit startled by this strange request, she assents at once. On the following morning, she instructs Smith to purchase a quarter pound of the finest Kweelong tea — from a reputable firm — and some sweets at the pastry shop recently opened opposite the cemetery by immigrants from Lyon. She is ready when the poet arrives at precisely the appointed time.

Mr. Browning takes no trouble to hide his curiosity about Miranda's abode when Smith shows him into the sitting room. He stands awkwardly in front of his hostess looking all about him as she proffers her hand. As if that gesture were of no consequence, he looks at her hand for a moment or two and then touches it quickly before withdrawing his own. She asks him to take a seat, but he ventures over to the silver on the mantelpiece.

"All that glitters is indeed not gold, wouldn't you agree, Mrs. Osborne?"

She smiles at this excuse for a witticism and asks him again to be seated.

He sits in the chair opposite and begins to quiz her: "I have heard you are a person of great wealth and I am therefore surprised to see you living," he glances up and down the room, "in such circumstances."

"I once had a large house of my own, Mr. Browning, and discovered that I did not enjoy its company. We parted from each other amicably."

He apparently does not take in what he is told. "All this silver! It must be of great value, worth many grand houses?"

"Perhaps you are correct. But I doubt you have come here today to talk of property."

Miranda's comment, frosty though it is, brings a smile to the poet's face, as if he had forgotten why he had asked to see her. "Of course. I am here to discuss that wretched impostor, Daniel Home."

Before she can offer a response, Mr. Browning informs her that his wife has long harboured the hope of communicating with the spirit of her dead brother. Having heard from Thackeray and others of Mr. Home's powers, she prevailed upon him to make the trip. It was at his wife's request that he had reluctantly appeared at Ealing on July 13. Only his wife's pleading could have persuaded him to remove them from the comfort of Tuscany to the gloom of London, which, he assures Miranda many times, is detrimental to his wife's poor health.

The selfless husband continues further, telling his hostess that he was well aware of the trickery being passed off in the name of science.

"Wherein lies the deception, Mr. Browning?"

Surprisingly, he is unprepared for the question. "It is obvious, madam."

"Not to me," she assures him.

"It is done with wires and the assistance of concealed assistants. Mr. Home manipulates some of the wires, and his confederates are hidden in the room."

"I saw no evidence of wires, and the Rymers would never allow any deception to be practised on their premises. They would have had to have been aware if any confederates were present."

The poet becomes impatient. "The Rymers may not be aware of how they are being misused."

"Mr. Home's arms and legs were plainly visible to all of us when the hand moved about the room. I don't think he could have been controlling any device."

The poet looks at Miranda as if she is a simpleton. "These fakers have many, many ways of manipulating the unwary."

"I do not doubt what you say, but I saw no evidence of what you claim. The table was lifted from the ground, the table shifted back and forth in the air, the accordion played the semblance of a melody, and the hand looked uncommonly human to me."

"Did you not observe my wife asking if the wreath could be passed to me, the wretched thing moving under the table and patting me on the knee and then quickly vanishing as Mr. Home went into another of his swoons?"

"I did not. Perhaps my attention was distracted."

"Madam, you have been badly used by a charlatan."

"Perhaps so, sir, but you have not proven that to me."

Having gained no ground, Mr. Browning shifts his argument. He had that evening, he assures her, arisen from his chair because he feared the hand might harm his wife. Miranda points out to him that there had been no evil in the outcome.

"Just so. But there might have been. Could have been." As he utters those words, the suspicion crosses Miranda's mind that the poet's outrage is centred on the wreath. At the time, she had been convinced that he had stood up to receive it as a tribute to himself. He might, she now wonders, have been mortified to see the garland delivered to his wife, no matter how much he loved her. Had he been enraged not to be recognized as the real poet? Is this the source of his quarrel with the medium?

Since she is not willing to join forces with him to denounce Mr. Home, Mr. Browning quickly concludes the meeting. As Smith enters the room with the tea, he rises to excuse himself. Miranda pleads with him to take some refreshment, but he refuses and is immediately on his way.

Men, she reflects, are such vainglorious creatures. My father found me of potential use many years after my birth; I served Mr. Osborne well but received little in the way of thanks; if I had assented to Mr. Browning's beliefs, I would have been his ally in assuaging his vanity.

As she thinks about it, Miranda becomes even more deeply annoyed with Mr. Browning, not only for his churlishness but also because he has forced her to revisit the Ealing séance. In the days following the event, amusement has given way to apprehension. I am someone who only believes in the world I can touch with my hand and gaze with my eye, she assures herself. Yet what if there is something else, a sphere upon which she has turned her back? Mr. Browning has forced her to reconsider the matter yet again. What if he is right? Of course, Daniel Home could be a consummate fake. That seems too easy an answer.

Had Mr. Browning stayed for tea, she might have told him about her recent visit to the British Museum in Bloomsbury. There is very little silver on display there, but she felt compelled to make her way to Great Russell Street two days after the event at Ealing. She inspected the gibberish written on the Rosetta Stone; she admired the marbles removed from the

Parthenon by Lord Elgin; for a while, she was transfixed by Sir William Hamilton's collection of ancient Greek vases. But she was, she knew, only postponing what was the real purpose of her visit. With some trembling, she made her way to the empty Egyptian sarcophagi that once contained human remains.

Although the Egyptians believed in the immortality of the soul, they took great care to preserve the body. Theirs was a culture centred on necrophilia. These thoughts, swarming in Miranda's head, almost caused her not to see the straggly young man heading in her direction. Quickly, she darted behind one of the giant winged Assyrian sculptures. From that vantage point, Daniel Home was in her sights as he inspected the habitations of the mummies.

Such an awkward, unprepossessing creature, she told herself, watching him move slowly from exhibit to exhibit, his head bobbing. Unlike that well-favoured rascal, Julian Wilson, he has no presence. Having reached that conclusion, another one forced itself upon her. If Mr. Home was a charlatan, he would have the style of one. Mr. Home may be many things, she realized, but he cannot be a trickster.

As Miranda looks around her sitting room that August afternoon, she takes comfort from the assemblage of silver pieces. They make so few demands of a frail woman.

~⌐

CHAPTER FIVE

AFTER MY OWN HEART

*A*lthough her husband has been dead only six months, it seems more like six years to Rhonda. In a half-year's time, she will have to remove her widow's garb, unless she wishes to attract undue attention. She would gladly remain in black.

She did not love Edward when she married him. After all, she scarcely knew him. Her family possessed a grand name, worthless land, and no money to speak of when the match was proposed by Edward, the Earl of Langdon, then a childless widower of fifty-one. Reluctantly, Rhonda's father asked her to consider the proposal. She was thirty-six years old.

From the time her father mentioned the possibility of her marriage to a man substantially older than herself, the thought that her husband would likely die before her had reluctantly crossed her mind. For the family, the marriage was seen as a necessity, although her father told Rhonda she could do as she pleased. Why then did she agree to marry — and later fall in love with a man so older than herself? After all, she had long settled into the single state. She suspects it was Edward's complete toleration — nay, understanding and acceptance — of her disability.

When confronted with any sort of emotion, be it sad or angry or joyous, Rhonda lets out whooping sounds that put every one in her company on edge. Her mother took all kinds of steps to rid her of this habit. She was strapped, she was sent to bed without food, she was confined to her bed-chamber for days at a time. No remedy worked. Her parents were embarrassed by her displays, which were sometimes fre-quent, often three or four outbursts on a single day. Her father ignored the horrendous sounds she emitted, although she hardly ever demonstrated them in his presence.

When Edward came to court Rhonda, he made polite con-servation on a variety of topics and, true to form, the awful sounds came unbidden, punctuating their entire conversation. Edward did not pretend not to have noticed these sounds, as most people did. Instead, he commented that she seemed to him to be a woman of such generous sentiments that, unbeknownst to herself, her body insisted in giving voice to those emotions. "Merriment seizes you unawares due to a surplus of good feelings within you." She was taken aback, both by his interpretation and by the fleeting suspicion that he was flattering her. At that time, she did not know that he was a man who in words and deeds always expressed the truth.

❧

Rhonda's friendship with Elizabeth Barrett has been long lasting. Perhaps, Rhonda often wonders, it is because of their shared, although very different, infirmities. Rhonda is one of the few people whom Elizabeth allows to call her by the childhood nickname of Ba.

The two women have been close companions since they were deemed tomboys by their parents. Of the same age — they are approaching their fiftieth years — they were raised near each other; Rhonda's family's estate bordered that of the Barretts at Hope End near the Malvern Hills. In those days, the two girls played outside as much as possible. Whether on the hunt for birds' eggs or climbing one of the smaller hills in the neighbourhood, their constant companion was Bro, Ba's younger brother by a year.

For Rhonda the Barrett mansion — more a castle than a house, inspired by all things Turkish — was a wonderful retreat, its tiny minarets and odd-shaped rooms providing the perfect setting for games of hide-and-seek. Mrs. Barrett was a warm, indulgent parent, and even the redoubtable Mr. Barrett was a genial presence in those early years.

Rhonda clearly remembers the day Ba, and her two younger sisters, Henrietta and Arabel, became deathly and mysteriously ill. The sick room at the Barretts was filled to bursting with the three youngsters. Henrietta and Arabel quickly recovered. Not so fourteen-year old Ba. The pain, which had begun in her head, travelled to her right side, just above the ribs. Then it invaded her back, then her shoulders, then her arms. She felt as if a tight cord was wound about her stomach and then broken. There were usually three attacks each day, some of which rendered her unconscious. Although Ba said she was being torn apart, no physician ever discovered anything wrong with her.

After his wife's death, Mr. Barrett became overly protective of his children, none of whom were allowed lives apart from him. Failure of the sugar crop in Jamaica, the source of his family's money, forced him to move the family to Fortfield Terrace in Sidmouth and then to Wimpole Street in London. Ba discovered that the smaller living quarters in London meant that she was now in the main confined to her upstairs room. The move from the country depressed her and worsened her ever mysterious condition.

Rhonda visited Ba two or three times a year, and their girlhood friendship maintained itself into adulthood. Ba seemed oblivious to her friend's shrieks, although the other Barrett sisters quickly absented themselves whenever their sister's friend arrived.

Rhonda heard at great length from Ba of her infatuation with the married Hugh Stuart Boyd, four years older than her own father. That hint of a romance was eventually transferred into a chaste friendship. Destined to be old maids, the compact between the two women was firm and unassailable. When the Earl of Langdon proposed to Rhonda, she sought out Ba's advice. Her friend's counsel was unflinching. "Since the Earl obviously adores you, his proposal is worthy of the closest scrutiny."

After her marriage, Edward and Rhonda called on Ba

regularly at 50 Wimpole Street, and they supported her determination to accept Robert Browning's secret proposal of marriage. How could they not be sympathetic, Rhonda recalled, to an invalid who once wrote to her with such pathos: "All the flowers forswear me, and die either suddenly or gradually as they become aware of the want of fresh air and light in my room." Of course they joked about the fact that they, two self-appointed spinsters, had proved themselves wrong, one by marrying a man fifteen years her senior, the other a man six years her junior. "Almost a quarter century separates our spouses!," Ba gleefully pointed out to Rhonda one day.

Rhonda never doubted Robert Browning's love for Ba, yet the incongruity between the poets astounded her. For one, Robert's fierce energy contrasted sharply with Ba's ready acceptance of her invalid fate. He was a man of the senses, she a woman of almost pure intellect. He had only seen her photograph when he declared in his astounding letter of January 1845 that he loved her verses with all his heart. Rather than holding back from such an advance, Ba welcomed it. Soon Robert was allowed, when Mr. Barrett was away at his office, to call on Ba in her chamber. Against all the proprieties, they were closeted together alone. Of necessity, their visits had to be short and much of what they wanted to tell each other was expressed in letters. Ba once told Rhonda that they had exchanged almost six hundred letters in the space of less than two years.

Rhonda's suspicion — one she is ashamed of — is that Ba and Robert might have tired of each other had not Mr. Barrett made it crystal clear to each of his children that they were never to marry. Then there was Ba's health. She was so ill that it seemed she had no hope of ever leaving home. Robert, who relished obstacles, was determined to have his way. Ba's streak of wilfulness then came to the fore. My old friend, Rhonda reminded herself, is both sly and steely when she is determined on a course of action. The emotional temperature in Ba's small, sedate room quickly became that of a greenhouse on a sultry summer day. Rhonda, who remained uncomfortable in matters of the flesh, was astounded when Ba took so readily to such pleasures.

Just before her elopement, she wrote Rhonda: "Before Robert, I lived on the outside of my own life, blindly and darkly from day to day, as completely dead to hope of any kind as if I had my face against a grave; a thoroughly morbid and desolate state it was, which I look back to now with a sort of horror. Then he came."

After the removal of the Brownings to Paris and then Pisa and finally Florence, the friends kept in touch by letter. When Edward died, Ba sent Rhonda comforting words, which Rhonda swiftly acknowledged. Then, just a few weeks earlier, Ba wrote to inform Rhonda that she was returning to England on a matter of great urgency. She had heard tell of the extraordinary powers of one Daniel Home and wanted to test his powers in order to get in touch with her dearest Bro, who had drowned fifteen years before at the age of thirty-three.

Although puzzled by her friend's interest in such other-worldly matters, Rhonda reflected that Ba suffered from the rejection of her angry father. Her wish to speak with Bro must have been inspired by a desire to reconnect with the happy parts of her childhood. Certain Robert would be averse to such an undertaking, she nevertheless knew him to be an indulgent husband.

In order to entice Rhonda to attend the séance, Ba provided evidence of Home's powers by telling her of the comical adventures of a mutual friend, the American connoisseur, James Jackson Jarves, who, after a séance, decided to spend the night with Mr. Home, hoping to encounter further manifestations of the spirit world. "As it transpired," Ba reported to Rhonda, "the demonstrations were so violent as to frighten even Mr. Home. The spirits, both female and unclothed, walked round the bed with distinct footsteps — drew the curtains backward & forward, lifted up the heavy four-poster bed into the air and did everything James asked them to do *except one*. He would not tell me what they refused to do, but he, as you know, is a person of a lascivious disposition."

When Robert was away during the afternoon, Rhonda recalled, Ba and her maid had experimented with automatic writing. "Wilson's hand goes stiff and cold," Ba reported, "while the pencil moves and vibrates on its own. She has not the least consciousness of what she has written. I took the pencil myself and felt it move in a spiral pattern, my fingers grew numb at the tips — but the force was not sufficient to produce a stroke even much less a letter." The poet teased her friend: "Rational people should not discount these wonders without examination." In her friend's humour, Rhonda could discern a lingering desperation. When Ba pleaded with her to join them at the séance at Ealing, Rhonda acceded.

❧

I have no interest whatsoever in the spirit world, Rhonda tells herself. I prefer the world I can hold and touch with my own hands. In fact, I rejoice that my little porcelain friends have been here to give me company.

Her father was a boy of twelve in 1772 when he and his father, while staying at the castle of the Elector of Saxony at Meissen, visited the factory where the finest hard-paste porcelain outside China was made. There her father and grandfather encountered Johann Joachim Kändler, then in his sixties. As a young man, Kändler had wanted to be a sculptor of animals and had diligently made life-like and life-size figures of some of the creatures in the Elector's menagerie. After the Elector's death, he applied his talents to porcelain. His red squirrels — their tails standing upright like pokers of fire, their faces filled with fierce determination — intrigued Rhonda's father. He was also taken with the parrots, opulently coloured in shades of harsh magenta, deep purple, and soft pink. The monkey orchestra, dressed in court finery, their simian energies harnessed to their instruments, enchanted him.

His eyes, Rhonda's father told her, opened even wider when they feasted on the various Harlequins from the *Commedia dell'Arte*. He liked the colouring of the flesh and of costume, the finely executed brush strokes of the hair, and the twisting movement of the figures, which makes some look as if they are about to topple. The faces were a bit on the severe side, he admitted, but that was simply a side of the personality of the sculptor.

"I saw the entire world in miniature, my pet," he told his daughter. "There is the fanciful side of existence in the imaginary animals that Kändler manufactured from his imagination. There is a delicate beauty in his shepherds and shepherdesses. There is pathos in his rendition of the poor. Ambition, greed, lust, pride: all manner of worldly pursuits and accompanying vices can be discerned in the court figures."

Her father returned to England with six small pieces by Kändler packed in a small butternut case her grandfather had made for the occasion. Although he did not return to the Continent until his nineteenth year, her father asked friends of the family to purchase pieces for him on their trips to Germany and France. He remained loyal to Kändler, but he purchased the finest examples available of the other great modellers, Höroldt, Böttger and Reinicke. By the time he was seventeen, he had acquired an astoundingly large collection of Meissen figurines. Her father was also well known to all the dealers in London, who introduced him to the rival claims of Bow and Chelsea. When he died in 1850, he had amassed the largest collection anywhere of eighteenth-century European porcelain figurines. At his funeral, one insensitive friend of the family told Rhonda that she was now the owner of a national treasure and must do something about making it available to the nation.

Truth to tell, Rhonda cares little for posterity. For the past five years, she has been a diligent custodian, nay, guardian, of her father's collection, but she has also augmented it substantially. She takes comfort spending hours at a time in sitting at her desk in the room the figurines inhabit. Some weeks she spends hours looking at the birds; at other times, the pastoral figures hold her rapt; she receives pleasure imagining the various disputes of Harlequin, Columbine, Pulcinello, and Scaramouche. She has the illusion of holding an entire world within her grasp, one in which no one rebels against her or tells her how to conduct herself.

Her other remaining comfort is Sutherland, a slightly smaller version of Marble Hill House, two houses away on Richmond Road in Twickenham, ten miles from the centre of London. The majesty and refinement of this Palladian villa is chastely augmented by the French park which surrounds it and the flow of the Thames on its borders. She remembers the happy days when Edward and she would take their carriage to nearby Eel Pie Island, mixing with holiday makers and feasting on the tavern's celebrated delicacy. Nowadays, of an evening, she sometimes walks to the back of the house to behold the broad, vivid, and lucid river.

Just the other night, the sinking sun was a deep, menacing red, raging as it met the water. Certain something is about to disrupt her secluded existence, Rhonda does not know whether to be happy or sad.

Although she accepted the invitation to dine at the Rymers, a wheel on her carriage came loose and by the time she arrived, all the guests, including the Brownings and Mr. Home, had gone into dinner.

She told the manservant who greeted her that she would simply await the end of the meal. He showed her into the large sitting room, where she promptly fell asleep and was awoken by Mrs. Osborne. That woman, she is aware, is accounted an outsider in Society. She is evidently far wealthier than all the landed families of Hampshire put together and yet supposedly lives in eccentrically modest circumstances. They know each other from the auction houses, although their collecting interests are dissimilar.

A tall, thin woman always garbed in deep black, brown, or blue, Mrs. Osborne looks forbidding, but in this particular case, Rhonda wonders, appearances may be deceiving. She knows that in the opinion of the fashionable world Mrs. Osborne is of no consequence. After all, she is not of distinguished birth and inherited her wealth upon the death of her husband, a merchant. Many women in a similar position seek to impose themselves upon Society, although any recognition they receive is a hollow mockery of what they desire. Rhonda observes that Mrs. Osborne has no interest in becoming what she is decidedly not and so shuns most of the trappings of wealth. Her one indulgence is her collection of silver, which Rhonda has heard tell is worthy of note. Like Rhonda, Mrs. Osborne has the urge to gather objects together, perhaps as talismans to ward off death?

At first, Rhonda feared her teasing had affronted Mrs. Osborne, but then the other woman seemed to relax considerably. They had embarked on a lively conversation when the Rymer manservant summoned them to the séance. On her way into the dining room, Rhonda hurried over to the Brownings. Ba, although her face was drawn much more tightly than usual, welcomed her cordially. Robert, who has always claimed

Rhonda to be a great favourite of his, seemed less enthusiastic. Obviously worried to see his wife so agitated, he was distracted and not displaying his best manners. Ba joked that Mr. Home had informed her that she would be presented with a wreath signifying her accomplishment as a poet, but, Rhonda noticed, Robert did not find the remark amusing.

About the séance itself, she had mixed feelings. Mr. Home may be simply a magician but, if so, she has no notion of how his various demonstrations are accomplished. His hands were nowhere near the vicinity of the veiled hand that glided deftly around the room. Home himself is best described, she decides, as languid. His voice creaks and his face is forever doleful, as if he carries the weight of the world upon his slender shoulders.

As the spirit hand made its way toward Ba, Rhonda was surprised that Robert interposed himself between the emanation and his wife. Was he protecting Ba from something he feared might harm her or did he wish to be bestowed with the garland?

Afterwards, when the guests were asked to leave the room, Robert was rude to Mrs. Rymer, almost to the point of accusing her of being in league with an impostor. Only after he had insulted his hostess several times did the poor woman make her way back into the dining room and return a few minutes later with her husband, who announced that the party was to be reconstituted. When Mr. Home's power subsequently elevated the huge dining room table, Robert seemed remorseful.

Rhonda was therefore not prepared for the incident the following week at the London residence of the Canadian bluestocking Anna Jameson, where the Brownings were staying. Rhonda had been invited to take tea and found the event hard going. Ba was distracted; Robert was determinedly polite but distant. Rhonda surmised husband and wife had quarrelled.

The maid entered the room and handed two visiting cards to Mrs. Jameson, who indicated that the visitors could be shown in. A minute later, Mr. Home, accompanied by Julian Wilson, the painter and dealer, made their way into the room. Rhonda recalled that the exceedingly handsome Mr. Wilson had been seated three or four places down from her at the séance.

Ba, rising to greet the two men, shook Home's hand warmly. In a flash, Robert was at his wife's side but refused the outstretched hand of the medium. With considerable flourish, he informed the young man that if he did not leave immediately, he would throw him down the stairs. Inserting herself between the two men, Ba apologized for her husband's ungentlemanly conduct but suggested that the two visitors might best do as he requested.

Mr. Home, whose face had turned deathly pale, made to remove himself. An irate Mr. Wilson would, Rhonda is sure, have struck the poet had Ba not bestowed a tender smile in his direction. He quitted the room after his friend.

Rhonda had never seen Ba in such a temper. She told her husband that she quite agreed with him that Mr. Home was not a manly person but that was no reason to conduct himself in such a discourteous manner. Obviously upset to be chastised in the presence of his wife's friends, Robert left the room, slamming the door behind him. Ba did not apologize on behalf of her spouse, but she asked Rhonda to stay a bit longer with her and Mrs. Jameson. "He will sulk for many hours," she observed. She explained that her husband had been furious about a rumour making its way around London — that the hand at Ealing had been that of Dante and that its bestowal of the wreath upon her signified that she was the great poet of her age just as the Italian had been of his. She scoffed at the preposterous suggestion.

Mr. Wilson's letter takes Rhonda by surprise. Somewhat reticently, he refers to the two occasions on which they have recently met. He is writing to ask if she might sit to him. Two years ago, Rhonda recalls, he had been the fashion among the new painters. Then nothing. He vanished from the public eye, reappeared as Julian Wilson the dealer, and, then, of a sudden, began painting portraits of Laura Bennett, to whom he was engaged. After Laura's horrendous death, he reverted to his second profession.

The canvases she has seen have aroused Rhonda's admiration. His landscapes and portraits are not rendered in the academic manner. His greens and blues in the Windsor Forest canvases are too vivid for most critics, who have labelled his colours unnatural. The huge rendition of Gabriel at The Green in Ealing overpowers Rhonda with its sublime grandeur. She finds the portraits of Laura Bennett deeply moving. Be she shepherdess, muse, or goddess, the sitter had, to Rhonda's mind, eyes of such intense beauty that she captured the considerable range of the emotions experienced only by members of her sex.

In his missive, Mr. Wilson writes that he had abandoned picture making in favour of picture selling because of enormous personal obstacles but has given thought in the last little while to reclaiming his original calling yet again and pleads for her assistance. As he recalls, no portrait of Rhonda has ever been put on public show. That is a misfortune because her colouring is ideal for a portraitist and her likeness should be made available for posterity. He proposes to paint Lady Rhonda in any costume of her choosing should she give him the considerable pleasure of granting his request, which he hopes she does not consider too forward. In addition, were she agreeable, on completing the portrait, Mr. Wilson would like to exhibit the resultant work before giving it to her gratis.

Rhonda writes immediately to express her gratitude but to deny the favour. After she seals the envelope, she remembers that her late husband had often lamented the absence of her portrait next to the full-length one of himself in the main sitting room at Sutherland. When she visits that room later that day, Edward's face looks particularly downcast, and she wonders if his loneliness would be eased if she provided his portrait with a companion? She tears up her letter and writes another in which she acquiesces to Mr. Wilson's proposal.

Mr. Wilson's grateful reply comes two days later. He will travel from London at a time convenient to her. "I shall take great pleasure in spending time in Twickenham, which I heretofore have known mainly from reading the works of its two most famous literary residents, Alexander Pope and Horace Walpole."

He then gets down to business, providing her with detailed

instructions. She is to choose a dress for the portrait. She must be prepared to sit for him for five days in succession, Monday through Friday, two or three hours each day. At the end of that time, he will remove the canvas with him to London for finishing. He reminds her that she will perforce have him as a house guest for almost a week and hopes that the trouble of that imposition will be rewarded by the finished product.

Rhonda is of two minds on how to dress for the sitting. Her first inclination is to appear in widow's weeds, but, if she were to do so, the resulting portrait would not match that of her husband, who is costumed in his forest green great coat and crimson vest trimmed with gold embroidery. She selects the frock she had worn when last presented to the Queen, an elaborate purple dress with a pale silver bodice. This assembly of colours and textures had been much applauded by her late spouse.

When Mr. Wilson arrives, he does not look exactly as she remembered. His colouring is much more florid; he moves with great agitation. Still, she must admit, he is exceptionally pleasing to the eye. They take supper together, but he says little, pleading his exhaustion from the journey. He observes that Rhonda's pastoral retreat must give her great pleasure. "There are no better views of the Thames than those seen here from these magnificent houses. The profusion of giant trees must be what Eden looked like." Rhonda smiles and tells him that now, in her widowed state, she feels isolated, even trapped. Shortly afterwards he retires.

The following morning, Mr. Wilson is brusque. He likes Rhonda's choice of costume but suggests that she might wish to add a bit of rouge to her cheeks to heighten her complexion. Almost immediately, he rescinds his request. "If necessary, I shall add a little colouring to the picture." Then, he checks himself: "When Nature has rendered something perfectly, it is an impertinence on the part of the painter to seek an improvement." When Rhonda blushes, his face turns a shade of lavender.

As Mr. Wilson works on his preliminary sketches, he asks her about the history of Sutherland. She begins to recite what she knows, but her hysterical laugh begins, in its customary way, to get the better of her. She asks him to excuse her, but he simply shrugs his shoulders. "It is of no consequence whatsoever."

"On the contrary," she rejoins, "it is the bane of my existence."

"I do not find it so. It seems the gateway to your soul."

"Of a very unsavoury kind!" she shrieks.

"Not at all. We all have feelings we feel compelled to conceal. Most of us do not show the discrepancy between inner and outer worlds. You are more honest than most."

The sky is so dark the next morning that the painter tells Rhonda he would prefer to paint in the afternoon, by which time he hopes that the sun might be restored. She offers to take him on a tour of the house, showing him all the paintings and sculptures that remain. They are in the midst of their promenade, when Mr. Wilson asks if he might see the Meissen. Of course, she replies but remarks that she thought they would be of little interest to him. "But," he responds, "I have been told that they are your passion."

As they make their way through the enormous room housing the collection, Mr. Wilson asks many questions about the pieces and, in the process, Rhonda observes that he understands at once the subtle differences between the various artisans, how one was more skilful with eyes, another with dress. He also discerns quite plainly that some were more sentimental than others in how they defined the human countenance. "Perhaps they put their own life experiences into the little creatures that they modelled? He who had married wisely and well was content with life and displayed that. Someone disappointed by life, on the contrary, allowed such sentiments to peep through."

When she sits to him in the afternoon, he returns to the pieces they had examined in the morning. "Before today, I had an aversion to porcelain."

"Why so?"

"They looked cold to me, and I thought their range of emotions limited."

"They are warm to the touch."

"Exactly what I noticed today." He then switches the direction of their conversation. "What about fakes? As a dealer I have always had to concern myself with that issue."

"Oh, there are many. There is a Parisian factory, owned by Mr. Samson and his family, that has been very successful in that regard."

"Have you ever been taken in by them?"

"I do not think so. But it would be of little consequence if I was."

He is startled. "Why so?"

"Because if I loved an object, I would not really care who manufactured it."

At their next sitting, the conversation drifts to the subject of collectors. Although he has no harsh words for his clients, Rhonda can tell the subject distresses him. Finally, he asks her about Mrs. Osborne, who had been present at the Ealing séance. "I once visited her at her strange dwelling above a greengrocer's and found her the strangest person imaginable."

"In what way did you think her odd?"

"She seems to have no concern but for her various pieces of silver which are strewn about and deprive her of much needed living space."

"I think the various silver objects provide her with a comfort she has never found in human companionship. In her heart, I suspect she is a loving person."

"I would not have criticized her had I known she was a friend of yours."

"More an acquaintance than a friend. We are both women fond of accumulating material treasures."

"Still, I had never thought to associate you with her."

She smiles. "I would be pleased if you did so."

Julian and Rhonda have carefully avoided any discussion of the Ealing séance. Both of them feel that it would be in bad taste to talk about mutual friends. They chance upon the topic when Julian remarks that Rhonda would make a perfect Saint Cecilia. He imagines a splendid composition in which, enmeshed in folds of white satin, her musical gifts would summon the spirits from the sky.

"In the manner of Mr. Home?" she jokes.

He blushes before responding. "I think both of you quite capable of summoning angelic spirits."

"Mr. Home knows of that world. I do not."

"Yet you are, like myself, painfully aware of your friend Browning's opinion regarding Mr. Home's gifts. Do you share his prejudice?"

"Not at all. I cannot explain what Mr. Home does, but I believe he is a honest person."

"I was positive you shared Browning's aversion to him."

"I am sympathetic to both men, divergent as their beliefs may be. Mr. Home is able to summon some sort of psychic force from beyond the grave. Mr. Browning, I am convinced, wishes to believe in that spirit world but is deeply frightened of it. As you know, his wife's health has been exceedingly precarious since youth. Robert loves Ba and wishes at all costs to preserve her for this world. He is afraid that she takes an undue interest in a world beyond ours."

"For this reason he despises Mr. Home and acts so badly?"

"That is my guess."

"What about the wreath?"

"Oh, on that score, we touch on something altogether different. I think Robert's vanity was wounded when the wreath was presented to his wife. He may adore his wife, but I doubt he wishes her to be the greater poet!"

"So the spirit's tribute offended Mr. Browning?"

"I think Mr. Home contrived with his spirit to compliment

the wife and thus please the husband. Robert's love for Ba may be enormous, but he is a proud man. To be honest, I do not think him fully aware of the complexity of emotions aroused in him that evening."

"He behaved very badly towards my infirm friend."

"I agree, but you must try to understand and forgive. Robert is a man with a good heart." Rhonda does not bother to add that she knows Ba to be much more ruthless than her spouse. Like most others, Rhonda reflects, Mr. Wilson sees only her gentle side. He has no knowledge of how completely Ba has bent Robert to her whim of iron.

The artist confesses that he himself is not certain of Mr. Home and other spiritualists. When all is said and done, their manifestations fly in the face of both logic and reason. The miracles of Christ did the same, Rhonda responds, and yet many people take comfort from them.

Rhonda has not been totally honest with Julian. In truth, she has been badly frightened by the Ealing séance. How dare the dead insert themselves back into the world of the living? Do they have any right to do so? Why would they wish to do so? Is my poor husband still present? Am I still married to him for eternity? If so, she reflects, that is both a comfort and an obligation. She reminds herself that in the midst of life we are surrounded by death. Never before has she taken that statement so literally.

The following afternoon Mr. Wilson is genial. Upon reflection, he confesses, he can see Rhonda's point of view regarding Mr.

Browning. He adds that he fully understands the sorrow that she has experienced after the death of her husband.

He still has not recovered from the death of his beloved a year before. Moved by his mention of his own loss, Rhonda admits to Mr. Wilson that widowhood is not something that suits her well. She confesses that ten days or so after Edward's passing, a melancholia deeper than she had ever experienced pierced her soul. Even now, this torpor often holds her in its sway. She does not mention that she has at times considered doing away with herself.

When she comes down to breakfast on the fifth day, the housekeeper informs Rhonda that Mr. Wilson left for London at half past six. He had explained that bad news had arrived by way of a messenger early that morning and that he must absent himself immediately. He requested Mrs. Langton to convey his regrets and apologies.

On the one hand, Rhonda is relieved that Mr. Wilson has abandoned her. In the next month or two, he will doubtless get in touch with her regarding the portrait. He will wish to exhibit it, and she will then insist on buying it from him at its market value. That will be the end of the matter. She revealed far too much of herself last night. He must remain a stranger.

Although his stay has completely unnerved her, it has had one unexpected consequence. During the past three days, her ungainly laugh has been absent — only in the company of her father and husband has she ever been offered such a reprieve. Reluctantly, Rhonda finds herself mourning Mr. Wilson.

For the past few days, Rhonda realizes, she has experienced the one passion that previously evaded her. Rather, she admits to herself, the one passion she has *evaded*. Mr. Wilson is a most attractive man, and she yearns to touch him. She wishes to be possessed by him — and to possess him in return. These are not feelings that Edward ever aroused, and now she is deeply angry at Mr. Wilson for making her aware of the needs of her body when she is desperately trying to address those of her soul. That wretch Home, she knows, is also responsible for this muddle. If the dead live, perhaps our bodies are always ready to catch the fire of lust? To her usual state of dry despair has been added the moist, uncomfortable state of desire.

To protect her sanity, she must move back into the living world, but the only sphere in which she is now comfortable is that of her figurines. I must have fresh air, she warns herself, or perish.

CHAPTER SIX

OUT OF HEART

*I*n February 1855, six weeks before the public display of the newly-discovered *Leda* by Leonardo, Julian Wilson had been summoned to the Duke of Exeter's rooms at the Albany, his London residence. Julian was familiar with the Duke from a distance but had never met him. Since any artwork of value had long ago been sold off by the impoverished Exeters and the Duke could not afford to buy anything, there was no reason for them to know each other.

The Duke's rooms are ample testimony to his impecunious state. The rugs are badly torn, the stuffed furniture has overstepped its boundaries. There is more than a little hint of squalor. Only one servant is in attendance. As soon as Julian is shown into the room, the Duke, who is standing by the door, pounces upon him, exclaiming how delighted he is to make his acquaintance.

The Duke is joviality incarnate. His conversation contains no wit, but he conducts himself as if it does. Perhaps with the force of his personality, the Duke hopes to counter the impression made by his greasy locks and frayed clothes. When he steps out of the way, Julian sees two figures at the end of the room. He recognizes them as Stephen Widdicombe and Lady Smythe but waits for the Duke to make the introductions. In contrast to the Duke, middle-aged Mr. Widdicombe is perfectly dressed but in the unusual colours that have brought him renown. Today his coat is a deep lavender, his trousers Prussian blue and his cravat canary yellow. Mr. Widdicombe is an American who speaks in the considerable drawl of the Southern states. Diminutive Lady Smythe, as usual, is clad in widow's weeds. Gossip has it that she and Widdicombe are lovers. Julian is taken with her refined features and her delicate, almost overly polite way of speaking. However, the lady manages few words this afternoon.

Mr. Widdicombe begins the meeting by outlining his claims to be a connoisseur of impeccable credentials. Although born in Georgia, his youth was spent in New England at the Phillips Andover Academy and, later, Harvard. After that, he left the United States for Europe and for many years now has been collecting art in Italy. He emphasizes that he is from a family of cotton growers and that he sometimes represents the interests of that group in the various courts of Europe. Mr. Widdicombe exudes prosperity. He is a man of independent means, his bearing declares, who has the wherewithal to collect anything he so pleases.

At this point, the Duke can contain himself no longer. "Yet the greatest treasure Widdicombe has ever uncovered lay for centuries unnoticed in an old storeroom at Arundel!"

Mr. Widdicombe nods assent. Yes, while visiting the Duke, whom he met last year when they were both taking the waters at Marienbad, he asked if he might scour the premises to see if anything of value might have overlooked the penurious eyes of the Duke's grandfather and father.

The young nobleman interrupts: "I did not have to think twice before giving permission. One has been down on one's luck for an exceedingly long time."

Widdicombe bestows a compassionate smile on the young nobleman and continues. "I think we have made a remarkable discovery." With that, he and Lady Smythe stand aside to allow Julian to see the small canvas placed on an easel directly in front of the mantle. Julian is startled to see Leonardo's lost painting, *Leda and the Swan*.

In addition to being raped and being blamed for the Trojan War because of the machinations of Helen, one of the twins born of Jupiter's lust, Leda has been a source of endless fascination. If, as in some accounts, she is compliant to the wishes of the god, she is morally lax — a slattern. If, as in others, she fights Jupiter off, she is merely one woman in a long series of females who have been unappreciative of male attention. In any event, the intrusion of the god was violent and unwelcome, and any painting of her carries the risk of having a pornographic edge.

Medieval and Renaissance man, Julian reflects, did not consider the Latin poet Ovid a teller of disgusting stories of sexual intrigue. Rather, Ovid's tales, even the one about the randy king of the gods making himself into a giant sex-crazed swan, were read, in a symbolical way, as instances of the transforming power of love.

In my age, Julian realizes, the artist who chooses to represent Leda and her giant bird-lover hazards anger and indignation. Even the work of artists as great as Leonardo and Correggio are now censured when they deal with subjects considered reprehensible by today's Society.

Correggio's *Leda* was painted in 1530 for Rudolf II of Spain. One hundred and thirty years later it was removed to Stockholm by Queen Christina of Sweden. Then the picture passed into the possession of several noble Roman families. One of these dismembered the painting, destroying Leda's head on moral grounds. Poor Leda arrived in a very altered and dishevelled state at the door of Frederick the Great in 1775. The Elector had the good sense to hire Charles Coypel to restore her as best he could. Fifty-five years later, the damsel was removed to the Kaiser Frederick Museum in Berlin, where she received a new head.

Like Correggio, Leonardo was fascinated by Leda and was pleased to have the opportunity to paint her. In his diary he wrote: "Then it came to pass that I executed a painting on behalf of Guiliano de' Medici. He wished to see the features of his inamorata mirrored so that he might kiss them without arousing suspicion." Yet the patron's conscience, and perhaps his wife, got the best of him because he subsequently returned

Leda to the painter.

The subsequent history of the canvas is difficult to trace. A rendition in the Gallery Borghese is a known copy. This version is thought to present a hillier landscape in the background than the original. There is another copy by Domenico Puligo in Brussels. There is a preparatory drawing owned by Her Majesty the Queen. There is even a version in Philadelphia in the United States. A second *Leda* by Leonardo hangs in Rome, but that painting has been the subject of debate: it might be by the master or it may have been begun by Leonardo and carried out in another's hand or it is a magnificent picture by a completely different artist. But the whereabouts of the original painting is not known.

Or not known until this late winter evening. The Leonardo was said to have once been, with the Correggio *Leda*, in the collection of Christina of Sweden, which that lady had fiercely declared to be the original.

Julian is not certain he is seeing the canvas that Christina so highly valued. He has many qualms about this painting. It is too unusually scrupulous in brushstrokes; it is also far more meticulous than any genuine Leonardo he has seen. On the other hand, the flesh of the woman is luminous, of a quality of workmanship only a genius possesses.

For the first time in a long while, Julian is thrown into a quandary by the authenticity of a painting he is asked to judge. He is of two minds. It could well be the famous missing Leonardo. Or it could be a fake. The overwhelming beauty of the woman, especially her coy smile, dazzles him as do all the other details in the picture, but he knows that Leonardo was a careless, sometimes lazy painter and this canvas has no mistakes. It is almost better than Leonardo himself could have produced.

Mr. Widdicombe and Lady Smythe do not dance attendance on Julian's reaction, but the Duke of Exeter cannot contain himself. "The canvas is to be presented to the world the month after next at a reception at the Royal Academy. We trust you will be there and, moreover, we hope that you will concur with us in celebrating this discovery."

Unwilling to declare the painting a sham but unable to confer the authenticity the Duke wishes, Julian declares it to be a painting worthy of the title of masterpiece. "But you agree with us that it is a Leonardo?" the Duke importunes.

"I cannot state categorically that it is the lost Leonardo, but I am willing to say it is worthy of the attention of all lovers of art." Julian will be of no use to the Duke or Mr. Widdicombe in fuelling the bidding among collectors. The Duke is put out and steals a glance at Mr. Widdicombe, who brushes the matter off by thanking Julian for attending on them.

At the Royal Academy reception, Mr. Widdicombe asks Julian if he has any further thoughts on the provenance of the *Leda*. He does not, but he offers one observation. "If the painting is a fake, it is an exceedingly strange choice for a forger."

"Why is that?" Mr. Widdicombe asks.

"Our age does not take kindly to Jupiter's antics. The painting is too frank for most people in this room, many of whom consider themselves lovers of art."

The American nods in agreement. "Yes, you may be correct, but a clever forger may have already thought of that. When all is said and done, the picture bears all the hallmarks of Leonardo."

Julian does not bother to add that Jupiter pretends to be a swan in order to have his way with Leda and that an astute faker may, in his choice of subject matter, be attempting to have his way with an unwary collector. That afternoon, the two men simply agree to disagree and wander off in different directions.

By late summer, Julian has all but forgotten Leonardo and his *Leda*. He has been preoccupied with his growing attachment to Lady Rhonda. How can he fall hopelessly in love with a woman old enough to be his mother? He is both relieved and alarmed when he receives a message from Lady Smythe summoning him to London. The Duke of Exeter has been murdered in his chambers in the Albany and the Leonardo stolen. She would not, she assures him, communicate this distressing information so urgently had not the description of the culprit, according to the police, borne an uncanny resemblance to the murderer of Laura Bennett. For this reason, she has taken the liberty of summoning him.

Mr. Widdicombe and Lady Smythe have removed themselves to the Savoy, where Julian meets with them. A hysterical Lady Smythe describes to Julian her encounter with a stranger the day before the Duke's murder.

"Two days ago, Hornby, the Duke's manservant, informed

me that on the day previous, a young gentleman had presented himself for an urgent appointment with the Duke. As his master was away at Newmarket, Hornby had told the man to return the following afternoon. However, the Duke had been delayed and the hour of the young man's appointment was now approaching.

"The next day, in the absence of Hornby, I let the young man in and showed him to the sitting room. He was small, of the slenderest frame nature ever allows to those of the masculine gender. His hair, which flowed to his shoulders in gold ringlets, was striking as were his emerald-coloured eyes. But what was most strange about the youth was his unfashionable attire, which consisted of an azure blue corduroy suit and bright green leather boots. In his hand, he held a peak cap, also of blue corduroy.

"He bowed in my direction and then excused his poor manners in seeking an interview without benefit of a letter explaining his purpose. I told him it did not signify and then asked what he required.

"'My lady, I have come at the behest of a mutual friend to ask after the Duke's state of health.'

"'Who is the mutual friend and why should he send you to inquire into such personal matters?' I inquired.

"'You will forgive me if I do not assign him a name. The Duke is at considerable risk.'

"'Sir, I am completely confused by what you say and do not know how you a stranger could be of any assistance to him. He is excessively corpulent, but that is of concern only to the Duke, not a matter for me and the likes of you.'

"'I am not speaking of the health of his body but of his soul. He is in grave danger. I come with a warning.'

"'Does someone threaten him harm?'

"'That is as may be. I can only speak with him.'

"Anxious to conclude the interview, I assured him I could be of no further use if he had no confidences for me to pass on to the Duke. With that, he smiled, bowed and showed himself out.

"On the following day, after the Duke had returned from Newmarket, I mentioned the mysterious young man to him. He had no idea as to his identity; he certainly did not seem the least bit dismayed when he heard what the young man had said. He was certain someone was playing a joke.

"That evening, Mr. Widdicombe and I went to the Haymarket to attend a performance of *Twelfth Night*. We invited the Duke to join us, but he declined, saying that he was fatigued beyond endurance from his travelling. When we left our rooms at half-past six, the Duke was reading in his sitting room.

"Several hours later, just as the play was finishing, a messenger sent by Hornby told us to hasten home without delay. We did so and were surprised to find Hornby and six members of the constabulary awaiting us.

"At about eight o'clock, the strange young man of the day before had knocked at our chamber doors and been admitted by Hornby, who was told to announce that Mr. Sydney Brown craved an interview with the Duke. Hornby showed the young man in to the Duke and then retired to his own room. About half an hour later, Hornby heard voices raised and headed for the sitting room. As he approached that chamber, he saw the door flung open and the Duke, like a beached whale, prone on the floor. Then he saw the putative Mr. Brown open the door to the chambers — the Leonardo canvas in hand — and let himself out. Hornby rushed to the Duke, who was already dead.

"Hornby quickly ran down to the caretaker, who was told to summon the police. On their arrival, it was discovered that the Duke had been killed by the insertion of an exceedingly small, wire-thin knife into his heart. There was a very small amount of blood on the carpet. The Duke of Exeter had died very quickly, so expert was the murderer in the use of his instrument. It was the attending policemen who informed Mr. Widdicombe and myself that the murderer appeared to be the identical person who had killed Laura Bennett and Bethany Sinclair."

The same demon, Julian agrees, had obviously slain Laura and Bethany. But why turn his hand against the Duke? What had they in common? Julian wonders if the murderer is an infernal spirit brought back to life by the likes of Daniel Home? Was this a way in which evil was loosened upon the earth? Could his new friend possess such powers, powers that he unleashed and then could not control?

Haunted by the presence of such evil and confused by his love for an unattainable woman, Julian Wilson determines to quit England. The wealthy American collector, Jarves, a resident of Florence, has invited him to assist him in the cataloguing of his huge collection. Perhaps in the warmth of Tuscany he can escape the sufferings that threaten to overwhelm him.

Daniel Home also seeks refuge in the same Italian city. Unable to forget his humiliation in London and anxious to leave England behind, Daniel eagerly accepts an invitation from Frances Trollope and her son, Adolphus, to stay with them at their villa in Florence. There, he is told, he need not encounter the Brownings, so large is the English community in that city.

Daniel is accompanied on his journey by Bendigo, the Rymers' eldest son. When they arrive at Dover for the crossing to Calais, the sky is clear, an omen that their passage will be trouble-free. The two men settle in their cabin, where Bendigo promptly falls asleep. There are many things Daniel does not know. He is unaware that Julian suspects that he may be a party to murder. He is oblivious to the fact that he is about to become the pawn of a ruthless villain. Instead, Daniel spends his time composing an inventory of his soul.

Anxious thoughts criss-cross his mind. He does not know why or how the spirits visit him. He has read all the theories: he is aware that many scientists speculate that the spirits of the dead are able, through the agency of mediums, to form raw matter — protoplasm — into recognizable small objects such as hands; he has read that many spiritualists use a form of group hypnosis to deceive their audiences.

Mr. Browning's display of anger reminds him of his Aunt Cook's. Once again, he feels as if he been made to drink from the cup of someone else's venom. He is filled with rage against the poet and all those who have labelled him a sham. He would like to strike out against them, proclaim his anger at such unjust treatment.

Just then, the ship rocks violently. Daniel rushes to the portal from where he sees the sky filled with lightning and thunder. The Channel has turned violent; the ship is tossed by huge waves. Despite the danger, Daniel feels exhilarated. For a few moments the sky returns to blackness; then everything is illuminated for a second or two as bright, violent shards fill the sky. The accompanying sound of thunder is deafening. The sheer magnificence of the spectacle becalms the young man's heart.

In the morning as they are taking leave of the ship, Daniel remarks to Bendigo that he must have been in a deep slumber not to have been awoken by the storm. His companion inspects him closely. "Mr. Home, I suffer from insomnia and can assure you I had not a wink of sleep last night. I rose twice and each time heard you snoring loudly. The crossing was completely uneventful."

PART TWO

FLORENCE

CHAPTER SEVEN

THE HEART'S DESIRE

On one side, the gentle Arno steals past beneath dark green foliage; on the other, the mountain leads the eye towards Fiesole, dotted with palaces and terraced gardens. The Duomo and Palazzo Vecchio tower above the trees. What other city can boast such a magnificent view as the Cascine bestows?

At this hillside vantage point, all parts of Florentine society converge in the winter of 1856. The great and the wealthy are here to mingle with each other. The equipages of the wealthy sit side by side. Phaetons, like fast frigates, shoot swiftly by in the sunshine-filled afternoons. Scandal holds court here. No one talks of frivolities such as politics or literature. The conversation is of the world — the last duel in Berlin, the witticisms current in Paris, the recent bankruptcies in London, the Russian ladies who have abandoned their husbands and families — and is conducted with great earnestness. Transgressions against good breeding, social gaucheries, solecisms of dress meet with sharp reproof, but graver offences such as murder and treason are often deemed of little consequence. The many visitors are Russians, French, German, and English, but all are called *Inglese*.

Even Julian's American host, James Jackson Jarves, is reckoned one of the *Inglese*, despite his broad, nasal-filled pronunciation. Yesterday, he insisted his protégé be introduced properly to Florentine society by attending the Grand Duke's Tuesday evening reception at the Palazzo Pitti, where upwards of seven hundred people are welcomed.

No court dress is required. The halls are divided into two by a very handsome and abundant supper at which Julian's countrymen, their usual pasty white faces turned bronze, behave abominably. Some of them seize plates of *bonbons* and empty the contents into their coat pockets. The Italians in attendance are more brazen. Large portions of fish, sauce and all, are packed up in newspapers and deposited in their pockets. Pieces of chicken share the same fate, sometimes without the benefit of a newspaper.

The Grand Duke is completely unprepossessing. He wanders about attempting to attract as little notice as possible. His clothes do not fit him, and he seems aware he has little or nothing to say. He does manage one semblance of a witticism when Mr. Jarves points out to him that his English tailor is in attendance. The nobleman shrugs: *"Qu'importe?* Everyone is welcome if they come to spend money in Florence." The Duke is the real figure of fun here, variously called *Grandoca* (big goose) and *Granciuco* (big ass).

The English notion of correctness obviously varies with country and climate. Here everybody is received without reference to their conduct, past or present. The warmer climate necessitates lighter clothing; this does not necessarily mean that the ladies must wear brighter colours or less clothing, but such changes are readily visible. A few of the English who settle here are obviously the refuse of Europe, persons who come for want of money or want of character. Most of the English are decidedly of the better class, people of refinement and money. Even they feel their ties to their mother country loosened, if not severed.

Tourism is a vital ingredient in the city's life. All the lodging houses are spruced up to the best modern standard; the shops stock goods from London and Paris; the galleries set their wares in the most attractive manner. Great is the joy in Florence at the advent of the stranger from abroad. But a very anxious question is posed to newcomers: "Here for the season, or going on to Rome?" The position of Florence on the highway to the Eternal City is the cause of many a sad slip between the cup and the lip.

Mr. Jarves, who dresses in the bright colours favoured by American society, has very little interest in the citizenry of present-day Florence. Very much in the manner of a Baedeker, he has a decided opinion on every church, palace, civic building, and residence in the city and admires only those built before 1500. Brunelleschi's colonnade for the Spedale degli Innocenti is "sublimity itself" because of the restrained classical design of pale browns and the blue roundels inserted between each opening; Michelangelo's huge pieces of funerary statuary (Night, Day, Dawn, and Dusk) in the New Sacristy at San Lorenzo are "vulgar" because they have a slight Mannerist touch to them. The Sala dei Gigli in which lilies, the emblem of Florence, cover the walls between Ghirlandaio's frescoes of Roman statesmen "hits the mark" whereas Vasario's courtyard of 1565, with its copy of Verrocchio's Pluto, is "insufferable." Jarves is an ardent collector of what he calls primitive Italian art, be it Etruscan, Roman, or Medieval. Very early Renaissance, before the laws of perspective were discovered, is most acceptable; in Jarves's opinion, the invention of depth in picture-making ruined everything. Jarves delivers all these opinions between puffs on his ever-present cigars. Julian suspects that many citizens of the city find his host insufferable, but he has plenty of money to spend.

Despite his proclivity for the ancient, Jarves's villa in the Oltrana district has standards of convenience and hygiene that match, as he puts it, the highest industrial standard. The interior, however, is packed with salvaged medieval masonry: carved doorways, chimney pieces, even portions of staircases. The walls are filled with paintings, while small and large statues, musical instruments, and ceramics nest among the architectural fragments.

Jarves has led a charmed life. He was born in New England and married very young. Then for health reasons (he had a spot on his lung), he and his wife settled in Honolulu where he grew wealthy as a businessman. During his stay, he also wrote the first documented history of the Hawaiian Islands. At the age of thirty-three, he and his family travelled to Paris, where the works of art in the Louvre came as a complete revelation to him. He then read Ruskin and, soon afterwards, after a sizeable inheritance from his manufacturer father was made over to him, made his way to Florence. He has been here for almost two years.

The American fears that the city is about to lose its heritage because of the intemperate attempts at modernization being introduced by the Grand Duke, who is the puppet of the Austrian Duke of Lorraine, the true ruler of the city. Unlike his friend Mrs. Browning, who writes in support of an independent Florence and a unified Italy, Jarves has little interest in what he calls "petty ideas of nationalism" but believes that, at all costs, the ancient buildings must be preserved.

Julian has been summoned to Florence to act as Jarves's authenticator. As a collector, the American has faced many obstacles, including a preponderance of forgers eager to take advantage of a wealthy collector. Deeply suspicious of some artifacts recently offered him, Jarves wants Julian to examine them. Chief among them is a *Madonna of the Veil*, attributed to Sandro Botticelli and done in his customary manner: the sweet-faced Madonna with her long, delicate nose, large, bony hands, pale blue eyes, and light brown hair searches the face of the onlooker; the child, also blessed with exceedingly refined features, looks upwards, as if lost in thought of heavenly things.

After even a cursory examination, Julian informs Jarves the painting is a fake: the blue of the Madonna's robe, which should be of a thickly applied and coarsely ground lapis lazuli or azurite, is made from Prussian blue, a pigment introduced only in the eighteenth century; the dark line of the lips of mother and son should be in thick pure transparent madder whereas they are rendered in black. The painting was not only not by Botticelli or a member of his school, it had been done within the year.

Deeply pleased that Julian has sniffed out a cheat, Jarves turns this discussion towards the undeniably authentic, the miracles worked by Daniel Home, whose séances Jarves had attended in the New World. At one, conducted on a Sunday afternoon, he beheld Home float to the ceiling, where, in a trance-like state, he had remained for at least ten minutes. During the interval, Jarves had risen from his seat and inspected the room thoroughly, checking for any mechanism that might be holding the spiritualist in place. He found nothing suspicious.

When Julian tells Jarves that he had been present at one of Home's séances the previous summer, the American's interest is aroused. He asks Julian's thoughts on what he witnessed. Julian confesses he has no explanation and agrees with him that Home is not a trickster. He rises in his employer's estimation for merely speaking what he considers to be the plain truth.

Jarves then relates a strange story: "Spiritualists have been in bad repute here in the past two months because of one Regina Ronti, a young woman who professed to be a medium, who seduced the elderly man-of-letters Seymour Kirkup. Well into his eighties, he has found himself saddled with the paternity of a baby girl, Imogen, whom he adopted when Regina died. On her deathbed, she told the gullible old man that he was the father of the little girl. Unfortunately, the outrage against Kirkham has led to a popular outcry against mediums of all persuasions. Home might be in danger of his life if he stays here too long."

Jarves adds by way of conclusion: "A more transparent case of imposture than Ronti is difficult to imagine. Home, on the other hand, can only be compared to the Nazarene in his ability to work miracles." When Julian points out that Home is a painfully shy, deeply insecure person, Jarves brushes this aside: "Christ sometimes displayed a reticent manner." Julian does not bother to point out that Christ had sought disciples whereas Home does not. He dares not confess that he himself has entertained some doubts about Daniel.

Of one person Jarves has decidedly negative feelings, his fellow American, Mr. Widdicombe, who, accompanied by Lady Smythe, has just arrived in Florence. His disdain is not centred on differences about works of art, for the two men share many of the same beliefs about early Italian art. Their disagreement is not sartorial for they dress very much alike. Rather, Mr. Jarves despises his countryman because he is from the South, which, Jarves is certain, will soon secede from the American union. The source of Mr. Widdicombe's wealth is the cotton obtained on plantations that are dependent on slavery whereas well-to-do Americans from the North gain their money from factories that offer gainful employment to immigrants from all over the world. According to Jarves, Mr. Widdicombe and his compatriots are exploiters masquerading concern for the backward slaves who, they improbably claim, cannot survive without them.

⤳❦⤳

Julian's days in Florence provide him with a welcome distraction from events in England. Despite the tragic circumstances, his abrupt departure from Twickenham was, he realizes more and more, a godsend. He did not wish to be drawn any further into Lady Rhonda's orbit. While residing in her home and perforce looking at her great beauty and speaking with her for hours on end, a sentimental attachment had formed. He disagreed with her defence of Mr. Browning and had reservations about some other opinions she offered. But, without doubt, his feelings had been aroused. Such an attachment, he realized, was dangerous to his peace of mind. Here in Florence, as much as possible, he hopes to forget Lady Rhonda and to blot out the memory of Laura Bennett and her murderer.

Jarves keeps Julian busy. He was even required the other night to attend Donizetti's *Lucia di Lammermoor* at the Pergola, the opera house. Attendance at the opera is a joke, since the wealthy visit each other's boxes during the performance to chat, laugh, and partake of refreshments. They all turned their backs on Walter Scott's poor heroine and the splendid *bel canto* singing of the soprano portraying her. The music was drowned out; the tragedy of the young woman ignored. A bemused Jarves informed him, "A box at the Pergola is an economical affair, as it saves the expense of receiving society under one's roof."

When he wishes to be alone, Julian takes himself to Doney's Café in the Via Tornabuoni, three salons filled with cream-coloured columns and marble-topped tables. Here there are the white uniforms of Austrian cavalry officers, noisy waiters, flower girls, and many *Inglese*. Julian sits alone by the hour pondering his gloomy prospects. His only companion is Burrasco, the whippet-like white dog who conducts himself like a needy, sponging dandy.

That animal haunts Doney's from morning to night. At breakfast, he is grateful for a slice of bread and butter; at lunch and dinner, he will dine only on meat, for which he waits patiently. Meeting a friend such as Julian, he greets him in the street with an empathic wriggle and barks furiously as if to say, "This is my friend, get out of his way or I'll bite you!" Burrasco takes his leave as soon as Julian has donated to him sufficiently from whatever meal he is taking.

From his employer Julian has learned that Daniel is in Florence and is not therefore surprised when he sees him at Doney's in November, about two months after his own arrival. Yet he almost does not recognize him when he catches sight of a tall, thin man in a nicely-cut Bond Street pale brown suit. The red curls in his hair are highlighted by the sun, his eyes glisten, and he walks with an erect carriage. In the open air and on a sunny afternoon, Daniel looks like so many of the *Inglese* who are sightseeing or shopping.

It takes Daniel takes a few seconds to locate who has hailed him. Finally, he catches Julian's eye, seems a bit startled and then smiles shyly. As he walks towards Julian, his gait slows and his shoulders begin to stoop. But when he reaches the table, he takes his friend's hand warmly and securely in his own. A man of exquisite good manners, he asks if he can join Julian. Daniel is not the kind of person to make any assumptions in social intercourse, no matter how trivial.

They both consciously avoid the topic of Mr. Browning. Daniel mentions he has travelled to Florence with Bendigo Rymer but is staying at Villino Trollope, even though Julian's friend Abigail Fanshaw had invited him to stay with her. When Julian mentions that he has been hired by Mr. Jarves to assist him with the authentication of some early paintings, Daniel discreetly mentions that the American had been extraordinarily kind to him when they knew each other in Massachusetts.

During their talk, Julian becomes aware of a side of the spiritualist he has never discerned before. As they speak of inconsequential things — the weather, mutual friends staying in Florence — he cannot help but notice how unadorned and plain a person Daniel is when removed from the spirit world. He even becomes jocular. His laughter, completely spontaneous, flows from a wellspring of good feeling and comradeliness.

The only hints of tension surface when Daniel finally mentions that he has heard that the Brownings, after an extended stay in Paris, have just returned to Florence. He obviously has no intention, he declares, of crossing paths with either husband or wife. He merely remarks: "Mrs. Browning is well disposed to the spirit world. Mr. Browning is not."

Julian cannot restrain himself: "His conduct towards you was unforgivable. I was on the verge of thrashing him."

Daniel's expression remains stoical: "The existence of the spirits can be disquieting to those who wish to live fully in the flesh and blood world. I suffered because I extended the hand of friendship and it was rejected. I now realize that I am, for him, the symbol of something that he does not wish to understand. My own wound was paltry and is now healed."

Daniel's ability to repress anger is astonishing and, Julian is certain, misguided. He sees no reason to dwell on the past, but such forgiveness strikes him as unnatural. Briefly, the harrowed look of Daniel Home reappears and then, as quickly, vanishes. Then the truth dawns. Daniel is pretending to feel no anger towards Browning. This is probably, Julian realizes, the only instance in which he dissembles.

At this point, the two men are distracted by the pleadings of Burrasco. As his friend feeds the demanding canine a piece of gravy-soaked bread, Julian notices a tall, angular woman exit from a shop on the other side of the street. Dressed in a green silk dress, her hair adorned in the latest Florentine fashion, she catches his attention. He is puzzled. He knows this person but cannot place her. Of a sudden, he realizes, just as she disappears, that the countenance belongs to Mrs. Osborne.

Daniel and Julian speak for about five minutes more. Daniel mentions that the interior of Mr. Jarves's home sounds even more opulent than that of the Villino Trollope and that he would like to call upon Julian to witness its marvels, but more importantly, to spend more time with him. They rise, shake hands, and go opposite ways.

Apart from Doney's, Julian's chief diversion is that treasure house, the Uffizi. Built in the sixteenth century as offices for Cosimo I's Tuscan administration, his heirs, shortly after his death, used the clerestoried upper storey to display the family's many treasures. Here, Julian spends happy hours looking at paintings by Giotto, Uccello, Piero della Francesca and Fra Fillipo Lippi. Visiting the galleries, crowded with ten times the number of canvases the walls can comfortably house and blocked with pieces of statuary, can be hard work, but the rewards are considerable. As a portraitist, Julian approves della Francesca's honesty in giving the Duke of Urbino his broken, hooked nose and in rendering the Duchess as a woman of noble ugliness.

Julian's hope is that he can find inspiration from what he sees at the Uffizi to begin anew, yet again, as an artist. Unlike many visitors to those crowded rooms, he never attempts to paint there. His time is spent staring at masterworks such as Giotto's *Ognissanti Madonna*, a work despised by Jarves because of its precocious use of perspective.

Lost in his thoughts one afternoon, he does not notice the Brownings until they are almost upon him. Quickly, he retreats behind the nearest piece of monumental statuary in order to let them pass. Unfortunately, they stop on the other side of the Jupiter, thus making him an eavesdropper on their conversation.

Their discussion centres on the statue that separates Julian from them. Unlike many of the English, Mrs. Browning wholeheartedly approves of the Uffizi's custom of displaying full nudity in paintings and statuary. Her husband agrees with her but thinks this statue in extremely bad taste.

"Robert, this Jupiter is the king of the gods, and he asserts his position magnificently."

"A bit too magnificently, my dear. The sculptor could have been more discreet."

"But Jupiter was very much a man for the ladies. Isn't that what is rendered before us?"

"He is shown in the most manly of terms and that is not a proper subject for any artist."

"I suppose you hold a similar opinion of Leonardo's *Leda and the Swan* and, like most of our countrymen, were well pleased when the painting disappeared yet again?"

"You cannot accuse me of being prurient about a canvas I have never had the pleasure of seeing!"

"But for you it would have been a source of agitation."

The poetess begins to twitter. A few moments later, Julian hears the poet begin to chortle, obviously at his own expense. Shortly afterwards, their attention taken by the Titian *Venus*, the Brownings move away and Julian escapes.

The mention of the Leonardo reminds Julian of the murder of the Duke of Exeter and, consequently, of the deaths of Laura and Bethany. Mr. Widdicombe and Lady Smythe have just taken up residence in Florence. As a courtesy, he should call upon them but cannot bring himself to do so.

Julian encounters Mr. Widdicombe and Lady Smythe where he least likely expects to see them. He arrives home at the villa to discover Jarves and Widdicombe huddled in the sitting room inspecting a thirteenth-century French ivory statue of a Madonna and Child. For the moment, Jarves and Widdicombe have forgotten their differences; in fact, Jarves does not recall that Julian and Widdicombe know each other. They shake hands and then inform their host that they have met on several occasions. "Oh, that unfortunate business with the Duke. It had slipped my mind," Jarves mumbles.

Jarves and Widdicombe take Julian into their confidence. The small statue, which has a line down its middle, opens to reveal the events surrounding the crucifixion, death and resurrection of Christ. "Most ingenious," Jarves proclaims the piece. "The mother and child open to unfold, as it were, the unhappy ending of the baby's life."

"Your comments are very secular. Many would disagree with your phrasing." The speaker is Lady Smythe, who has been hidden from Julian's sight in one of the room's dark corners. As she steps into the light, Julian is again struck by her quiet, luminous beauty. She advances to allow Julian to take her hand, which he kisses. "Christians would describe it differently. The outer shell shows the infant who has come to redeem the world. The inner depicts his death, which culminates in his resurrection and the promise of eternal life to all his followers."

Mr. Widdicombe looks displeased. "We are not here to discuss theological niceties. We have come here to ask Mr. Jarves's opinion of this statue, which has just been offered to me. Lady Smythe is of the opinion it is a fake. I am certain she is wrong."

"There is something very mechanical about the carving, as if it has been made to look deliberately archaic. It has no spontaneity. For me, it lacks conviction."

Lady Smythe and Mr. Widdicombe are obviously repeating a conversation that has taken place before. He flatly contradicts her: "Medieval man was mechanical. Those craftsmen, who professed a belief in their God, had no conception of themselves as artists. Their work has no individuality. If one found a hint of a sensibility in this statue, it would be a fake. My companion has little knowledge of early primitive art."

The scorn in his voice is palpable. Julian is uncertain whether he is witnessing a genuine argument or a performance for his and Jarves's delectation. Jarves, whose specialty does not encompass medieval ivories, has no decided opinion.

After holding the piece in his hands for several minutes, Julian realizes that the visitors are looking in the wrong place to make an attribution. "The piece is a fake but that cannot be detected from looking at the carving. Rather, look at both sets of hinges. They are extremely old, but the holes for them have been drilled by a modern machine." As his listeners take turns examining the object again, they nod agreement with Julian's clever detection.

Jarves, jubilant that the issue has been resolved under his roof, invites all three to take a glass of port. As soon as they are seated before the fireplace, Lady Smythe remarks that she is happy to encounter Julian under much happier circumstances than those at the Albany. Widdicombe interrupts her: "That unfortunate young man is dead and buried. He is of no consequence. Of more importance is the *Leda* that has gone missing once again."

"The Duke was a poor young creature gone astray," Lady Smythe observes, staring straight ahead at her companion.

In an attempt to change subjects, Julian mentions that he has encountered Daniel Home in Florence. "We have all

witnessed the work of this master of undoubted authenticity."
Mr. Widdicombe disagrees with this observation. "I think my
friend Browning is correct to be suspicious, although I have no
evidence with which to challenge the medium. In my opinion,
he is a brilliant illusionist."

"My dear Stephen, you are in a very suspicious frame
of mind today. You have eyes but do not believe what they
show you." With a hint of malice in her voice, Lady Smythe
continues: "I stand corrected in the matter of the ivory; I did
not know why it was a fake. I do not bow easily in the case of
Home. There is scientific evidence that validates his powers."

"I do not understand how Daniel accomplishes his wonders," interjects Julian, "but he is a person of great sincerity and
integrity." Jarves immediately concurs. Widdicombe, knowing
that he is the lone agnostic in a room of believers, simply
observes that on this issue he remains on Mr. Browning's side.

"Then, my dear, you are not on the side of the angels," his
lady friend observes. "Daniel Home is a true original. Ours
is an age in which the authentic has become confused with
the fake."

"You are aware," says Widdicombe, "that many Florentines
are convinced that Home is a necromancer who raises the
dead to life?" He pauses. "Such people are, according to my
manservant, capable of rousing dead murderers and other
criminals so that they can commit yet more crimes." Lady
Smythe pleads with Widdicombe to stop speaking nonsense. A
crimson blush crosses Julian's face as he hears the American
gentleman voice sentiments similar to those he himself has
entertained.

In an attempt to change subjects, Jarves remarks that the marriage of the Brownings has evidently suffered a decline since the Ealing séance. Julian, recalling the couple in conversation at the Uffizi, observes that he has seen them in high spirits and such gossip is probably wrong. Mr. Widdicombe says he hopes that is the case. "In any event," he observes, "domestic tranquillity is always best accomplished if the female follows the lead of the male." Lady Smythe is displeased but holds her tongue.

As they walk back to the villa after seeing the couple off, Julian asks Jarves about Lady Smythe. The American knows very little about her. At the age of twenty-one, the youngest child of a country doctor and his wife, she became a governess in the home of Sir George Smythe, a widower. Jarves thinks her surname may have been Brown. They were evidently a happy couple, but the Baronet, in France on business, died in a stagecoach accident. About two years ago, Lady Smythe began to be seen in company with Widdicombe.

Thoughts of Lady Smythe lead Julian to reflections centred on Lady Rhonda, another woman who has difficulties following male leads. He knows he was an emotional coward in not getting in touch with her before leaving for Italy. He thinks of penning a letter to her, but he decides that she is one of his young life's many bygone opportunities.

CHAPTER EIGHT

AN ABUNDANCE
OF THE HEART

*F*rom the moment Miranda boarded, she realized the *vetturino* had been a terrible mistake. The rascal who drove her party was a perfect torment. He began each morning at whatever time he pleased, halted whenever he liked, usually at the worst wayside inns, where the meals consisted solely of rye bread, sour wine and stewed garlic. He rarely urged the horses beyond a trot. If anyone dared complain, he would stop in a public place and appeal to the bystanders about the wretched *Inglese*. The immediate result was that a ferocious crowd would surround the carriage and harangue the innocent passengers with invectives and insults and menacing gestures. On reaching an inn at night, the driver would give such a negative representation of his charges that they were denied admittance or given the privilege of paying for all services in advance. The wretch fumigated the travellers with his tobacco, and his dog, an ugly Spitz, stood on the roof barking all the way to each destination.

In such an outlandish, preposterous, and expensive manner does Miranda Osborne travel to Florence. Being a complete innocent in foreign travel, she paid for the second most expensive type of travel and received precious little value for her money. She could have gone cheaply, using a combination of diligences and railways but had been warned that waifs, strays, opportunistic young bachelors, and common thieves were rife. She could have hired her own carriage from London to Florence, but that is inordinately expensive. Having selected the middle way and being but one of six passengers — four within, two without — in the great heavy carriage, she arrives in Florence subdued and tired.

Her beleaguered condition makes her more apt than ordinarily to follow Signora di Cenzo when she presents herself. A mite of a woman dressed in a bright orange frock, her eyebrows twitching and tiny sunken eyes blazing, Signora di Cenzo heads directly for Mrs. Osborne. Paying no attention to those who had accompanied Miranda from Paris, the family of three or the aged spinster, armed with a wide variety of guidebooks, or the elderly lawyer who has papers to be signed and would be leaving immediately afterwards, she asks in her primitive English if the solitary English lady has accommodation arranged? When Miranda shakes her head no, the Signora nods her head sagely and offers her own humble abode, priced most reasonably, which is within easy walking distance from where the party has disembarked. So it comes to pass that

Miranda is soon settled on the via del Presto, opposite Santa Margherita de'Cerchi, where, the Signora informs her as further testimony to the worthiness of her establishment, Dante married in 1285.

Miranda has no regrets for having acted so precipitously.

She has a large drawing room, a large bedroom, three smaller rooms, an ante-room, and a good kitchen. All of these rooms are well furnished: five sofas, plenty of easy chairs, large and small tables. Besides, she has indulged herself in what is called *Servizia*. Her bed is made, rooms cleaned, and breakfast prepared. For all this, she pays very little: 15 crowns a month. For an additional small sum, Signora di Cenzo prepares her midday and evening meals. Food is plentiful and cheap — butter and milk, sent up with ice, large plates full of fruit, fine cherries and ripe apricots. Her principal expense is an open carriage, the horse, and the driver.

If Miranda owns up to it, a touch of collector's mania has uprooted her for the next few months. She has abandoned her silver, Smith, and her lodgings — in that order of importance — in pursuit of the Holy Apostles' chalice made early in the thirteenth century in Cologne. This elaborate piece, made of gilt-silver, depicts the apostles in low relief along its rim; the filigree knob holding the top and bottom together is rendered in exquisite detail; the bottom has four roundels in high relief depicting scenes from the life of Christ. In truth, the object has never been seen, but there are woodcuts of it. For her, the acquisition of such an object would be a monumental accomplishment, the crowning achievement of her life as a collector.

Even information about the present location of this grail is hard to come by. Elderly, trustworthy Gabriel Hermeling, formerly of Cologne, but now the proprietor of a splendid shop in London, confided to her that the object has recently surfaced in Florence and could be had by the right person for the right price. Too old to travel himself, he suggested she send Smith to negotiate with the owner, but Miranda did not feel that her servant would be the right person to send on such a delicate mission. Hermeling informed her that she or Smith would have to be prepared for a considerable stay in Italy, since the owner of the piece craved anonymity and would probably open negotiations slowly. He also thought it might take considerable time to reach an agreement as to price and thus prise the object free. He advised her not to advertise the nature of her mission lest other collectors follow on her trail. So Miranda has blithely put it about that she is travelling in order to broaden her horizons. That explanation — by Smith — means nothing to Miranda, but everyone to whom she mentions this purpose nods his or her head sagely.

Although she does not wish to admit this even to herself, Miranda has been influenced by the Ealing séance and Mr. Browning's subsequent call upon her. Although not of a religious temperament, Miranda has begun to wonder if there is a force hidden beyond the material and mechanical that governs life. She did not like Mr. Browning even a little bit, but some of his intensity has brushed off on her. Moreover, that frail-voiced Daniel Home has had some sort of malignant influence on her. After all is said and done, chalices are connected to Catholic rite, that hodgepodge of Popish superstition that rules Florence. She is too old to change horses in mid-stream. Yet she is conducting herself like some demented medieval knight in pursuit of Christ's chalice.

Shortly after Miranda has settled in at Signora di Cenzo's, that inestimable lady calls on her during the middle of the afternoon, that portion of the day reserved for napping. After apologizing profusely for having disturbed her lodger, she inquires if she can assist in any of her endeavours. Miranda assures her that this is not possible, since she is in Florence awaiting a message from an unknown person. Without intending to do so, she arouses her landlady's curiosity and then has to explain that she is attempting to purchase a rare work of art and expects to be approached by the owner or his representative in the next little while.

In her broken English, the Signora tells Miranda, with great precision and gentleness, that if the person in question intends to approach her in a public place, perhaps it would be best if Mrs. Osborne blended into Florentine society a bit more assuredly than she does at present? The Signora informs her that the dark colours she wears makes her stand out a bit too much as an *Inglese*. If she were to wear the brighter colours usually chosen by Tuscan ladies, she might be less conspicuous and, in the long run, more successful in fulfilling her mission. The matter is handled with such tact that Miranda is not insulted. In fact, she sees the logic of her landlady's argument.

On the following day, she and the Signora visit the shops of the Villa della Studio, where the Englishwoman purchases three dresses. Miranda, also at the Signora's insistence, puts her hair up in the style favoured by Tuscan ladies.

Having made these changes, Miranda waits for someone to contact her with word about the chalice. Since her mind is completely taken up with the prospect of her new acquisition, she is both startled and displeased when she receives a note from Mrs. Browning asking if she might call the following day. She assents reluctantly.

Signora di Cenzo volunteers to prepare a proper Florentine tea for the great woman, who is venerated by many for her republican sentiments. At the appointed hour, the Signora shows the poetess into Miranda's reception room. The woman Miranda had seen some months ago in English twilight looks very different in Italian sunlight. She does not stoop as before. Here she carries herself with great assurance and energy. However, the lines that etch her face run far deeper than Miranda's, although they are approximately the same age. She shakes her hostess's hand warmly and expresses regret at not having had the opportunity to exchange greetings with her at Ealing.

Mrs. Browning does not waste time in small talk. "I realize that Robert visited you at Highgate."

Miranda nods.

"I fear he may have been rude to you."

"I would not say that. He may have been a trifle brusque. I did not give it a second thought."

"That is very kind of you. As you know, my husband considers Mr. Home a fake."

"He made that clear to me."

"I daresay he did. I disagree completely with him. On this score Robert has angered me considerably." She then goes on to relate how their friend, the American writer and diplomat, Nathaniel Hawthorne, had marvelled recently to both her and her husband at Home's skills as a medium.

"I have become of Mr. Hawthorne's persuasion," Miranda declares.

"Indeed, so am I. I am sorry that Robert attempted to turn you to his side in an unseemly manner."

"The matter is forgotten."

"I wish I understood my husband in this matter. It is the only hint of a cloud in our usual domestic sunshine."

"From my experience, your marriage is a very successful one if the matter of Mr. Home is its only impediment."

Mrs. Browning then changes subjects, telling Miranda of an adventure she had enjoyed in Florence shortly before the Ealing séance. One day, her husband told her that some fine paintings had been discovered at a local monastery not open to women. The poetess and two of her friends decided that they would view the pictures. The three of them dressed like schoolboys in loose trousers in the Turkish manner. As they approached the monastery, Mrs. Browning became fearful of being discovered, taken to jail and thus ridiculed in the newspapers. Just then, Mr. Browning appeared in a carriage and insisted the three ladies get in. The poetess had cried in gratitude to her husband for protecting her from herself. In a similar manner, she is implying, Mr. Browning had tried to shield her from Home.

Mrs. Browning asks if she can do anything to make her fellow Englishwoman's stay more comfortable. She takes her leave, as the rules of etiquette dictate, after an hour. She promises that she will, if Miranda is still in Florence after she and her husband return from Paris and London, invite her to the Casa Guidi, where, she trusts, she will finally encounter the real Robert Browning.

Two days later, Miranda finally receives a message from the owner of the chalice. They are to meet at three in the afternoon on the following day in the small courtyard of Santa Maria Novella.

Since Baedeker highly recommends this Gothic church, Miranda arrives just after one o'clock to give herself ample time to view it. The famed Masaccio painting of the Holy Trinity appals rather than edifies her, and the red devils in the frescoes of the Spanish Chapel strike her as childish. On the other hand, the interplay of white and brown surfaces on the church's façade gives it a splendidly playful appearance, as if one is entering a gingerbread house; Filippino Lippi's fresco of St. John raising Drusiana from the dead she judges worth seeing. In it, the fashionably costumed lady stares gratefully at the saint, who seems to have in a single stroke given her a new life and, perhaps, a new identity. Would that such miracles happened in ordinary life, Miranda reflects.

At the designated hour, she enters the small, sombre courtyard where four tall yew trees, planted within a small square at its centre, are the only decoration. The courtyard is deserted, so she sits on the small bench positioned along the exterior wall. Patiently, she waits for almost ten minutes until a woman, who apparently had been hidden behind the yews, walks in Miranda's direction. The visitor is dressed completely in black and a veil obscures most of her features. Miranda barely makes out that her eyes are large, her mouth delicate, and her general appearance pleasing. In her hands she holds a wooden box. Without any preliminaries, the woman sits next to Miranda and asks if she would like to view the chalice. The Englishwoman nods assent, whereupon the other opens the box and, without further ado, hands her the object of desire.

On close inspection, it proves to be exactly what Miranda had hoped for. The prints had depicted the chalice accurately. It is in perfect condition and blazes with splendour in the sunshine. The hallmarks are as they should be. When Miranda indicates that her inspection is complete and that she is satisfied as to authenticity, her visitor peremptorily removes the vessel from her hands. If she wishes to purchase the chalice, the price will be three thousand pounds. This is a much larger sum than Miranda had envisioned. Nevertheless, carried away by the moment, she does not haggle. When Miranda informs her visitor that she can have the money within a fortnight, the vendor declares herself satisfied, assures Miranda she will be in touch by messenger, stands up, and vanishes, presumably into the nave.

Miranda has agreed to pay an exorbitant amount for the chalice, but she is certain all the time and trouble taken to unearth the treasure has been well spent. She is filled with a delicious sense of happiness as she makes her way back to via del Presto. Opposite Doney's, she is startled to see Mr. Home and Mr. Wilson in close conversation. Neither of them, she is certain, spots her as she darts into a shop and pleads to be allowed to exit out the backdoor.

On the day following her assignation with the lady in black, Miranda writes to Smith, giving her detailed instructions for Messrs Coutts, the bankers, to transmit the three thousand pounds to a corresponding bank in Florence. Not having much of anything to do that day since she has visited most of the churches recommended by both Baedeker and Cook, she instructs her driver to take her to Fiesole, where she can take supper and see the celebrated view from there of the sunset over Florence.

She leaves at two in the afternoon and arrives an hour later at the Duomo of San Romolo in the piazza. After setting Giovanni free and instructing him to meet her at the same place at eight, she roams to the front of the Palazzo Communale, returns to the church and then heads down the Via Dupre to the Roman amphitheatre. That structure, surviving only as heaps of ruins carelessly tossed together, depresses her. Distracted by the heat — it is an uncommonly hot day for February — and the plaintiveness of what she has witnessed, she regrets her decision to take a meal in Fiesole, although she reckons the view of Florence five miles below will be sublime.

Having found a restaurant that provides a good view of the city and thus, she hopes, of the sunset, she asks to be seated outside. As she waits for her food to arrive, she notices a distracted-looking Lady Rhonda wandering in her direction on the other side of the street. In London, Miranda would not have hailed her, but in Italy it seems the right thing to do. Startled, Lady Rhonda looks around several times before her eyes come to rest on her friend. She returns the greeting and crosses the street.

Lady Rhonda is delighted when Miranda asks if she will take supper with her. She is, she informs Miranda, staying nearby at the ramshackle villa of the writer and trouble-maker Walter Savage Landor, a dear friend of her late husband. In her excitable way, she describes how this residence is almost bare of furniture but that the white-washed walls are even more crowded than those of the Uffizi and filled with pictures of every kind imaginable. The only common denominator, she howls, is their departure from both fashion and good taste. "Like us, he is a collector but, not by my reckoning, a connoisseur!"

Miranda mentions that she has seen Julian Wilson and Daniel Home conversing together at Doney's. They must, she remarks, be friends, although they are such dissimilar young men.

"I don't know about that!," Rhonda interjects. "They both fancy themselves young Hamlets!"

"You mean they are prisoners of indecision?"

"Yes. Mr. Wilson cannot decide whether he is an artist or a dealer. Mr. Home wishes his all too frail flesh would melt away."

Miranda has formed very decided opinions about these two men. "Mr. Wilson is a man of flesh and blood. He has the capacity to find happiness on this earth. Mr. Home will always be divided between the spirit world and the one in which he lives. Earthly existence will always be an extraordinarily difficult trial for him." She pauses: "Mr. Wilson has had the opportunity to make choices. No such option has been granted to Mr. Home."

"You speak with great conviction."

"Like me, Mr. Home is a loner. He will find his salvation in isolation. Not so Mr. Wilson. He is a gregarious creature, who, even when he dislikes someone, like myself, is the embodiment of charm."

Lady Rhonda decides to change the dangerous drift in the conversation. "What about Mr. Home's manifestations? Do you trust him?"

"Implicitly, although I cannot speak with any logic on the matter." Since she has not arrived in Florence in the middle of the winter season, Miranda inquires the purpose of Rhonda's sojourn. She is, she replies, a good friend of the Brownings and is visiting with them. This is strange news because, as the poetess herself had told Miranda, the Brownings had returned only briefly to Florence and were, at this very moment, en route back to Paris and thence to London. When, in turn, Lady Rhonda inquires the purpose of her stay in Florence, Miranda is about to tell of her search for cultural enlightenment. She does not understand why, but she confesses her quest for the grail.

At first, Lady Rhonda is facetious. "Like Mr. Tennyson, you are intrigued by tales of Arthur and Camelot." Then her mood shifts, darkening considerably. "You must be careful as a single woman travelling alone that you not put yourself in any danger. There are many rogues in this city. I have heard tell of pieces — usually very valuable canvases — being offered simultaneously to three or four wealthy collectors. After each, unknown to the others, has paid a handsome sum, he receives nothing in return or, sometimes, a pitiful copy of the original. Mr. Hermeling is a reputable dealer, but in this instance he may have been hoodwinked."

Miranda thanks Lady Rhonda for her advice and readily owns up to having considered this possibility. "I have determined," she assures her, "not to hand over any monies until the chalice is safely in my hands." Not satisfied, Lady Rhonda cautions her to exercise prudence. "That is a virtue often in short supply with many a hungry collector."

The women admire the unusually spectacular sunset. First, the sky fills with alternating streaks of purple, lavender and pink. Then, the fiery sun blots out all these colours, leaving the two women alone with a dark sky and a small assortment of bright stars. Of a sudden, a crescent moon asserts itself, casting its clear light down upon them. When they part, Lady Rhonda and Miranda agree to meet in Florence within the next little while.

Lady Rhonda's warning does not go unheeded. With some trepidation, Miranda takes Signora di Cenzo into her confidence. The Signora's small eyes open wide when told of the scheme. She immediately volunteers to be her guest's coadjutor, suggesting that Miranda inform the mysterious vendor that any exchange of money for merchandise be done in her sitting room. At the appointed time, she will be certain to be at home below, within easy range to be of assistance.

Five days later, one day after the money has arrived from London, a message from the lady in black arrives in the afternoon. Two days hence, at ten in the morning, she announces her intention of calling upon Miranda. Signora di Cenzo is on full alert, but the transaction goes smoothly. The lady, clad as before, arrives on time, accompanied by the chalice. She asks if Miranda wishes to inspect it again. After Miranda has done so, she politely inquires if indeed she still desires to purchase it. Miranda assures her that this is the case and hands her the envelope with the money. The vendor grasps it but does not open it, instructs her that she should find a safe spot for her new acquisition, thanks her buyer for her patronage, bows and then walks out the door and down the stairs. Both Miranda and the Signora are amazed by how wonderfully everything transpires.

That evening, Miranda informs the Signora that she will remain in Italy until the end of March. The weather, she observes, is much more accommodating than what she is used to in London, and the Signora assures her that her new possession will be safe in her home until she returns with it to England.

Miranda now settles into improving herself for the remainder of her stay in this exquisite city. Some days when she wanders about, she imagines herself as living in a bygone age, so antiquated are the buildings, so intense is the presence of the past.

At Doney's, she is welcomed into a small circle of English ladies, the chief of whom, Abigail Fanshaw, is a woman of considerable intellect. A short, squat woman of early middle age, she is always dressed, like some of the Italian widows, in deepest black. However, she introduces Miranda to her husband the second time they come upon each other. Later, Miranda is told by a mutual friend, Mrs. Conway, that Mrs. Fanshaw has been in mourning since the death of her son some years before.

On the following afternoon, when they are taking tea at Doney's, Abigail, seeing Home pass by on the street, speaks of him as a modern messiah, a true miracle worker. When Miranda asks how she knows him, she is told of the strange circumstances surrounding the séance Abigail had attended a year earlier when her little lost son had been momentarily restored to her through Mr. Home's agency.

Abigail then relates another story, chilling her listener to the bone. The Countess Cotterell, a dyed-in-the-wool sceptic, had attended a séance in Florence the previous week. While the hands of all seven people, including those of Home, were placed in plain view on the table, there appeared the apparition of a frail, womanish hand and forearm that ended at the elbow in a white mist. The hand made efforts to reach a fan lying on the table. The Countess, recognizing the hand of a dead aunt she had disliked, exclaimed, "Fan yourself as you were used to do, dear aunt!" The hand picked up the fan and wielded it with a menacing gesture in the direction of the Cotterells.

A gentleman at the table felt what Home told him was the hand of his dead child. It patted his cheek and arm. The distraught father took hold of the hand, which he exclaimed was warm and small. He would not loosen his hold until it seemed to melt out of his clutch. Then, the really harrowing experience took place. Lady Cotterell felt her dead baby, who had died seven years earlier, on her knee. The child remained with his mother for fifteen minutes, during which time the mother asked her son: "Darling, won't you give your hand to Papa?" The matter-of-fact Lord Cotterell swore he felt his infant son's hand placed in his own.

After that séance, Lord Cotterell turned his back on Home, although he confessed to his friends that he thought the manifestation genuine. Like Mr. Browning, he may have feared that the medium was in danger of asserting too much power over his spouse. Mr. Browning had complained of the rasping sound of the medium's voice whereas Lord Cotterell has deemed it effeminate.

Mrs. Fanshaw despises what she called the "masculine conceit" of Lord Cotterell and Mr. Browning. According to her, both men had asserted that such a master of the "unnatural" as Home must also be "unnatural" in other aspects of his life.

Signora di Cenzo advises Miranda on all things Florentine and declares that she has become an ideal citizen of the city-state.

Her sincerity and kindness touches the Englishwoman deeply. On the evening Miranda tells her that she has written to Smith announcing that she would soon return to her native land, the Signora pleads with Miranda to stay longer.

There are, she informs her, many things in life besides silver objects. Eagerly assenting to this proposition, her guest points out that she is also, like herself, a creature given to obsessions. Perhaps so, the landlady agrees. But how does the English lady know this? Miranda informs her that she has gathered from her companions at Doney's that her landlady is an ardent patriot, a fierce enemy of the Austrians. Yes, the Signora agrees, she wants to see Florence as part of a unified Italy.

"In fact," Miranda declares, "I think you will do anything, within reason or even outside its borders, to bring that about." In response, the Italian looks at her quizzically.

"Madam, you are such a true patriot that you will pass off a fake such as the Cologne chalice and think nothing of it."

A great actress, the Signora looks at her accuser in a startled fashion before assuming her more normal appearance.

Miranda does not mince her words. "I began to suspect that the chalice was a sham only after I had handled it several times here after I purchased it. Each time I beheld it I grew to love it more and more. The craftsmanship is outstanding, and the religious fervour of the craftsman palpable. But, during my time here, I have inspected many medieval works of art, although only a few were ever done in silver. I could see no kinship between these objects and the chalice. For one thing, the roughness so evident in medieval art is lacking. I also think

that the personality of the maker is embedded in this particular sacred vessel. My eyes tell me such feelings had no part of
thirteenth-century art."

The Signora gulps as Miranda continues: "I have not been
able to determine if you are the artist. Surely the young woman
in black, perhaps your daughter, is the craftsman I have to
thank for such a miraculous piece of work?"

Mistakenly, the Signora thinks a touch of sarcasm has
invaded what the Englishwoman says. She begins with an
apology and an explanation. She and her confederates had
circulated the story about the discovery of the lost chalice
among the highest class of sellers of silver in London, Paris,
and Berlin. Miranda had been the only person to succumb to
the bait. The chalice had been made directly from the old
woodcuts. Only the finest materials had been employed; the
maker was indeed her daughter, Stella, whom Miranda had
met twice. She knew from her son in London, who worked for
Mr. Hermeling, that Mrs. Osborne was planning the trip to
Florence; she had been on the lookout for Miranda for three
weeks before she finally arrived.

At this point, the Signora begins to weep. The proceeds
from the forgery have already been given over to the patriot
cause, but she offers to recompense Miranda in due course.
She had never suspected that she would form a sentimental
attachment to her guest.

She is flabbergasted when Miranda informs her that she
need not think of recompensing her. She had spoken truth-
fully when proclaiming her love of the chalice. "Of course, I

have paid far too much for it, and I hope you will abandon the path of deceit. As far as I am concerned, the matter is closed. I am a satisfied customer." The Signora is not a woman who likes to show surprise, but, on this day, she displays it in abundance. Miranda tries to conceal her own astonishment at the words that have escaped her lips.

CHAPTER NINE

LOSING ONE'S HEART

This autumn the pastoral delights of Twickenham offer no solace. The figurines may depict life, Rhonda knows, but they themselves are empty of it. She seldom troubles them with a visit. She has been tempted again these past few days to instruct Hunter to prepare the phaeton for a trip to London. Just as she is on the verge of issuing the order, she thinks better of it. On the following day she instructs Hunter to be ready at ten the following morning. Her once strong resolve has been broken. She has returned to the gaming table, a setting she has avoided for almost twenty years.

As a young, unmarried (and she thought unmarriageable) woman of noble birth with a great deal of time on her hands, she had passed many days and evenings at Lord and Lady Ponsoby's, where the drawing room had been made to resemble a professional gaming house, complete with hired croupiers and a commercial faro bank. Indeed, the Ponsobys charged faro-dealers fifty guineas a night for the right to set up tables. That noble couple also engaged a small orchestra, which played into the small hours of the morning. Like other ladies, she became addicted to faro, a game of chance, which, like roulette, overwhelmingly favours the dealer. Gaming was to her class what gin was to the poor: it ruined families and corrupted lives.

Her mother paid no heed to what the daughter in whom she was so disappointed got up to. Her father pleaded with Rhonda to abandon this dangerous activity: "Let me entreat you to beware if gaming is mentioned to you any more and decline to take part." Seeing that she paid no attention to his sensible advice, he wrote again: "Play at whist, commerce, backgammon, trictrac or chess, but never at quinze, lou, brag, faro, and if you are pressed to play always make the fashionable excuse of following my advice. In short I must beg you, my dearest girl, if you value my happiness, to send me in writing a serious answer."

She did not favour her father with a reply. She simply continued on her unsteady course. Not only did gambling pass the time, it also provided a setting in which, at long last, she could fit in. There was so much drinking of spirits that no one paid the slightest heed to her ungainly laugh. Some of the habitués at the Ponsobys must have simply assumed that she made such noises only when inebriated.

Her life of dissolution continued for seven years, until she reached her thirtieth birthday. On that day, she received a stern missive from her father: "You must learn to respect yourself, and the world will soon follow your example. While you herd only with the vicious and the profligate you will resemble them — pert, familiar, noisy and indelicate. You will be lost beyond recovery." This admonition did not bring her to her senses, but her mother's sudden death three days later did. She hastened back to Herefordshire, where she remained for the next six years until she married.

If Edward had known of her career as a gambler and of the terrible expenses to which she had put her father, he never mentioned it to her. After she met him, she never for a moment gave any thought to the pleasures of faro.

Last evening she reached, she is certain, the nadir in her tortured existence. She was at Lady Ailesbury's where the guests play faro according to the strictest of rules: no borrowing from the bank. She arrived, flushed with excitement, so certain was she that she would finally recoup all her losses from the past fortnight. She sat down to play and then realized her purse was empty. She cried and made an inordinate fuss until Lady Gray lent her ten guineas. Having gained her way with that noble lady, she insisted the bank lend her a further sixty. A very distressed Lady Ailesbury allowed her house rule to be broken. Luck was with Rhonda, and she won over two hundred pounds. Triumphant, she scooped up her winnings and made for the door. All of a sudden, there was a series of loud coughs. She looked back to see both her lenders staring hawk-eyed at her. Aghast and with many apologies and the usual horrible exclamations, she repaid both loans.

She cannot relive her sordid past, she reminds herself. Nor can she evade the revelations of that mysterious night at Ealing. Her return to the faro table reminds her that she gambled away her youth. Home's reminder of the claims of the dead forces her to consider that she has never fully lived her life. Is that why Mr. Wilson poses such a threat to me now, a woman of fifty?, she asks herself.

Rhonda determines to quit England. She will make her way to Meissen in hopes of purchasing a few new animals for the porcelain zoo in which she has largely lost interest. En route back from Germany, she will take the waters at a spa.

Unfortunately, the weather in Baden-Baden proves deplorably bone-chilling. She sees no benefit accruing from her treatments here. She could venture south to Tuscany, but she would have to avoid Florence in order not to encounter Mr. Wilson, who has been there, she understands from Ba, several months.

She is in a state of paralysis. I do not wish to see Mr. Wilson, she tells herself, but a warmer climate would be most satisfactory. She writes to Mr. Landor, who is in England this winter, in hopes of securing his abandoned villa on the outskirts of Fiesole. If she winters there, she could keep close to home and not have to venture into Florence. Mr. Landor may be an old reprobate, but he is kindness itself to Lady Rhonda. The villa, he writes, is at her disposal. She sets off for Italy the next morning.

Rhonda ventures no further than Fiesole. The villa, she soon discovers, is an awkward, inconvenient place, its walls filled with the most humdrum pictures imaginable, the rooms virtually empty of furniture. She misses Julian Wilson more than she cares to admit.

Her view of the world has turned topsy-turvy. Why should I be attracted to that young man, she asks herself? Why am I so haunted by the night at Ealing? She used to think that human beings lived and then simply died. She is no longer certain of that truism. Daniel Home, she decides, is either an angel or a devil.

Very much to her surprise, at the end of a long walk into Fiesole, she comes upon Mrs. Osborne, with whom she takes her evening meal. Mrs. Osborne is much altered since Rhonda saw her last. For one, she is dressed, à la mode de Florence, in a red chiffon frock. This is much different from her habitual London attire. Her colouring, now a healthy pink, is much improved. Her hair is done with an eye to fashion. She could be said to glow. When Rhonda remarks on the metamorphosis, Mrs. Osborne simply observes that the sun of Italy is very abundant when compared to that of England.

When, in turn, Mrs. Osborne asks Miranda the purpose of her trip, Rhonda prevaricates by telling her she is visiting the Brownings. She can tell immediately from the frown that momentarily crosses Mrs. Osborne's face that she knows that Rhonda is lying. In an attempt to change subjects, Mrs. Osborne mentions having seen Mr. Home and Mr. Wilson at Doney's. She even speaks with some passion about the two men. She sees Mr. Home as a solitary like herself whereas she considers Mr. Wilson a person made for earthly joy.

Rhonda's face turns crimson at the mention of Wilson.

Mrs. Osborne then declares that she is now convinced Home is an angel. She may be a very wise woman and an excellent judge of character, but Rhonda is not sure if she agrees. Mrs. Osborne also replies strangely when Rhonda, toward the end of the meal, inquires if the Ealing séance has in any way altered her life. Mrs. Osborne looks her straight in the eye and then slowly announces, *"I am like Lazarus raised from the dead."*

After Mrs. Osborne confides to Rhonda her real purpose in visiting Florence, the noblewoman instructs her to exercise great caution. Mrs. Osborne seems completely heedless of the dangers that she might be subjecting herself to in the pursuit of such a treasure.

A few days later, Rhonda instructs her driver that she will visit the Biboli Gardens, sufficiently out of the way in the city that she is unlikely to encounter any *Inglese* she does not wish to see.

She and Edward had come to this spot on three previous visits to Florence. For them, it became hallowed ground. They particularly admired how the neatly clipped box hedges give way to the wild groves of ilex and cypress. Try as they did at Twickenham, they never achieved a contrast between artifice and nature to rival this one.

Rhonda dismisses Hunter at the entranceway, instructing him to return in three hours. It is another uncommonly warm and sunny day, and she opens her parasol. She wanders off to the Amphitheatre and that most mannerist of follies, La

Grotta Grande. She saves the best for last, although a deep sadness overtakes her as she strolls down the Vittolone, the majestic avenue of cypress, out of which appear, from time to time, the statues of ancient Roman gods and goddesses. She is just about to reach the end of the avenue and walk into L'Isoloto when she espies a tall gentleman in a cream suit, obviously an Englishman, walking in her direction. As he approaches her, a tentative smile crosses his brow. She has come face to face with Julian Wilson.

He shows no surprise in encountering Rhonda, almost as if this were an everyday event. She cannot dissemble her feelings, a composite of joy, relief and embarrassment.

"Mr. Wilson, how strange to encounter you here of all places!"

"You didn't know I was in Florence?"

She lies. "I had no idea. I am staying for a few weeks in Fiesole and have not ventured into Florence as yet."

"Well, I have been here for some months assisting our mutual acquaintance, Mr. Jarves."

"I have not been in touch with him for some months."

Julian asks about her health and other routine matters, but Rhonda can see the cloud of uncertainty residing behind his pleasant smile. She is about to conclude their conversation, in the hope that she can shake off the disquiet the artist arouses in her, when Mr. Wilson mentions that he has brought her portrait with him to Florence, intending to complete the canvas. Of course, he had not known she would be here, but, if she were to sit to him one more time, perhaps he could bring it to a successful fruition?

She considers her response carefully. "I would be willing to do so if I can take possession of the portrait upon completion in the next week or two." In that way, she reasons, she could permanently rid herself of Mr. Wilson. Her request, issued in an abrupt manner, seems to take him by surprise. However, he readily agrees to her condition, and they arrange to meet at Mr. Jarve's in a week's time.

Since Rhonda needs no longer conceal her presence in Florence, she ventures out the next day to take lunch and decides, on her way back, to stop at Santa Maria del Fiore. Having paid her respects to the Duomo and Campanile, she reaches the east doors of the Vestry, where she encounters another difficult, self-satisfied, handsome young man, John Ruskin, whom she has met at exhibitions in London.

His air of pedantic superiority, she admits to herself, puts Mr. Wilson's in the shade. Just before her arrival, he gloats, he had come upon an English cheesemonger and his wife who had exclaimed before Ghiberti's doors — those which Michelangelo said were fit for the gates of Heaven — "How dirty they are! Oh, quite shocking!"

Having encountered someone he vaguely knows, Mr. Ruskin expresses the full range of his disdain for the Florentines: "It is the most tormenting and harassing place to lounge or meditate. Everyone here is idle, and they are always in one's way. The square is full of listless, chattering, smoking vagabonds who are always moving every way at once, just fast enough to make it disagreeable. You cannot have a moment's peace. In fact, it is dangerous not to be on guard, for the Italian carts always drive *at* anyone who looks relaxed."

Having launched himself on a favourite topic, he proceeds to talk at Rhonda: "In the galleries you can never feel a picture, for it is surrounded, if good, by villainous copyists, who talk and grin, and yawn and stretch, until they infect you with their apathy. One can sometimes get a perfect moment or two in the chapels or cloisters of the churches, but the moment anyone comes it is all over. If a monk, he destroys all your conception of monks; if layman, he is a lazy Florentine who saunters up to look at what you are doing, smokes in your face, stares at you, and spits at what you are studying."

His peroration becomes apoplectic: "Taking them all in all, I detest the Italians beyond measure. They are Yorick's skull with the worms in it, nothing of humanity left but the smell." Once he tires of his invective, she asks if it is simply a case of *margaritas ante porcos*?

"Pearls before swine? You may be correct, Lady Rhonda."

She does not bother to point out to him that the Florentines see many of the *Inglese* as barbarians who have no appreciation of the beauty of their city. Having heard reports of the many difficulties in Mr. Ruskin's marriage to Effie Gray, she can easily understand why. When Mr. Ruskin proposes lunch, she is glad to inform him that she has already taken her midday meal.

After giving Mr. Ruskin the slip, she encounters Mr. Home at Doney's, where she is taking her afternoon tea. She could have cut him when he walked in her direction, but, goodness knows why, she hails him so that they cannot possibly miss each other. The smile that crosses his face is so genuine that she knows she has not made a mistake in being so brazen. Indeed, she asks him to sit with her, although unsure of any safe topic of conversation that could pass between them.

Having never travelled to Tuscany before, Mr. Home observes how burnished the landscape is in this part of Italy. They pass the time politely on such inconsequentials when, rather to her own surprise, she is brave enough to question him about his reaction to Robert Browning's impolitenesses. Shrugging his shoulders, he says that he is used to such behaviour by now, having experienced it often enough. There is no point in dwelling on such bygones. In the warmth of Italy, he hopes to devote his attention to more pressing concerns.

Now completely heedless of the consequences, she asks him what those are.

"The nature of the love. The importance of the passions."

"Those are grand topics, Mr. Home," she teases. "Do the spirits have opinions in such matters?"

"That is the point. They return from the dead precisely because they do feel strongly. That is why they speak to the living. They worry about their loved ones who are often ruining their lives with their obsession with the dead. By their very presence, the spirits remind the living to take advantage of their lives on this earth. They confess their love for those that remain behind while, at the same time, urging them to get on with the business of living."

"Do you listen to your spirits, Mr. Home?" Her question is in earnest, although she fears he might still think she is teasing.

He looks at her directly. "That is a great difficulty. I am the messenger who often ignores the import of the messages he delivers."

"What is the full import of that message, Mr. Home?"

"It is Horatian. Seize the day!"

As they speak that afternoon, Home's face becomes so animated that he is transformed into quite a different young man from the one she has met before. His countenance gleams, his manner is passionate. Then, suddenly deflated, he observes: "My despair is that I know what I must do but seem incapable of carrying it out."

Rhonda points out to him that the tragedy of so much of human existence seems to lie in the difference between the active and the passive. Sometimes, she admits, she sees the advantages of living an unexamined life. Otherwise, you run the risk of squandering your existence. Daniel nods his head sadly. A few minutes later they take their leave of each other.

Jarves's studio at the back of his villa at Oltrano is large and filled with sunshine. Julian positions Rhonda in front of the windows at the end of the long room and sets his easel back a greater distance than he had at Twickenham. On her arrival, Julian kisses Rhonda's hand a bit too fervently for her liking.

During the sitting he is not talkative, wanting, he claims, to make all the final adjustments to the portrait. This procedure occupies him for almost two hours and, having held her head in the same position for that length of time, she is well pleased when the session comes to a close.

Rhonda asks if she might take a look at the portrait, which she had never even glanced at in Twickenham. Obviously having hoped she would not pose such a question, Julian wrestles with himself for a few moments before agreeing. He walks down to her, takes her hand and accompanies her back to his place in front of the canvas.

The glint in the dark green eyes, the large brow, the pink inhabiting the cheeks, the angular trim to the nose, the deep red of the hair, the thin colourless lips, all these she recognizes and approves. Yet this woman, shown full-length staring away from the viewer, is lost in thoughts melancholic. She is a deeply troubled person.

At first, Rhonda is tempted to compliment the artist on how lifelike the representation is but to admonish him for making her look so hopelessly forlorn. Instead, she tells him that he has captured her very soul.

CHAPTER TEN

STABBED TO THE HEART

*T*he Villino Trollope, on the corner of the new Piazza Maria Antonia, is renowned for its marble pillars surrounded by statues of grim men in armour. Inside is a wide assortment of majolica, old bridal chests, carved furniture, a celebrated terracotta of a Madonna by Orcagna, and at least a hundred cinquecento *oggetti.* The library is a wonder. More than five thousand books, many of them illuminated or enriched by costly engravings, spill over every surface of the room. The garden, which stretches all the way from Via del Podere to the ancient walls of the city, has huge pillars, a tessellated marble floor, inscriptions and coats of arms; bas-relief adorns its walls, here and there a niche devoted to some saint. There is even a house specialty: a squash drink from the lemon trees which grow in great pots in a colossal shed in the winter and are then moved out into the garden in the summer.

Sparrow-like Frances is resourceful and overly-opinionated; Adolphus has an amiable disposition and has no hesitancy in declaring his brother, Anthony, as the more talented writer; Adolphus' wife, Theodosia, dislikes her mother-in-law, whom she considers to have turned Adolphus into a namby-pamby, an expression she uses tiresomely.

From the start, Frances insists Daniel call her Fanny, a privilege reserved for intimates. She tells him in exhaustive detail about her troubled life and her subsequent triumphs over adversity. He now knows more than he wishes about her late husband, the pedantic lawyer, Thomas Trollope, who was not only incompetent but unpleasant. Improbably, he was also a man of a romantic turn of mind, who, when a friend wrote glowingly of America, thought briefly of emigrating there. As it turned out, it was Fanny who was determined to make the family fortune in the New World, where she was accompanied by one son, two daughters, and a French painter by the name of Hervieu. Adolphus and Anthony were sent away to school with the result that Thomas had the family house to himself.

"I need not tell you, Dan, about the rigours of the New World," she would preface one of her monologues and then proceed to tell him of her adventures with considerable relish. After a series of incredible difficulties and mishaps, Mrs. Trollope and her party arrived in Cincinnati, Ohio, the furthest frontier town in the United States in 1827. There, she and Mr. Hervieu built a Greco-Moro-Gothic-Chinese palace, an emporium devoted to the selling of art and fine workmanship to the barbarous inhabitants of the Wild West. Unfortunately, the cost of building their edifice overwhelmed any hope they had of financial success. The building became known locally as Trollope's Folly and, eventually, ended up as a bordello. Fifty-one years of age, dependent on the earnings of the good-natured Hervieu, and saddled with the expenses of three children, Fanny applied to Thomas for assistance. He replied querulously that he did not see that she required funds of any kind. Bit by bit, she sold everything she owned and began to scribble. Having completed her book, she and her party returned to England, where the caustic *The Domestic Manners of the Americans* became a runaway success.

When yet further financial difficulties ensued, Fanny, to escape her creditors, settled in Bruges, where, in succession, a daughter, a son, and, finally, her husband — who took refuge with her — died of consumption. During this time, she developed a curious regimen. From nine o'clock every morning till eight in the evening, she attended to the sick beds of her various charges. From eight in the evening until about three in the morning, she sat at her desk writing the light-hearted novels for which she has become famous. A stranger to aesthetic concerns, she judges her mighty output solely on its commercial success. She determined to settle in Florence twelve years ago because of the city's affordability.

Unlike his mother and brother, Adolphus is a writer of a more elevated turn of mind, having turned himself into an Italian nationalist. In fact, the Villino is rightly suspected by the Austrians to be a centre of good-natured contempt for the Grand Duke and his government. A tall wispy man with long white hair and an accompanying beard, Adolphus is something of an item of curiosity to all who live or visit Florence.

The most prepossessing of the Trollope trio is Theodosia, a slight woman with huge grey eyes, irregular features and a dark olive complexion. Her lineage is most curious: she is the daughter of Joseph Garrow, the offspring of a British officer and a Brahmin lady. At the age of twenty-five, Garrow married a rich Jewish widow of forty-eight. That lady, celebrated for two things, her agreeable musicianship and her disagreeable temper, gave birth in 1825 at the improbable age of fifty-nine to Theodosia.

Of a deeply self-introspective character, Theodosia proclaimed herself a poet at the age of thirteen, spent her childhood at Torquay and in 1844 came to live in Tuscany. Walter Savage Landor said of her — she repeats this innumerable times — "Sappho was less intense, Pindar less lively." At the age of twenty-three, Theodosia married the thirty-eight year old bachelor, subsequently inherited money from her mother and purchased the Villino.

Since her daughter-in-law is her landlady, Fanny has to be extremely careful about not offending her and, of course, Adolphus is dependent upon his wife's financial resources. As a result of these complicated forces, Daniel has been thrown into a lion's den.

Theodosia, although amazed by the manifestations of the spirits who have visited her home, is convinced that Home must be a fraud. She has bluntly informed him that she considers him to be the most gifted trickster ever to assume mortal form. Although she avoids confronting her dominating mother-in-law, Theodosia is not afraid of expressing her disdain for all mediums and spiritualists directly to Daniel's face. In turn, Frances becomes angry at Theodosia but airs her displeasure at her son, who has, understandably, come to regret having invited the medium to stay. Daniel has destroyed his domestic tranquillity.

In a morning, all three Trollopes write in the large sitting room. Frances's writing desk occupies the space to the right of the mantelpiece; Adolphus sits at a desk pinned between two huge book cases along the south wall; Theodosia's sits with her back to him. No talking of any kind is permitted in the room from eight to five each day. A guest can sit and read in the middle of the room, although it is difficult to move about so encumbered is the space with furniture.

Every day Daniel feels more uncomfortable and unsettled at the Villino and feels he must soon obtain sanctuary elsewhere.

Daniel begins to frequent the Villa Colombaia, a former monastery occupied by Major Charles Samuels, formerly of the 13th Regiment of Light Dragoons, a veteran of Waterloo, an event about which he talks about non-stop. One room of the Villa is entirely given over to a recreation of that famous battle: the thousands of toy soldiers were purchased from a shop in Piccadilly; everything else has been reconstructed by Samuels himself. Also at the Villa are Mrs. Crossman, the Major's widowed sister, and her two daughters, Miss Crossman and Mrs. Baker.

Mrs. Crossman, an incredibly small, shrunken, white-haired woman, is, as her brother observes, a hypochondriac. Her chief complaint, however, concerns her bedroom, which opens on to a staircase leading down to what had been the monastery's chapel. Every night when she retires to bed, she experiences an intense cold that cannot be dispelled by a large fire or shielded against by any amount of blankets. She has become convinced that she is not alone in the room, although no voice ever speaks to her nor are there any rappings or sounds of a presence.

Daniel agrees to perform a séance in Mrs. Crossman's bedroom; the only other person in attendance is Mrs. Baker. As they seat themselves around a table, a heavy chair moves itself forward, as if someone is joining them. The sound of the sweeping of heavy garments can be heard followed by a scraping noise like nails on wood. Then the cloth of the table next to Mrs. Baker rises up, as though a hand is pushing through from below. Soon afterwards, Mrs. Baker and Mrs. Crossman declare they can endure no more, and the session concludes.

On the next evening, the party is augmented by Major Samuels and one of his military friends. Everyone in the room feels the temperature drop precipitously. A stiletto Mrs. Baker uses as a penknife is pulled out of its sheath and flung about; a table is lifted and pushed violently across the room, stopping at the head of the staircase. The group follows the table and once they have been reassured that it is quiescent, they return to their places and wait as Home descends into a trance. Mrs. Baker's elbow is grasped by a hand with long, yellow, skinny fingers. She whispers to the spirit, and through Daniel it replies, in Italian, that he is most unhappy and needs her assistance. Mrs. Baker asks after the spirit's identity in Italian, and it responds in what is evidently an archaic dialect. In his hypnotic state, the medium is able to speak perfectly in a language of which he has no knowledge beyond the most rudimentary expressions and pleasantries.

The spirit identifies himself as a Franciscan monk by the name of Giovanni, who, having murdered several members of his own order, died in Mrs. Crossman's room. When Mrs. Baker asks if he wishes masses to be said for him, he replies that he does not require such intervention, but he nonetheless requests her prayers.

After that evening, the temperature of the room stays normal, and Mrs. Crossman is able to sleep comfortably, although her multitude of other symptoms persists. When she complains to Daniel that he has not alleviated them, he reminds her that he is not a physician.

In January 1856, five months after Daniel's arrival in Florence, Signor Landucci, Minister of the Interior to the Grand Duke of Tuscany, requests that the medium not leave the Villino after dusk. The injunction, he is told, is for the safety of his person and for all the expatriate community, as he has made enemies among the ignorant populace, some of whom are bent on taking his life. Daniel has been accused of playing upon the superstitions of the peasantry, claiming to administer the seven sacraments of the Catholic Church to toads, and of raising the dead to life through these and other practices of the black arts. Landucci assures Daniel that the government believes him innocent of such charges, but that Daniel's resuscitation of Giovanni, the homicidal monk, has worsened the situation.

For obvious reasons, the Trollopes are deeply upset by this injunction, feeling that their persons and property are in particular danger. Luckily, Daniel has recently been introduced to Count Branicka, a Polish nobleman, who, impressed by the medium's powers, has asked him to accompany him and his family as far south as Naples and then back to Rome.

Daniel determines to accept this invitation. On the evening of the third of February, as Daniel prepares to retire, he is delivered a message by an otherworldly voice. His powers as a medium are to be suspended for exactly one year. When he asks the reason, none is forthcoming. Certain that the Count's interest in him is based solely on his powers as a medium, Daniel unhappily informs Branicka the following morning of this news, convinced that the invitation will be rescinded. The Count immediately replies that he values Daniel for himself even more than for the strange gift he possesses. He urges Daniel to leave Florence with him as planned. Daniel replies that he will most gratefully join the party.

In the midst of the agitation caused by the loss of his powers, Daniel disobeys Signor Landucci, wandering out the following night to the centre of the city. For many years, Daniel has seen his gift as an encumbrance, but now knowing that he will lose it, he wonders who he is apart from that dubious talent. He is, he assures himself, a person of some natural intelligence; he can make conversation readily with all sorts of persons; he is a loyal and persistent friend; he can express heartfelt gratitude to those who have assisted him; he has never been a charlatan. Having compiled this list, he still sees himself as a person of absences, a man without qualities. Since Edwin, he has had no close friend; he has never been intimate with a woman. His ability to summon the spirits has denied him a character of his own because he is called upon to express the feelings of others. Those thieves have also stolen his physical well-being.

They drain all his energy. He must rest in order to receive them; he is a wreck after their visitations. Having rendered him unfit for any respectable profession, they are harsh masters. He, the ungrateful servant, powerless to rebel against them, hates them and despises himself for following their dictates.

Finally, exhausted, Daniel walks down via Giorgio la Pita and comes to the entrance of Giardino dei Semplici. Determined to rest there before returning to the Villino Trollope, he sits down at the first bench he comes upon. Anxious thoughts continually leaping to the forefront of his mind, he moans loudly.

"Mr. Home, you are distressed?" inquires a woman's voice.

Startled, Daniel realizes that a figure is sitting on the other side of the bench.

He apologizes for his unseemly behaviour. The voice answers: "You need not do so. Especially to one who has marvelled at your skills."

"Madam, I do not recognize your voice," he responds in confusion. "When did we meet?"

"I am Mrs. Osborne. I was present at the séance at Ealing last summer. We were not introduced."

"Yes. I remember you. I did not know you were resident in Florence."

"I have spent two months here and have heard of the exorcism you performed at the Villa Colombaia. I understand some of the locals have taken against you. Is that what has so agitated you?"

"No. I am in a strange state. A spirit has announced to me that my powers will be suspended for a full year."

"Has this occurred before?"

"Never. The suddenness of the annunciation has confounded me."

"You are saddened?"

"I am not certain what I feel. That is part of my anguish."

"Yours is a great gift."

"It is also a great impediment to a normal life. I often feel a simulacrum of a human being."

"My experience of life is that we must grasp what we are given. If we are disappointed, we must be patient. If we meet hindrances, we can only remove those we have the power to eradicate. Any other path is folly."

"So we must accept our individual lots, good or bad?"

"We must do our very best with them. We must be as human as we can be in husbanding them in our own service."

"I am of two persuasions. I am delighted to be rid of the so-called gift, which has made me into an oddity. On the other hand, my life has been dominated by this force and it is my only claim to distinction."

"You have a clear idea of the obstacles that confront you. That, in itself, is a blessing."

"I have no clear path to follow."

Mrs. Osborne laughs gently. "You are young. For you, time will take a long time to run out."

This middle-aged woman's candour, so different from his own reticence, disarms Daniel. He tells her that Robert Browning's abusive behaviour still distresses him.

"He acted impulsively, perhaps to protect his wife."

Daniel, sensing she knows more of the matter than she admits, reveals that he has often thought of avenging himself upon the poet. But he has decided such an act would do no good. Besides, he has no idea of how to revenge himself on anybody. Then he confesses something to her of which he is deeply ashamed.

Just before the Ealing event, Daniel had met the elderly Sir David Brewster at several séances. At each of those sessions Daniel had been successful in obtaining the co-operation of the spirits and Brewster had confessed his belief to him in the unknown forces in attendance, yet he later branded Daniel a liar and a fake in the public press. Three days after that obnoxious piece had appeared in the *Morning Advertizer*, Daniel had encountered Brewster in Pall Mall. Rather than avoid him, Daniel confronted the elderly man and demanded an explanation. Brewster, regarding him with some contempt, replied that, after considerable soul-searching, he had decided that he had been witness to the activities of a very clever conjuror.

"A cold rage filled me, and I told the old man he was nothing more than a Pharisee. I accused him of trying to discredit me because the appearance of the spirits made a mockery of all the scientific experiments to which he had devoted his life.

"He looked stricken by my vehemence and walked away. He died the following day, and I have been beset by regret and guilt ever since."

Mrs. Osborne is firm: "Sir David's death and your encounter with him had nothing to do with the other. We must allow for coincidence. I suspect the only contrivance you have ever practised in your young life is to mask the anger that boils up when you are attacked by Brewster, Browning, and their ilk."

With that, the lady rises. Daniel asks if he can accompany her to her lodging. She assents, and they walk the short distance to the via del Presto. As they talk, he recovers a distinct memory of what Mrs. Osborne had looked like at Ealing. If she had not told him who she was, he would never have recognized her. After they part, Daniel heads home.

Approaching the Villino, Daniel sees a slender young man detach himself from the shadows of one of the adjoining houses opposite. A few moments later, a violent blow to his left side throws Daniel, breathless, into a corner of the doorway. Another blow follows the first, this one to his stomach. Then a third one in the same region. The assailant runs off, shouting, "Dio Mio! Dio Mio!" Daniel sees the gleam of a blade in the villain's hand.

No one responds to his frantic knocks at the Villino. So, as quickly as he can, he makes his way along the wall to the door of a neighbour, who admits him. Daniel is in a state of shock and does not know the nature of the injuries he has sustained. As it happens, they are not serious. The first blow had been parried by the door key he carried in his breast pocket; the second by the overlapping folds of his fur coat as he crumpled in the doorway; the third blow has penetrated his clothes and made a small wound to the stomach, which bleeds slightly.

The awakened Trollopes, concerned that they might be attacked by the same mysterious assailant, grow even more unfriendly than before, even though Daniel assures them that the miscreant is simply a street rogue. Within the hour, a messenger arrives at the Villino: Mr. Widdicombe, the American gentleman, has been murdered on the street, presumably by Daniel's assailant. Mr. Widdicombe, who was renting a villa a short distance away, had informed his companion, Lady Smythe, that he would take the night air briefly. He had just left his villa when his companion heard him cry out. He was dead by the time she reached him.

On his last afternoon in Florence, Daniel determines to visit the Brancacci Chapel at Santa Maria del Carmine. Many of those attending his séances in this city have recommended this site because, they claim, Daniel's life is similar to the incidents in the life of St. Peter celebrated in the Masolino frescoes. In that cycle, the chief apostle heals the sick and the crippled and, most significantly, raises the Emperor's son from the dead. The frescoes are astonishing in their graceful, elegant beauty. The setting is Florence, not the Near East; St. Peter is easily distinguished by his cloak of orange, an especially wonderful use of that colour.

Like all visitors to the Chapel, Daniel is most struck by the work of Masaccio, Masolino's pupil. Masaccio's given name was Tomasso Cassai. He was called by the nickname of Masaccio

(The Impetuous One) not because, as Vasari explains, he was a bad or spoiled person but because of his lack of attention, from an early age, to the things of this world. He was totally absorbed by the matters of art. At the age of six he moved with his mother from San Giovanni in Altura, a small village, to Florence; at the age of twenty one, he enrolled at the Arte dei Medici e degli Speziali. Four years later he assisted Masolino and then went to Rome and Pisa. He returned to Rome on a commission and died there, in mysterious circumstances, at the age of twenty-seven.

When life was taken away from Masaccio he was only four years older than Daniel, who spends two hours scouring all the panels, trying to understand how Masolino's refinement had given way to Masaccio's roughness. The older man was a consummate artist of exquisite detail; the younger man looked at life as it was. His beggars and cripples are repulsive, castaways who have no place in the everyday commerce of the world.

At the last, Daniel stops before Masaccio's *Expulsion of Adam and Eve from the Garden*. Their bodies are heavy, going to fat. They have already suffered a great deal from the consequences of Original Sin. Adam, completely ashamed of himself, hides his face from the viewer's gaze. Eve covers her breasts with her right hand, her pudenda with her left. Her face is wracked with misery and the pain of self-knowledge. Nevertheless, there is about the couple a handsome majesty, of persons who recognize the errors of their ways. For the fraction of a second, Daniel sees himself as a similarly dishevelled, hapless Adam, but he promptly dismisses the fancy.

The artist who created the middle-aged Adam and Eve died young. Perhaps he had to pay for his genius with his life? He was a man possessed of boldness and yet he surrendered to death at such an early age. In contrast, Daniel sees himself as having been given a talent — if such it can be called — of no artistic or lasting value. For many, he is simply someone who provides amusement. Yet, sometimes the lives of those in his audience are deeply touched. But, he has the temerity to ask, what about myself? What have I been given? He cannot answer that question and is, once again, filled with dispiriting unease.

He lacks, he decides, the steady self-centeredness that accompanies genius. He might have the sensibility of an artist, but he has been provided with none of the character flaws to become one. Nor does he possess the ruthlessness required to become a genuine impostor. If only Mr. Browning understood this about him. Since all great writers by necessity must spin the fabric of life into lies, the poet should know Daniel incapable of the deceit of which he accuses him.

He hurries back to the Trollopes to finish packing. Three hours later, the Count's carriage draws up to the Villino. In a gesture of face-saving politeness, all three Trollopes are at the doorstep to say good-bye. As he steps into the carriage, Daniel greets the Count, his wife, and their son. For a few moments he does not recognize the other person tucked into the corner, a small, beautiful woman dressed in black, her eyes red and tear-soaked. Then he recognizes and greets Lady Smythe, for whom the city of Florence has likewise become a place of menace.

~~~~~~

CHAPTER ELEVEN

FEELING HEARTS

*H*aving succumbed to love, Julian Wilson and Lady Rhonda are warmed by each other's embraces. For most of their acquaintances, things have come to an awful pass. Four persons have been murdered. Lady Smythe has lost her lover. Daniel's powers have deserted him; some Florentines suspect him of murder. A great deal of money has been filched from Mrs. Osborne.

Cynthia Wilson's heart seemed to stop beating when she heard of her son's marriage to Lady Rhonda in Baden-Baden. She was aware that her daughter-in-law — how she detests being forced to call her such! — had sat to Julian last August. In fact, the last time he visited his parents, after his sojourn in Twickenham and an overnight stay in his rooms in London, he looked, as her husband put it, like a lovelorn calf. Julian refused to talk about what had occurred between the Lady and him, soon removed himself back to London, and later wrote to inform them he had taken employment with Jarves in Florence.

Mrs. Wilson does not hide her feelings from her husband: "Our son is not only ungrateful, he is perverse. He has married into the highest reaches of the aristocracy (in itself usually a laudable objective) in such a way as to make himself a *persona non grata* in Society."

Florence, in Mrs. Wilson's view, is the refuge for a certain kind of person who is unwilling or unable to conform to the pleasantries that make life in England so worthwhile. In the past week, she has heard that the outrageous Mrs. Osborne, who has been living in that city for some months, has determined to settle there; in fact, she has arranged for her serving woman to travel to Italy with several carriages in tow containing her hoard of silver.

Mrs. Wilson's suspicions about Florence were first aroused when Elizabeth Barrett, after abandoning her doting father, settled there with Mr. Browning. That woman, always of a delicate condition, soon enough conceived a child and evidently now wanders all over the continent with her husband and son. How has Mrs. Browning managed such a recovery, Cynthia asks her husband? Not from her consultations with the spiritual world but, according to a reliable source, through large helpings of morphine, for laudanum no longer suffices. Evidently she is completely addicted to that nefarious substance, which though relieving her physical sufferings in the short run, will eventually take its toll.

She has also learned that Mr. Home, the sometime toast of London society, has been accused of being a necromancer and has abandoned Florence in favour of Rome and Naples. If a man of such dubious character finds that place troublesome, she can well imagine how it was the perfect setting in which Lady Rhonda could seduce her gullible offspring. That place is also, as the papers tell her, a place where a gentleman like Stephen Widdicombe could be easily murdered.

1858

Abigail Fanshaw still feels despondent about Daniel Home's abandonment of Florence two years earlier. She rejoices, however, in the most recent news she has had of him. His powers, after precisely one year, were restored — *God be praised!* she exclaimed. Although he took the lamentable step of becoming a Roman Catholic, fortune has cast her most favourable eye on him. He has become a great favourite of the Empress Eugénie and thus, perforce, of Napoleon III. He is also engaged to be married. His bride, called Sacha, is of the Russian nobility, the sister of Countess de Koucheleff. "Imagine the conjugal furniture floating about the room at night!" she jokes with Miranda Osborne. That lady has become an active participant in the life of Florence, sharing as she does the nationalist sympathies of persons like Mrs. Browning, who now receives her regularly at Casa Guidi.

From Mrs. Osborne, now a close friend of the Brownings, Abigail has discovered that the poet is freshly agitated by his wife's interest in things spiritual. This time he has encountered an even more formidable rival in one Sophia May Tuckerman

Eckley, a rich American lady. Like Mrs. Browning, she is a poet, although her verse is cumbersomely allegorical and theological. Mrs. Eckley showers her new friend with expensive presents and provides her with communications from her dead brother. Mr. Browning considers his wife's new friend a charlatan and leaves the house whenever she presents herself at his door. However, he cannot threaten to throw her down the stairs! Mrs. Browning confides to Mrs. Osborne that "intercourse with the unseen makes me calm and happy, full of hope and understanding." The poetess's metaphor is interesting, given the fact that rumours are rife of a Sapphic relationship between her and Mrs. Eckley.

The Browning household is now an unhappy one. Mrs. Eckley professes to hear loud voices that no one else does and claims to convey messages from the spirit world. She and Mrs. Browning spend hours doing automatic writing; they also communicate by means of telepathy. Mr. Browning intends to put a stop to what he calls "this nonsense," but he seems powerless to do so.

Miranda Osborne writes regularly to Lady Rhonda, who now lives in Switzerland with her young husband. Lady Rhonda's embarrassing laugh, much to her surprise, has completely vanished.

1861

As Elizabeth Barrett Browning is dying, she moves in and out of consciousness. At times, her mind wanders, and her husband fears she no longer recognizes him. He takes her in his arms, supporting her head with his own, and shuddering when she coughs. After a second abscess pierces her trachea, she is silent. She passes away in the early summer.

When Miranda writes to Rhonda, she can barely hold her pen from grief. She tells her friend: "I shall write again in a day or two, but I shall answer the question in yours of June 20. Yes, I was the person who, five years ago, told Julian you were resident in Florence and intended to take a trip to the Biboli Gardens. From what he later confided in me, I gather that he waited for you on two separate occasions before *accidentally* coming upon you! I am disappointed in Julian: he assured me we would keep that secret to ourselves."

1862

Miranda Osborne's energies remain consumed by the movement to liberate Florence from the Austrians. Her nieces and nephews are furious that she has squandered a substantial part of her fortune in contributions to the cause. Miranda, who now rents Mr. Landor's villa, has removed all the paintings from the wall, installing in their place huge cabinets wherein she arranges her collection of silver. The only piece that graces her sitting room is a splendid chalice, which she claims is her favourite piece. She often jokes about its mysterious origins, calling it her holy grail.

No one would ever believe that twenty-eight years separates Julian and Lady Rhonda. They do not venture back to England but live in Montreux in the French-speaking part of Switzerland, where Mr. Browning and his son Pen visit with them. Mr. Browning and Mr. Wilson tolerate each other for the sake of Lady Rhonda. Mr. Wilson's canvases are increasingly sought after. Yet Mr. Wilson claims happiness has robbed him of ambition. He now paints as he pleases.

Daniel's young wife Sacha passes away in July near Périgueux. Mr. Browning and Mr. Home are now widowers with young children to raise. Gregoire is but a babe of three whereas Pen is thirteen and evidently of an intractable disposition, very much his father's son.

Daniel Home finds it difficult to accept any kind of assistance, such a solitary figure has he been since childhood. His great gift has been of incalculable benefit to others but remains a heavy burden to him. A guiding light to many, he is cast into the darkness.

PART THREE

WASHINGTON,
DISTRICT OF COLUMBIA

CHAPTER TWELVE

BEING OF GOOD HEART

*T*he city is humid, smelly and unsightly. The District of Columbia in May 1863 is not, as Daniel has heard it described, "a city of magnificent distances," but more like a grab-bag of close-pressed squalor. The unfinished Dome of the Capital, which he can see from his hotel room, has become a symbol of everything that is wrong in the no-longer United States. Black scaffolding sits uneasily around the unfinished shell, like a monster looking down warily upon the deformities it has created.

The place is a jumble of majestic white marble buildings and brown, dusty streets filled with soldiers, civilians, and hawkers. Goats, cows, chickens, and pigs clog the thoroughfares. A wide assortment of livery stables, bordellos, and saloons border Willard's Hotel, where Daniel is lodged. Long wagon loads of the wounded pass up Fourteenth Street as he steps out for an evening stroll. Some mornings he sees cavalry forces riding by, led by bands of buglers and drummers, heading to battle. Many of the men will be dead within a few hours.

The stench from the nearby canal, filled with drowned cats, rotten garbage, and whiskey bottles, overwhelms him every time he has to venture outside. The needle that is Washington's Monument is only a third of its planned height. Like Horatio Greenough's much-mocked statue of George Washington as Jupiter on the east portico of the Capital, it testifies to ambition thwarted by war and corruption. The District of Columbia was envisioned as a monument to American ambition; like Vienna, it is a city constructed to announce its inhabitants' intention of ruling the world. For Daniel, the place is an uneasy mixture of decadence, frivolity and pretentiousness. A village with the ambitions of empire.

Washington is also a place of rumours. The Confederacy is about to disintegrate. The Confederacy is about to receive full military support from England, which desperately needs cotton for its mills. Lincoln is in grave mortal danger; at least seven assassins are stalking the president.

Union supporters are reminded that careless talk can undo the war effort, but, as Daniel notices, almost every resident of the city could be a spy since they all speak with the drawl he associates with the Southern states. That is, he realizes, because the District of Columbia is really more a Southern city than a Northern one. Absent here is the sense of purpose he had witnessed as a youth in Hartford and Boston, where commerce is king. In this place, it is gossip that is manufactured, retailed and purchased as the very stuff of life.

Except for the fact that he seems doomed to be a wanderer on the face of the earth, why has Daniel returned to the country he abandoned in his early twenties? Ostensibly, Daniel has volunteered his services to the Union cause. He will be offering public recitals of American and English verse on behalf of the Soldiers' Aid Fund, a group whose mandate is to provide comfort for the wounded and disabled soldiers who have returned to every town and village in the Union. In Daniel's case, he is to perform at the many makeshift hospitals in the Washington area.

The real purpose of his journey is much more devious and is not of his own making. Since his marriage to Sacha, Daniel has become much more confident in public forums. Inspired in large part by his wife, he now speaks with considerable vigour and assurance. For Daniel, this is play-acting, but he can now manage such roles easily.

Six weeks ago, in March 1863, Daniel, a resident of Paris, is summoned to the British Ambassador's residence on the Champs Elysée. Mr. Crow, many years in the service of his government and plainly embarrassed to have to deal with the likes of Daniel, assumes all the graciousness at his command as he invites the medium to take brandy with him.

Crow's narrative, as diplomatic communications usually are, is filled with circumlocutions and obfuscation, but, eventually, he begins to explain why Daniel has been summoned for this interview. Willie, the much-beloved son of President and Mrs. Lincoln, died of a typhoid infection in February 1862. Although desolated, the President has soldiered on. The same claim cannot be made for Mrs. Lincoln, "a lady of extreme emotions," as Mr. Crow labels her. Moreover, Willie's death has caused considerable difficulties for Her Majesty's Government, which is already viewed by the North as sympathetic to the South.

A mystified Daniel waits patiently for the diplomat to unfold his story. In an attempt to obtain the assurance that her son survives in some manner beyond the grave, Mrs. Lincoln has called upon several spiritualists for assistance. None of these ladies and gentlemen has been of help. Unfortunately, one of these persons has done considerable harm, and that gentleman — Mr. Crow's enunciation of that word conveys both irony and disgust — is an Englishman.

The person in question calls himself Lord Colchester, although he is not a peer of the realm. He conducted séances at both the White House and Soldiers' Home, the president's summer residence. At those gatherings various sounds, supposedly heavenly in origin, could be heard. At his last performance, the room was in complete darkness and a banjo played when, all of a sudden, the lights were turned on. Colchester was discovered holding the musical instrument in his hands. Moreover, he was, under further inspection, found to have electrical instruments of various kinds strapped to his biceps. The scoundrel was escorted out of the presence of the Lincolns but, on the following day, Mrs. Lincoln received a letter from Colchester, threatening her with dire consequences if she did not procure for him a War Department pass to New York City. Lord Colchester was deported and is evidently now resident in London, where he has resumed his dubious practices.

As he listens to this dismaying story, Daniel still cannot fathom why he has been summoned by Mr. Crow. Having finished his tale, the diplomat invites his guest to smoke a cigar with him. Daniel declines, but his host removes one from the nearby humidor, chops its head, and proceeds to light it.

"My dear boy," Mr. Crow seems to be speaking sincerely, "the Home Office is of the opinion that you could do a great deal to help Her Majesty's government ease some of the diplomatic tension resulting from Colchester's outrageous behaviour." He puffs on the cigar. "Your wonderful, some say, miraculous, talents, testified to by some of the crowned heads of Europe, including the Empress Eugénie, might be of assistance to the Lincolns in their hour of need." Another puff. "Should you agree to assist that distraught couple, you would be performing an invaluable service for your native land."

Daniel explains that he can never make any guarantees. The diplomat purrs: "Success seems to follow you wherever you go."

He will not listen to Daniel's protestations. Instead, he outlines the story that will explain Daniel's presence in Washington. Mr. Crow has gone so far as to make arrangements for Daniel to leave Paris and sail from Southampton within the week and explains that a factotum employed by Mr. Pinkerton, the head of the American secret service, will meet Daniel's boat in New York City and travel with him by train to the American capital.

Mr. Crow does not bother to ask Daniel's consent to the scheme that he has hatched. Instead, he thanks the medium for his service to Her Majesty and indicates that the interview has reached its conclusion. Time, after all, is awasting. So, four weeks to the day of his meeting with Crow, Daniel is a guest at Willard's.

At the outset of this return voyage, Daniel's memories of his first trip to America and of his Aunt and Uncle Cook are at best scanty. He even finds it difficult to recall their faces. He only clearly remembers Fitzroy, the tiny drowned dog, especially his delicate, narrow grey muzzle. Then his memory darts ahead to how completely desolate he was when he returned to England as a young man. He wonders how much he has changed in the intervening years. Misery has always liked my company, he thinks to himself.

But then his thoughts are flooded with his dear Sacha. He remembers meeting the seventeen-year-old beauty in Rome in the winter of 1858, two years after the debacle in Florence. She is a lithe young creature, full of energy. He recalls her clear white skin, her rose-red lips, her swan-like neck; most of all, he recollects her gentle laughter. Twelve days later, they have agreed to marry. That heady time is hard to recall in detail. He does have a clear memory of their first quarrel. She tells him she has no belief in spiritual things and asks him to abandon the practice of what she calls magic. He assures her there is no conjuring in what he does. Moreover, his poor health suits him for no real profession. He tries to be straightforward: "I do not understand what happens during my meetings, but I feel compelled to assist those who ask me for help."

Her eyes fill with tears: "If your mission can bring consolation to others, I shall not stand in your way." She adds: "If I can assist, I shall." Over the next two years, his beloved develops some capabilities as a medium. He is no longer isolated. There is a purpose to his existence. He has a soul-mate. Then in May 1859, his son Gregoire is born, a beautiful, healthy, happy child. Can his happiness be more complete? Within a year, his wife is bed-ridden, suffering from the tuberculosis that kills her in July 1862.

Daniel's great joy in life has been cruelly ripped away from him. His wife's wealthy family is split down the middle: some adore him, others hate him. Her estate is the subject of endless litigation. Friends with small children of their own look after Gregoire when Daniel travels.

This crossing to the United States is completely uneventful. When his boat docks in Manhattan, he decides to face his challenges head-on. He will try to put aside his introspection, which, he feels, is excessive. As much as possible, he wishes to rid himself of the spirits. Yet his so-called mastery over those forces has brought him to America. In order to be of any use, he must resolve to be selfless. That is the only worthwhile remedy.

Daniel's determination is almost overwhelmed by what he witnesses on his first day. Most of the hospitals are filthy, mud-encrusted tents put up higgledy-piggledy wherever a free space exists. Harewood Hospital, on the outskirts of the city, has three thousand beds. Lincoln Hospital is a motley assortment of tents stretched across wooden frames on the marshy plain east of the Capital. Armoury Square and Judiciary Square are, as the Secretary of War, Mr. Stanton, puts it, state-of-the-art. They are constructed on a pavilion plan that consists of separate wards radiating from a central corridor. Douglas, where Daniel is assigned, was once a private mansion and is the handsomest of the Washington hospitals.

The water here is infected, the food contaminated by faeces, and the mosquitoes ever present to feast upon the sick. Typhoid fever, malaria, and diarrhoea are a greater threat to the soldiers than the wounds that brought them there in the first place.

The befuddled physicians use meaningless terms such as mephitic effluvia, sewer emanations, lack of nerve force, cholic temperament, odour of horse manure, and poisonous fungi in the atmosphere to explain the rising death toll. They employ a dazzling array of medicines, most of them ineffective or harmful: laudanum, ipecac, camphor oil, silver nitrate, turpentine, belladonna, castor oil, and calomel. When these fail, and they usually do, the physicians resort to bleeding, cupping, blistering, leeching, binding and chafing. This is the era of heroic dosing, whereby the patients float in a miasma of treatments and cures.

The great medical discoveries about bacteria and antisepsis are still a few years away. Amputations are performed at an alarming rate because the wounds inflicted by the .58 Minie bullets are staggering: the wounds are huge and jagged, bones are shattered, and bodies bleed copiously. A soldier surviving a gruesome wound on the battlefield faces a painful surgery (even though chloroform is now in wide use), the almost absolute certainty of a major infection, and the strong possibility of being killed by the drugs prescribed to treat him.

Daniel enters this chaos in order to fulfil his announced intent of reciting to the wounded. The doctors and attendants have no time for him. No one knows who is in charge. Daniel quickly determines that he must simply pitch in. Many of the soldiers are illiterate; some are blinded; some are too ill to concentrate enough to read anything. Daniel sits down beside them, comforting them as best he can. Some men wish to talk of their sweethearts, others to talk about the deaths that soon await them. Most of them are Christians who wish to be reassured about the future of their immortal souls. Some take great comfort from having Tennyson read to them; others enjoy Browning's monologues. Daniel does whatever will assist the poor wretches he encounters.

Thomas Haley, a twenty-year-old cavalryman in the 4th New York, emigrated from Ireland to enlist on the side of the Union. When Daniel meets him, a bullet is still lodged in his lung. He lies there with his chest exposed; the tan on his cheeks and neck has yet to fade and imparts a misleading glow of health. But pain clouds his face, and the stimulants which he is constantly fed have reduced him to a shy, frightened animal. He looks at every object and person forlornly. Daniel sits next to him when, all of a sudden, the youth opens his eyes, gives him a long, steady look, turns away and falls asleep again.

John Mahay, shot through the bladder, lies in a constant puddle. Sometimes his pain is so great that tears pour from his eyes and the muscles of his face contort hideously. A boy in age but old in misfortune, Mahay was placed in infancy in a foundling hospital in Manhattan and bound to a tyrannical master. One afternoon he shows Daniel the scars from the regular beatings he sustained.

Some of the rooms where the wounded are left to recover or to die have a sickly, sweet smell. Sometimes, the odours are riper. Gangrene has its own repugnant scent as do bedsores. Often Daniel can still smell the rank, sour stink of urine and dysentery long after he has left the hospital.

If he had to choose, Daniel would say Douglas was an inferno rather than a purgatorio. He can see no reason for this suffering, even though he knows that the slaves have been cruelly used by their Southern masters and that this civil insurrection is being waged in part to liberate the blacks.

Daniel goes about his appointed rounds. He writes letters on behalf of many soldiers, but the men are often at a loss for words to describe the grim reality of their situation; Daniel has to invent entire paragraphs in order to both inform and comfort the recipients. What surprises Daniel most is the outpouring of guilt from these men, torn apart by the fact that they are often fighting against and killing members of their own families.

Another frequent visitor to the hospital is a man who embodies Daniel's idea of an old Southern planter. He dresses in a wine-coloureded suit, a white shirt, a carelessly knotted tie, black Morocco boots, and an oatmeal-coloured, wide-brimmed hat with a gold and black drawstring. The man's nose is too broad for his face, his eyebrows are cunningly arched, and his beard is pure white. His piercing blue eyes are what attract Daniel's attention. That, and the slow, slouching way in which he moves from bed to bed. He brings all sorts of gifts to the inmates, even checks off a list as he bestows his offerings of liquorice, pipes, pouches of tobacco, horehound candies, toothpicks, combs, even servings of rice pudding.

Late one afternoon, as he is leaving Douglas, the old man catches up to Daniel. He introduces himself as "Mr. Whitman of Brooklyn in the State of New York." Daniel is startled: "The poet?" In his turn, the man is amazed. "You know of me?" Daniel tells him he is a great admirer of *Leaves of Grass*.

If there is any shred of shyness or hesitancy in Walt Whitman, it now vanishes. He informs Daniel that he has come to Washington to minister to those who have given of themselves so valiantly in the Union's cause. In order to support himself while in Washington, he works in the Paymaster's office most afternoons; he is lucky to have friends, who provide him with room and board. Every spare cent he has he spends buying presents for the patients. "I try to bring comfort to their souls, but I know full well the value of earthly pleasures." His speaks in a sing-song voice, very similar to the cadence of his verse.

As they talk, Whitman's enthusiasm soars. The War had to be fought in order to preserve the wholeness of The Nation. Mr. Lincoln is purging America of terrible diseases: slavery and the pride of those states that seek to separate from the Union. When Democracy was in danger of being slain, Mr. Lincoln presented himself to the nation as the avenging angel who would put things right.

"What a volume of meaning, what a tragic poem there is in every one of those sick wards," Whitman exclaims. His conversation becomes a rambling monologue. America is filled to bursting with limber-tongued lawyers, dyspeptics, slave-catchers, body-snatchers, gaudy men with gold chains made from the sweat of common, hard-working people. The rulers of the world are greedy and corrupt. Since they have no respect for themselves, how can they show any to the poor whom they trample under foot? The captains of industry do not even know they have bodies, so divorced are they from their real selves.

Daniel agrees with much of what his companion proclaims, although he has never been one to put matters so bluntly. He interrupts Whitman: "Do you think our paltry efforts at Douglas are of any benefit?"

Whitman is astounded at his companion's naivety: "Of course. You remember the words of the Nazarene, 'If you do anything for the least of my children . . .'"

Daniel finishes his companion's sentence: "'You do it for me.'"

"Precisely."

"But what if one is not a believer in the Gospel?"

"You do not need to be a Christian to understand the effects of good works."

Daniel informs Whitman that he agrees with him, but his own questions about the nature of evil are more philosophical than theological. The poet responds decisively: "Of philosophy as a discipline I have a very negative opinion."

Since they are strangers, never likely to meet again, the poet confides to Daniel that he wants to write a book of verse to be called *Drum-Taps* about his experiences in Washington. After that, he intends to abandon poetry for the business of life. Although he has long proclaimed his intent to be the great American bard, the War has robbed him of that ambition.

"The suffering of those glorious young men has moved me to a new level of consciousness." Daniel does not feel capable of such grand feelings. What he has seen has left him depleted rather than energized. But he burns, as never before, with a love of his fellow man.

The following morning, Daniel has a conversation with Timothy O'Sullivan, who occupies a room near his at Willard's. Mr. O'Sullivan, who is twenty-three — seven years younger than Daniel — bears a strong resemblance to him. In fact, they met because the porters at the hotel often confused the one with the other.

His family had emigrated from Ireland to escape the potato famine when Timothy was two. His early life in the Bowery was filled with poverty, his youth with frequent stays in jail, and his young manhood with driving ambition. At the age of eighteen, he was apprenticed to Mathew Brady, the photographer. For two years, his work consisted mainly of readying the wet plates for his master. As the sitter held rigidly still (aided by an invisible harness at the back of his neck), O'Sullivan would insert the plates he had saturated with chemicals into the camera while Brady exposed them. O'Sullivan would then rush back to the darkroom and develop the plates before they had a chance to dry. He was a year into his apprenticeship before Brady allowed him to take any photographs of his own. In fact, he only received that opportunity when his employer was asked to shoot some cityscapes. Although he is good at keeping it a secret, Brady has terrible eyesight and has a difficult time even taking studio photographs. Outside work is really beyond him. All of O'Sullivan's early photographs were, of course, sold as the work of Brady.

In the late 1850s, Brady was the most fashionable photographer in the United States; his huge showroom and studio on Broadway even became a tourist attraction. Most visitors could not afford a formal sitting, but Brady did a huge trade in quickly made *cartes de visite*, tiny photographic portraits that could be used in place of business or calling cards. When the war came, Brady, according to O'Sullivan, went soft. He no longer cared about the studio and its profits. He decided that he wanted to photograph the war and use this new medium to record the greatest event in American history. Painters had taken full advantage of the Revolutionary conflict; photographers could now immortalize the war with their art.

According to O'Sullivan, this patriotic "horseshit" was quickly seized upon by Lincoln and his cabinet, men who knew the value of propaganda. Soon afterwards, Brady travelled to Washington, opened a new studio there, and put one Alexander Gardner in charge. O'Sullivan was sent south to assist Gardner, who split from Brady a year later in 1862. Mr. O'Sullivan has been working for Gardner for just over a year.

O'Sullivan is not an overly talkative fellow, but, when he does speak, he is boastful. He also holds many opinions that are controversial in the District of Columbia. Daniel is his rapt listener as they sit at the bar for a drink.

The photographer is not really interested in the outcome of the war, although he assumes the North will win. He also thinks that compassion for the slaves and states' rights are not the issues that led to the conflict. He is of the opinion that the industrial North, being the gateway for immigrants, had no need to keep slaves after 1820. In fact, many wealthy Northeners began to feel guilty about exploiting their dusky brethren. That guilt, and the accompanying shame, led them to censure their cousins in the South. Of course, the South, being an agrarian economy, could not pay the wages of the European immigrants and depended on the labour of the blacks to survive. In O'Sullivan's view, the Southern slave owner has a great deal of respect for the work of slaves whereas Northerners have a very low opinion of coloureds.

O'Sullivan points out to Daniel that Mr. Lincoln has never held the black people in very high esteem. In order to be elected to the highest office in the land, the President, taking advantage of all the divisions in the Democratic Party, had to court the Abolitionists. That is what put him, a Republican, in office, and it was Lincoln's alliance with the Abolitionists that led to the formation of the Confederacy.

O'Sullivan's ruminations may be politically astute, but Daniel decides that he is much more comfortable with Mr. Whitman's sometimes far-fetched brand of idealism.

CHAPTER THIRTEEN

FROM THE BOTTOM OF ONE'S HEART

*A*n entire week passes before Daniel receives a note from John Hay, one of the President's secretaries, requesting his presence at the White House at ten on the following morning. The exterior of the large residence of the American President is suitably impressive, but Daniel is struck by the tawdriness of the interior. He has read in the English press that Mrs. Lincoln was shocked by the shabbiness of the living quarters when she first viewed them; she evidently spent many thousands of dollars to rectify the situation. But as he passes through a rabbit warren of small offices and catches glimpses of some larger rooms, he notices that large squares have been cut away in the carpets and that many of the curtains, window sashes, and furniture have also been vandalized. Unlike the residence of the British Prime Minister, tourists are encouraged to visit the White House and, obviously unsupervised, they have collected souvenirs aplenty. Daniel wonders if a republic, by its very nature, must, unlike a democracy, indulge its citizens in such excesses.

As he is reflecting on the differences between the two forms of government, his guide indicates that they have arrived at Mr. Hay's office. Daniel is ushered into a dark and windowless room. Mounds of books and papers are piled so high before the desk that Daniel cannot see beyond them. He is greeted by Hay, a young man of excessive and chilly refinement, who guides him to a chair. The atmosphere is claustrophobic; Daniel feels as if he has been placed in a trench.

Of medium height and handsome in a conventional way, Hay makes it clear from the outset that he disapproves of all spiritualists. His narrow eyes search Daniel's countenance rudely. "I believe you have been told about our problems with Colchester," he asks belligerently.

Daniel admits to being familiar with that unfortunate incident.

"The trouble is that Mrs. Lincoln is not the kind of person who learns from experience, no matter how harsh the incident or painful the lesson."

When Daniel does not reply, Hay continues: "If the President has a failing, it is that he indulges that woman so completely."

"What do you mean by indulgence?"

"He is willing to attend a further séance to determine if a genuine communication can be established with his dead son."

"Are you telling me that the President has no belief in the spirit world?"

"No. I am telling you that the President, a man of generous sentiments, is willing to entertain the possibility that the dead exist in some form."

"You are not a man of such generous sentiments?"

"Exactly so."

"Mr. Hay, I should like to remind you that I am not here of my own volition. I have not requested an audience with the President or his wife. I do not make any claims or guarantee success. And I am furious that you think you can insult me so brazenly."

As far as Mr. Hay is concerned, the interview is going very badly. "We are grateful to you for answering our summons. The President and Mrs. Lincoln are eager to meet with you. In my office, I must defend the President's time and many are of the opinion that I am too zealous in my manner of conducting business."

"I am in the camp of your critics."

Mr. Hay decides it is best to ignore that remark. "If possible, Mrs. Lincoln would like to meet with you tomorrow morning. I think that the best time for the séance would be on the following evening, if that schedule is agreeable to you?"

Daniel nods his head yes.

"If you would be so gracious, Mr. Nicolay, the President's other secretary, and myself would like to be present at the séance."

"I have no difficulty with doubters of any kind attending."

The young secretary, who had broken into a sweat, is now

grateful for Daniel's acquiescence. He would have had a lot of explaining to do had an enraged medium stormed out of their conclave. The two men exchange polite sentiments about looking forward to seeing each other in the very near future.

That evening, Daniel fulfills a long-standing wish. Mr. Hay, perhaps in reparation for his ill-advised comments, has left a ticket to Jenny Lind's recital at Ford's Theatre. President Lincoln, a great admirer of the Swedish Nightingale, was to attend in his box that evening but cannot because of an emergency meeting of the War Cabinet. His loss becomes Daniel's gain.

Daniel is familiar with Lind's history and sees the parallels between their lives. As a young girl, Lind was sent away by her cruel mother to live with relatives. When she returned at the age of nine, she took comfort in singing to herself. One day a passerby overheard her and soon afterwards Lind, a Cinderella no longer, was sent to study at the Royal Academy in Stockholm at the government's expense. By the time she was twenty-four, she was the most famous entertainer in Europe. Once Queen Victoria delayed her departure to Balmoral so that she could hear the famous voice. Six years later, P.T. Barnum lured her to America, where she has became an even greater sensation. Although much loved, Jenny Lind has not escaped censure. Her critics accuse her of being a mere trickster who, with simple gestures, a moderately attractive voice and great cunning, gives her listeners the impression that she can reveal to them the mysteries of the universe.

A woman of mild temperament, Lind never rebelled against the tyrannical Mr. Barnum. She has never replied to her critics. Often, however, she is simply unable to perform. Her upper notes suddenly lose their sweetness, and she must patiently wait for her powers to be restored. In private life she is now Mrs. Otto Goldschmidt, the wife of the Boston musician and conductor. Now in her forty-third year, she performs rarely and only in the service of charitable causes. The money raised this evening is for the Washington hospitals.

In London, Daniel has heard Adelina Patti, a larger-than-life performer who walks on to the stage with considerable swagger, magnificently costumed. Although Lind's hair is beautifully coiffed and garlanded with myrtle, she is simply dressed in a white silk blouse and a red velvet skirt that touches the ground. She patiently accepts the tributes of the audience before nodding to her accompanist to begin.

Daniel notices that her nose is immense and broad; her throat is large to accommodate her huge larynx; her eyes are small, a glaucous grey. Unlike Patti, Lind does not rely on a pyrotechnical display of cascading high notes. Her voice is, quite simply, sweet.

From the box, Daniel can study the soprano carefully. He can see how much of what she does is purely mechanical. Often, her mouth is held in odd positions; her tongue moves rapidly to control her output. So these are some of her secrets, Daniel thinks to himself. Yet the effect is magical. He does not care a whit about how the notes are produced so beautiful are the sounds.

Like everyone else in the audience, he is deeply moved

when she concludes the evening with Handel's setting of "I Know That My Redeemer Liveth" from the *Messiah*. In rendering the most famous song in her repertoire, she is transformed into the diva who dwells in paradise with the angels.

Even more than Jenny Lind or Queen Victoria, Mary Todd Lincoln is the most written-about woman in the world. She is known under various sobriquets such as Madame, Delilah, the Hellcat, Her Satanic Majesty, and The Lady-President. The invention of the telegraph has made the transcontinental spread of information easy; it has also created an intense demand for gossip. The reclusive widow, Queen Victoria, does not provide sufficiently interesting copy for the growing number of journalists plying their trade in England and the United States; Jenny Lind lives quietly in Boston.

Every movement of the volatile Mary Lincoln, a person inclined to express extremely undiplomatic opinions in public, is carefully scrutinized and often presented in the worst possible light. When she visits the best couturiers in New York City in search for a dress suitable for the inaugural ball, she is labelled a heartless spendthrift completely unaware of the restraint that should be practised at a time of great crisis. When she attempts to restore the interior of the White House to a semblance of dignity worthy of the President's status, she is accused by Unionists of insensitivity to the plight of the slaves.

Even her husband, it is claimed, is annoyed by his wife's excessive "flub-dubs for this damned old house, when the soldiers cannot even have blankets." Mr. Lincoln is known for describing himself and his wife as "the long and short of it." In whimsical moments, he will maintain that although one *d* was good enough for God, the Todds required two.

The lady's most insignificant actions earn notoriety. One afternoon, a woman journalist notices "the presidential coach with its purple hangings and tall footman" outside a dress shop in Manhattan. Curious, she follows the First Lady into the shop, where she beholds Mrs. Lincoln bargaining with a sales clerk over a pair of black cotton gloves. Mrs. Lincoln is dressed in a red silk dress, garishly embroidered with flowers and trimmed with laces, ribbons and other pieces of furbelow. Her cape is made of black lace, her hat trimmed with flowers, feathers, and tinsel balls; she carries a pink parasol. The First Lady has "a short, broad face with a sallow, mottled complexion, light grey eyes, with scant light eyelashes, and exceedingly thin pinched lips." In sum, this woman is a haughty "self-complacent" creature with a scornful expression.

In the North, Mrs. Lincoln is suspected of being a traitor; in the South, she is accused of being a turncoat. Although husband and wife were both born in Kentucky, Mary, unlike her husband, is from a wealthy, slave-owning family. Although she sacrificed many comforts when she married the struggling young lawyer, she has standards that she puts into practise when she goes to live in the White House.

At her insistence, Robert, her eldest son, attends Phillips Exeter Academy and, later, Harvard. When her husband and his advisors suggest Robert volunteer for the Army, she intervenes because she cannot stand the prospect of losing yet another child. That interference makes her even more suspect in the North. Then, there is the fact that some of her brothers and brothers-in-law are fighting and dying for the Confederacy. She even brazenly receives her sister, the widow of a Confederate officer, at the White House.

Even the most intimate details of the Lincoln marriage are fodder for the newspapers. What about the President's first love, Ann Rutledge? Wasn't Miss Todd a very poor second best? There is the fact that the Lincolns were first engaged in 1840, broke off their engagement for almost a year, and then married in 1842. A close friend of the President has let it be known that Mr. Lincoln jilted Mary Todd at the altar and that she later married him only to exact revenge. In truth, despite their occasional public squabbles, the couple love and respect each other.

Mrs. Lincoln, it is now widely rumoured, is going mad with grief over the loss of her son, Willie. There is some truth to that claim. In February 1850, the Lincolns' second child, Edward, died, at not quite four years of age. Willie, born in December 1850, was conceived to replace the loss of his brother. Of the couple's three other sons, Willie was the most mischievous and loveable. Soon after moving into the White House, he convinced Tad, his younger brother by three years, to convert the roof of their new home into a circus to which they charged five cents admission. There, the audience saw Willie dressed up in his mother's lilac gown and Tad, in blackface and wearing his father's spectacles, singing their father's campaign song, "Old Abe Lincoln Came Out of the Wilderness" at the top of their lungs. Willie also organized

"Mrs. Lincoln's Zouaves," with himself as Colonel, Tad as drum major and their friends in subsidiary positions. One day the brothers wandered into Washington and could not be found until dark. Willie claimed, "we had decided to see how far we could go. We went down steps pretty near to China and when there weren't any more, Tad dared me to explore and we did and got lost." To a journalist who once quizzed him about living in the White House, Willie was extremely candid: "I wish people wouldn't stare at us so. Wasn't there ever a President who had children?"

When Willie died in February 1862, his mother was so stricken that she could not attend his funeral service in the East Room. Unable to control her emotions, she could not visit Tad, who was seriously ill with typhoid but recovering. After witnessing one paroxysm of sobbing, the President led his wife over to a window. He pointed to the insane asylum in the distance and warned her that she must control herself or that would be her fate.

Daniel knows a great deal about the pathetic history of Mary Lincoln when he arrives for his interview. The same functionary as the day before leads him to the Conservatory, the First Lady's grandest accomplishment in her White House renovations. As they head down the corridor, two women, in close conversation, advance in their direction. One woman bears a passing resemblance to photographs Daniel has seen of Mrs. Lincoln; the other woman, who smiles at him, he is certain he has met before. He asks his guide the identity of these women. The aide tells him that the taller woman is Emilie Helm, Mrs. Lincoln's widowed sister; her companion is Lady Smythe, a resident of Georgia.

Of a sudden, as the floodgates of memory open, Daniel realizes how much that noble lady has aged in the seven years since he has seen her. He recalls hearing that she had immigrated to Georgia in the United States to assist the widowed Mrs. Widdicombe, the mother of Stephen.

The two men reach the door of the Conservatory, and the overwhelming, sickly-sweet smell of lilies puts the encounter out of Daniel's mind. The lilies are obviously Mrs. Lincoln's favourite flowers, perhaps because they are harbingers of resurrection and rebirth.

Newspaper accounts have not prepared Daniel for his meeting with the First Lady. She rises when he enters the room and extends her hand timidly. This famous woman is often described as short and dumpy and, although these adjectives are accurate, they do not taken into account the clarity and directness of her eyes, her regal bearing, or her radiant countenance. Her hair is worn with braids intertwined at the back of her head; her dress is a delicate pink.

When they are seated opposite each other, Mrs. Lincoln thanks Daniel for travelling to the United States to assist her and her husband. Politely, Daniel says the matter is of no consequence. Mrs. Lincoln brushes such conventionalities aside: "I am sure you have been much inconvenienced, and I suspect that guttersnipe Hay was rude to you when he met with you yesterday!"

Daniel does not offer any comment and so she takes his

silence for a yes. "I am surrounded by my enemies here in this fish bowl where Mr. Lincoln and I are on constant display." She abruptly changes the subject. "You are prepared for tomorrow evening?"

Daniel assures her that he never prepares for his séances; anything of significance that might occur will simply happen. "It is all by happenstance."

"Your manner is completely different from any other spiritualist I have ever encountered. I feel I can put my complete confidence in you."

"I hope it is not misplaced."

Suddenly, Mrs. Lincoln's brow looks deeply troubled. "I am certain the ministering angels of the dead will be kind to a troubled woman such as myself."

"Madam, I very much hope so."

So directly does she look him in the eye that Daniel witnesses the rage and sadness that are eating her from the inside. She may have a histrionic side, to which so many inches of newsprint have been devoted, but she is just a mother who has been deprived of a much treasured son. Such love cannot be counterfeited. She gives Daniel a kindly look, rises to bid him adieu but is overcome with emotion. He takes her hand in his, kisses it, bows, and leaves the room.

On the following evening, Daniel is decidedly nervous. His greatest fear is that Mr. Lincoln will be displeased with him, much in the manner of Robert Browning. When Daniel arrives at the White House, Mr. Hay is waiting for him in the foyer. They walk to a room on the west side, near the living quarters. Mr. Nicolay is already there. He is a short, extremely thin man of sharp angles. He mentions to the medium that the room has been emptied of all furniture except for a small table, five chairs, and a wide, ornate floor-to-ceiling mirror that is too heavy to move. Daniel informs him that the room needs more light. Nicolay instructs Hay to see to the spiritualist's needs. A few minutes later, Hay returns with some servants who install the requisite lamps.

A few minutes later, Mrs. Lincoln enters the room. She pays no heed to the two young men, but she greets Home warmly. "If we are ready, I'll fetch the President," Mr. Nicolay announces and leaves the room. No one engages in any small talk. After a quarter of an hour, the door is opened by Mr. Nicolay, who leaves it open and takes his seat. Almost immediately, the President enters the room, shutting the door behind him.

Daniel has seen countless photographs of Mr. Lincoln, but he is not really prepared for the spectrally tall, gaunt, bearded man who walks over to him, his arm extended. His face is densely scored with lines not seen in his pictures. It is the soft amiability of the man that makes its deepest impression on Daniel. The President is reckoned a great orator, but the warmth of his speaking voice is astonishing. He expresses his thanks to Home for travelling so far to be of service. He then turns to his wife. "Mother, are you ready?" She nods. "Yes, Mr. Lincoln, I am prepared."

As he always does, Daniel asks the group to join hands. He

takes Mr. Lincoln's in his right, his wife's in his left. He asks the group to maintain complete silence, and he reminds them that he cannot promise any results.

Slowly, Daniel feels himself descending into a familiar reverie. At first, he is immersed in a blue substance much thicker than water. He glides easily through it, using his outstretched arms and hands to steer himself. A feeling of blissful well-being fills him. Then, he notices the shore to which he must direct himself. That beachhead is of thick, black volcanic sand. How he hates to leave the kingdom of the water for the rigours of the earth. He glides towards the shore, lifts himself up and proceeds to walk into the forest a few hundred yards ahead. His way forward is not encumbered, but his self-assuredness has been replaced by a gnawing anxiety. The way ahead is too difficult. He is tempted to turn back, but he knows he carries within him a terrible responsibility. He forces himself forward.

The forest is gradually replaced by a treeless incline that he must ascend. He begins the climb reluctantly and soon all his limbs threaten to rebel. He finds it hard to breathe. He feels his heart pulsing loudly. His lungs threaten to give out. Only gradually does the terrain level out.

He walks forward, now with some ease. Ahead is a small, hooded figure, awaiting his arrival. The hood vanishes as Daniel reaches the figure and looks into the eyes of a young man. After searching his face, the youth beckons him forward. In a minute or two, they reach the edge of a new forest into which his companion walks. Daniel follows. The glade is black, and walking through it is difficult, as if the two companions are pushing themselves through onyx. Suddenly, a tranquil yellow light surrounds them, allowing them to proceed with ease. The young man turns around and in his arms is a young boy. Daniel now becomes aware that someone is standing behind him. He turns around and looks for the first time since her death into the eyes of his beloved Sacha.

The Lincolns and the two secretaries observe Mr. Home entering into what looks like a trance. They sit patiently for about ten minutes. Mrs. Lincoln's eyes betray her fear that nothing will happen. Her husband, seeing the anxiety on her face, becomes concerned. Mr. Hay and Mr. Nicolay are bored.

Suddenly, Home pulls his hands away from the Lincolns and gets up from the table. He walks with great hesitation, almost limping, until he reaches the large mirror on the other side of the room. He peers into the glass for a moment or two. Then, the audience of four is startled to see that Home's reflection in the mirror undergoes a change. Myriads of tiny blue lights swarm his ears, eyes, mouth and hair. After a few minutes, they notice a hooded figure in the mirror approach the medium. When this person slowly removes the hood, all four gasp as they recognize Willie Lincoln. He turns away from them and slowly dances away; he returns carrying a young boy whom both the Lincolns recognize as Edward, who died thirteen years before. Then, at the side of Home, a slim, dark-haired woman appears.

The four figures in the reflection glance in the direction of the small audience. Then Willie, Edward and the woman vanish. A few moments later, the lights in the mirror disappear. Home slowly walks back to his place at the table and takes the hands of the Lincolns. A few minutes later, he awakens.

Mrs. Lincoln is so completely overcome that she quickly excuses herself. She takes the medium's hand and thanks him from the bottom of her heart. If they are impressed or touched, Mr. Nicolay and Mr. Hay do not admit to it. They take their leave shaking Home's hand. They wait for the President, but he signals for them to go. After they close the door, the President walks over to the medium, stands before him, places both his hands on his shoulders for a few moments, and then embraces him. "God bless you, Sir, for your great kindness!"

On the drive back to Willard's, Daniel is filled by a sense of elation he has not experienced for a long while. He is jubilant that the Lincolns have had the opportunity to see their two dead sons and to know that they are safe in the great beyond. But far greater is his own exultation in being reunited with his dead wife, who has never before appeared to him. He remembers Tennyson's words: "Far off thou art, but ever nigh;/I have thee still, and I rejoice;/....I shall not lose thee though I die." Used to suppressing his feelings, Daniel waits until he is alone in his hotel room before allowing salt-filled tears of joy to run freely down his face.

CHAPTER FOURTEEN

A HEART TO HEART TALK

On the morning after the séance at the White House, Daniel receives a message from Lady Smythe. If he is agreeable, she proposes to call on him that evening at Willard's. Perhaps they can take supper together?

When he sees her for the second time, he is again amazed how much Lady Smythe has aged. Her frame is still wiry, but her hair is now completely white, her face wizened, and her back stooped. No wonder he did not immediately recognize her the other day. She has read about Daniel in the newspapers and expresses her sympathy about Sacha's death.

Daniel brings her up to date about some of the people she knew in Florence.

Miranda Osborne has been completely rejuvenated by the Republican cause; when she speaks in Italian, no one can detect a foreign accent. All her listeners are amazed at the force of her feelings. No *Inglese* ever spoke like that, Daniel has been told. Her face having burnished a deep brown under the Italian sun, she is often mistaken as a native of her beloved Florence.

Lady Rhonda still sits to her husband, and those portraits continue to make him the most eagerly-collected painter in Europe. Theirs is a contentment reserved for few mortals. Happiness, Julian has confided to Daniel, has so robbed him of ambition that he now has become a genuine artist. The joy that radiates from the face of his wife in his various renditions of her is something witnessed before only in the sweet-faced women of Botticelli and Leonardo. Lady Rhonda's continual sadness is that she could not conceive a child with her second husband.

While Daniel speaks, Lady Smythe notices how remarkably vigorous he now appears. His nose has become broader, his moustache thicker, his chest more filled out, even his hands look larger. His voice, once so thin, has been transformed into a magnificent baritone.

Recently, he confides, a journalist, in the midst of an audience with him, was caustic in expressing his scepticism about the profession of medium. Daniel replied that he himself did not fully understand the spirits, and then he fixed his accuser with steely eyes: "There are more things in heaven and earth than are dreamt of in your philosophy."

Lady Smythe applauds Daniel's response to his interrogator. When Daniel asks about Lady Smythe's present circumstances, she tells him that she settled in Georgia in order to minister to Mrs. Widdicombe, Stephen having been that poor lady's only child.

"I am now numbered among the outcast Rebels," she observes. When they met the other day, she was accompanying her friend, Emilie, Mrs. Lincoln's sister. Emilie, though a Rebel, can cross to the Union from the Confederacy because of her status as Mr. Lincoln's sister-in-law. Lady Smythe is the perfect travelling companion because she remains an English subject.

Daniel thinks back to the crisis in Florence, especially the unkindness of the Trollopes, the attempted murder, and the loss of his powers. He remembers how agitated he was when he entered the coach on that last day and encountered Lady Smythe. He was glad to put his own sorrows aside and console her for the loss of Stephen Widdicombe. He remembers how small and vulnerable she looked. He took her tiny hands in his and kissed them. She was so desperately grateful for the small kindnesses he bestowed.

As all kinds of niceties are exchanged, Daniel is battered with the most unsettling images and voices, which veer in and out of his consciousness. So powerful are these that Daniel, impolitely for one so versed in society's conventions, veers the conversation in a new direction by exclaiming: "You are the murderer of those four people!"

If she is surprised, Lady Smythe does not betray it. She looks him straight in the eye. "I have always thought you uncommonly kind to a person who has misused you grievously. I assumed you knew I had been your assailant in Florence."

"I have never been a clairvoyant, Lady Smythe. I had no

idea until this moment when some spirit voices informed me."

Having been unmasked, Lady Smythe is not reluctant to relate the entire story of her past life. After all, she observes, the Unionists have no interest in her past and will be delighted to see her leave for Atlanta early on the following morning. In fact, she is eager to confess her sins.

Lady Smythe was born Sylvia Brown in a small Yorkshire village; her father was a country doctor, who specialized in surgery. She was orphaned at the age of ten, sent to live with an unfeeling aunt and eventually deposited by that unkind relative in an orphanage. At the age of twenty-one, Sylvia went into the service of Sir Roger Smythe, a man many years her senior.

"My biography bears many resemblances to the life of Jane Eyre as immortalized in Miss Brontë's recent novel, but there was no madwoman in my husband's attic. Indeed, we were happily married until he died in a fatal accident. I was distraught when he passed away. Eventually, I recovered my equilibrium, rented the manor house and went into London society."

For some years, Lady Smythe sailed, as she put it, on the surface of things. She was unhappy but not deeply so. She did not feel she was drowning until she met Stephen Widdicombe, a man ten years her senior. When she fell desperately in love with him, he tolerated her. What little fortune she had, he helped her spend. He had been raised by a black mammy who did everything for him and he came to have similarly high expectations of all women in his life. Besotted with her lover, Lady Smythe followed wherever he led. When she discovered he had taken a mistress, she could not contain her fury, a passion directed not at Mr. Widdicombe but at the object of his affection, Laura Bennett.

Lady Smythe smiles wearily as Daniel's face registers his shock at this piece of information. She continues with her narrative. Miss Bennett put off her known lover, Julian Wilson, by pretending to a general dislike of men. This was merely a cover to conceal her illicit liaison with a man of whom her parents would have completely disapproved. Claiming to be a messenger from Mr. Widdicombe, Lady Smythe, clothed as a young man in a costume and wig designed to attract the attention of the residents of Saxe-Mundy, obtained entrance to the cottage from her victim. There, using skills learned as a child at her father's side, she drugged and then stabbed Laura Bennett.

The subsequent murder of Bethany was necessary because Widdicombe owed a great deal of money to Mr. Minsky, who had threatened to drag Widdicombe to court. That murder, a warning to the father, was instigated by Widdicombe, and she had carried it out in a manner virtually identical to the first homicide.

When that death was under investigation, Widdicombe became worried that Minsky might reveal to Bethany's mother the identity of the man responsible for the murder. In order to investigate this possibility, Lady Smythe assumed another disguise. She presented herself to Mrs. Sinclair as Sylvie, a woman from Yorkshire, experienced in the trade. She was immediately taken on and stayed at that establishment for three weeks until she was certain that no information had been leaked by Minsky to his former mistress.

During that time, Sylvie, unbeknownst to him, witnessed

Mr. Wilson in the room of one of her fellow prostitutes. "I also saw you, Mr. Home, when you called on Mrs. Sinclair. Having eavesdropped on your conversation with my employer, I became convinced that she knew nothing and posed no danger. Since her life was safe, I vanished from Half Moon Street the next day."

Seeking to make money when his funds from the South began drying up, Widdicombe, a faker of prodigious gifts, had embarked on the Arundel Leonardo in league with the impoverished Duke of Exeter. The Duke, on slim evidence, became convinced that their fraud was about to be uncovered and threatened to expose Mr. Widdicombe. Lady Smythe acted once more. This time, again in concert with Widdicombe, she waited until the Duke had gone to the races at Newmarket. In the disguise used on two previous occasions, she called on the Duke's manservant, left her message and departed. Two days later, she called on the Duke again, was let in by the unsuspecting Hornby, committed the murder, and made sure the manservant saw her escaping with the canvas in hand.

Widdicombe destroyed his Leonardo, and the two departed for Florence, unsure of what speculations in which to involve themselves. Mr. Widdicombe had an ambition to sell a fake to Mr. Jarves. He began by consulting his fellow American about an ivory about which he said he entertained grave suspicions; Julian Wilson quickly identified it as a forgery.

All in all, she was elated, convinced that her subsequent existence would be trouble-free. Unfortunately, Lady Smythe discovered soon after her arrival in Florence that her lover had taken a new mistress, an Italian woman of aristocratic birth, and planned to throw her over. When, outraged, she threatened her lover with exposure, he laughed in her face. In condemning him, she would be putting a noose around her own neck.

Knowing of the animosity against foreigners rampant in Florence and aware in particular that many natives of the city were convinced Daniel Home was a necromancer, she hit upon the idea of attacking and wounding Daniel and then, as she headed home, creating enough of a disturbance with her shouts of "Dio Mio!, Dio Mio!" to draw Widdicombe outside to investigate. She knew him well: he did exactly what she anticipated, and she stabbed him to death outside the door to the villa they shared.

Lady Smythe had counted on the Florentine police, a disorganized group at the best of times, to be completely perplexed by the nature of the attacks. They would assume the assailant was male — she had not yet burnt the "costume" and wig. She hoped that the authorities would assume that the culprit was a xenophobe who, not having killed one Englishman, would wreak vengeance on another strolling in the area of the botched attack. In order to make the crime appear as Florentine as possible, she used a blade Widdicombe himself had purchased in the city a few weeks before.

"I was well aware you were in the habit of wearing a thick fur coat, Mr. Home, and I was reasonably certain that I could stage a convincing attack on your person without causing you real harm. That is exactly what occurred, thank God! My surprise was the amount of grief I felt for Stephen, despite the despicable way in which he had treated me. In the coach the next morning, my tears were genuine. Your kindness at that time touched me, and I regretted that I had used you as a stalking horse."

Lady Smythe's subsequent career, as she points out to Daniel, is largely a matter of public record. Overcome by remorse for her dreadful deeds, she decided to leave England and settle in the United States, where she took up residence with Widdicombe's mother, where she oversees the plantation. When she journeys to Washington, she carries information from Mr. Davis, the President of the Confederacy, to either Mr. Lincoln or Mr. Steward, his Secretary of State. The messages she exchanges are concerned solely with the conditions governing the exchange of prisoners and their treatment.

The wickedness of Lady Smythe amazes Daniel. At the same time, he is astounded by the force of her feelings for Widdicombe. Daniel deeply loved his dead wife, but he would never have been capable of the sublime purity of jealousy to which Lady Smythe fell victim. He has never been capable of such emotions. Does one have to experience such feelings to be fully human? How does one continue to conduct one's life when one has given in to such feelings in a criminal way? How could her fakery have so completely escaped him? Not only had she misused him badly, she had also played a particularly heinous game of cat and mouse with Julian Wilson. Having been accused so often of being an impostor, he has, of course, always been reluctant to throw stones at others. But in this instance, his blindness, as it were, dazzles him.

"You have paid a price for your crimes, Lady Smythe?"

"By the reckoning of the law, I have escaped scot-free."

"That is not what I am referring to. Your life here has been one long penance."

"I have always known you to be a charitable man, Mr. Home, and this evening you do not disappoint me. Passion made a complete monster of me. When I killed him, I still loved Stephen. In the past seven years, my existence has been, as much as I can make it, in the service of others. I hope that God will accept my acts of penance as atonement for my horrible deeds."

Daniel promises that she can rely on his discretion. "I can assure you, Lady Smythe, that your secrets will not be uncovered by me. No useful purpose would be served."

Lady Smythe announces that she must return to her friend, Emilie Helm. They have a long journey to begin early the next day, she reminds Daniel. The two walk to the entrance to the hotel to await her carriage. As it draws up, they embrace and take leave of each other.

CHAPTER FIFTEEN

THE EDUCATION
OF THE HEART

*W*hen Daniel returns from the hospital to Willard's the following evening, there is a note from O'Sullivan asking him to come to his room at the earliest opportunity. The door is open when Daniel arrives, the photographer's clothing and equipment piled up in front of the bed.

O'Sullivan is terribly agitated. There has been a skirmish about twenty miles outside the city limits, the closest action to the capital in a very long time. Gardner wants O'Sullivan to head there at daybreak, but the appendix of the boy who assists him has burst that afternoon. The doctors are not even sure he will survive. O'Sullivan recalls that Daniel, who has four days left in Washington before he takes the train to New York to catch his ship to Southampton, had mentioned that he would like to travel outside the city to see the countryside.

Would Daniel join him on this excursion? His duties would be relatively light. "A strange way of sightseeing to be sure, but you might enjoy it." Daniel accepts the invitation.

Instead of using a picture wagon as most war photographers do, O'Sullivan has converted an army ambulance, substantially bigger than a wagon, into a travelling photographic studio. At the outset, he points out to Daniel that they are not venturing into a battle zone; they are visiting the aftermath. "We are not able to take pictures of the battles, of course; our cameras are too heavy for that. But we can show what the land looks like and, of course, all the officers and their men want souvenirs."

As they ride along, the land that they view in that portion of Virginia re-conquered by the North is largely empty of inhabitants. The landscape is pretty in a quiet, unsensational way. In Washington, although the lilacs, magnolias and azalea have ripened into full bloom, Daniel has not paid them much notice. He has been vaguely aware that their bright pinks and purples provide a glaring contrast to the bleakness that has seeped into every aspect of the city. Here, in the open countryside, the air is heavily perfumed, forcing him to notice the flowering shrubs and trees. Every so often he and O'Sullivan see a farmhouse in the distance. Once or twice they come upon youngsters, usually boys, who have been sent by their parents to deliver messages to neighbours a mile or two away.

Their progress is especially slow because the two horses have to be rested frequently, so heavy is the load they are carrying. Not until dusk do they reach the area of the battle. "We are probably a mile or so away," O'Sullivan announces.

"The light is no good. We'll stay here the night and then set out early in the morning. It'll take an hour or two to take the photographs, and then we'll be on our way. We'll be back in Washington by tomorrow evening."

They eat their meal and then get ready to bunk down. O'Sullivan has never spoken to Daniel about what it is like to take images of the dead. Daniel, who imagines it must be a dispiriting experience, asks his new friend if he finds it unsettling.

"No. It's as if they're all asleep when I see them. Like lost babes in the woods." He pauses. "That reminds me. I reckon my work is along the same line as yours."

Daniel doesn't see any resemblance.

"Well, we're both interested in the dead and we both bring them back to life. Of course, they manifest themselves to you; I have to go out searching for them.

"There's another thing. If you look at an undeveloped negative, you don't see anything. The ghosts are there and are only called back to life by the chemicals that fix them forever. We're both of us interested in the strange business of immortality."

O'Sullivan continues to wax philosophical. "I guess you can't arrange things in advance at your séances. Or at least you're not supposed to. I have to do a lot of planning to get my pictures, make them right."

Daniel doesn't understand what O'Sullivan means. "Well, we sometimes move the bodies around to get the best possible exposures."

"You don't drag corpses from one place to another?"

"Hell, yes. Do you recall that photograph from the third day

of Gettysburg, where the Rebel corporal is slumped against a
tree at the bottom of an embankment?"

Daniel recalls being touched by the image.

"Well, three of us dragged that fellow two hundred feet
from the battlefield to position him there. No one's interested
in pictures of men lying flat on the ground."

"But by altering the evidence, you're faking history."

"That's as may be. But I'm an artist when I use that camera
of mine. I've got to get the best possible picture."

Daniel spends a restless night, turning and twisting on the hard
ground. His back hurts so much that he decides to get up and
walk a bit. Darkness still covers the land, the stars are dim, but
the moon is bright. Without meaning to, Daniel moves at a
brisk pace. He can manage to see ten feet ahead, enough to
know the terrain is free of obstacles. All of a sudden, a large
white object blocks his path. He advances slowly until he comes
upon the prone corpse of a white stallion, its saddle still tied to
its back. The eyes of the beautiful animal remain open, staring
piteously at Daniel. Moved by the sad end of the mighty beast,
he pats its mane and moves on.

Just as dawn is about to break and the mists begin their
slow ascent, Daniel reaches the edge of a precipice. The earth
at his feet falls away sharply to reveal a deep hollow sculpted
vigorously from the land. The sight is sublime: tops of trees
compete with each other for a share of the sky, the land rolls
irregularly, and an array of soft greens adorns the ground. As
the mist disperses, Daniel sees dozens of corpses costumed in

dark blue and silver grey in the bottom of the bowl. Death has had its way with many. Near him, a Union soldier lies slumped against a tree, as if lost in restful sleep. The small bullet hole on his brow indicates his is a never-ending rest.

Stumbling a bit, Daniel descends slowly to the bottom. He notices the thick wedding band on the left hand of a Rebel. Although his other hand has been blown away, there is a smile on the face of this tall blond fellow, perhaps because he thought of his beloved as death took him. A few feet away is the long torso of another Rebel dressed in a makeshift uniform: only his trousers are of Confederate Army issue. No socks or boots cover his feet; his head has been blown away. Daniel crosses to the other side of the valley and comes upon the corpse of a youngster who could not have been more than fifteen years of age. His Union uniform is pristine, his cap sits squarely on his head, the leather of his boots gleams. Only a trace of melancholia lingers on his handsome, inexperienced face. He obviously accepted death with considerable grace, perhaps equanimity.

In his mind's eye, Daniel can see the slain men ascending heavenward. He imagines all the questions they will have about the meaning of their lives, the fates of their loved ones. He knows the messages they will wish to convey to those they have left behind. He realizes he might be called upon some day to speak with some of these men and hopes that he will be able to bestow some words of hope or consolation on those they left behind.

As he looks up into the surrounding land, Daniel knows he is neither soldier nor statesman nor artist. For want of a better word, he is a seer, a man who communicates with the dead and gives their feelings flesh and blood. A very strange profession, one he would never have chosen for such an ordinary man as himself.

ACKNOWLEDGEMENTS

Transformations is very loosely based on some incidents in the early life of Daniel Home (1833–1886). As its sub-title indicates, Elizabeth Jenkins' meticulously researched biography, *The Shadow and the Light: A Defence of Daniel Douglas Home, the Medium* (1982), provides a favourable, sympathetic assessment. Robert Browning's venomous hatred of Home is discussed in all biographies of him. I found Julia Markus's *Dared and Done: The Marriage of Elizabeth Barrett and Robert Browning* (1995) particularly helpful and informative. Giuliana Artom Treves' *The Golden Ring: The Anglo-Florentines, 1847–1862* (1956) is a treasure house of fascinating information.

Attitla Berki copyedited this book with precision, sensitivity and imagination. Once again, I am deeply grateful to Marc Côté for his enthusiasm, support, and intelligence.